W9-ANN-078

KING SHAKA

— ZULU LEGEND —

LUKE W. MOLVER

© Copyright Luke W. Molver, 2019
All rights reserved.

No part of this book may be used or reproduced in any manner whatsoever without written consent from the publisher, except for brief quotations for reviews. For further information, write to Catalyst Press, 2941 Kelly Street, Livermore CA 94551 USA, or Jive Media Africa, PO Box 22106, Mayor's Walk, 3208, South Africa, or email info@storypressafrica.com

Published by **Story Press Africa**, an imprint of
Jive Media Africa (South Africa) and **Catalyst Press** (USA).
Website: www.storypressafrica.com

Jive Media Africa
P O Box 22106
Mayor's Walk, 3208
South Africa

Tel: +27 33 342 9380/2
Email: admin@jivemedia.co.za
Website: www.jivemedia.co.za

Catalyst Press
2941 Kelly Street
Livermore CA 94551 USA

Tel: 001-925-315-5970
Email: jlpowers@catalystpress.org
Website: www.catalystpress.org

Illustrated by: Luke W. Molver
Written by: Luke W. Molver

Acknowledgements: This work has drawn on
Myth of Iron: Shaka in History by Dan Wylie, *The Assassination of King Shaka* by John Laband, and *Emperor Shaka the Great* by Mazisi Kunene

Fonts in the graphic text by BlamBot, used with licence.

Library of Congress Control Number: 2018967172

Trade Paper ISBN 978-1-946498-93-9
Trade Cloth ISBN 978-1-946498-90-8

FIRST EDITION

10 9 8 7 6 5 4 3 2 1

FOREWORD

It is an honor and privilege to write the Foreword for this book, which follows on King Shaka's emergence as a leader in **Shaka Rising** and recounts the ambitions and challenges of his reign as king.

The story of the legendary King Shaka, King of the Zulu people, has fascinated ordinary people and scholars for nearly two centuries in Africa and around the world. His legacy as one of the greatest African military tacticians of the 19th century is rich with complexities, myths and ambiguities.

This book succeeds in communicating King Shaka's story because it locates him within a historical context. He was both product and shaper of the changes that were occurring in southern Africa during the late 18th and early 19th centuries. The story equips the reader with knowledge about a wide range of social and political issues including belief systems, leadership, accountability, nation-building, gender relations, diplomacy, patriotism, loyalty and strategy. This empowers the reader to comprehend the socio-economic and political developments of the early 20th century.

In addition, King Shaka's story gives the reader a better appreciation of settlement patterns in south-eastern Africa at that time, particularly in the present-day KwaZulu-Natal and Eastern Cape.

While scholars continue to debate King Shaka's role in state formation in southern Africa, there is general recognition of his role in the transformation of military strategies and the consolidation of communities in what later came to be known as Natal and Zululand. King Shaka's story is a reminder of the fluidity of ethnic and linguistic identities.

His legacy lives on – that of the distinguished leader who founded the Zulu nation – and it will continue to influence the perceptions of present and future generations.

Dr Sibongiseni Mkhize
Chief Executive Officer,
South African State Theatre, Pretoria

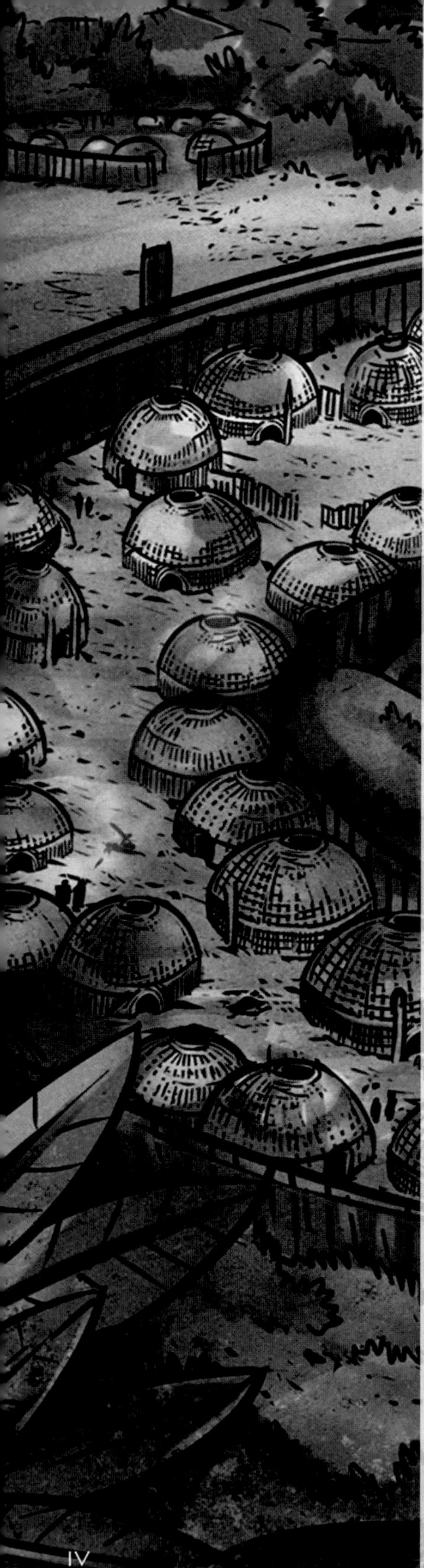

THE CHARACTERS IN

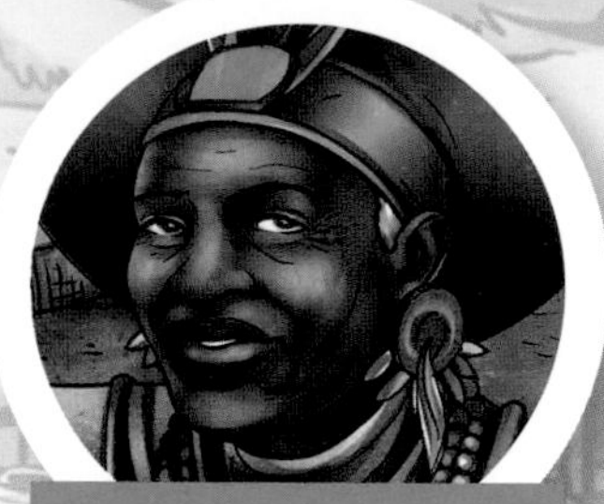

NANDI
("The Great She-Elephant")
King Shaka's mother and
high-ranking *inkosikazi*

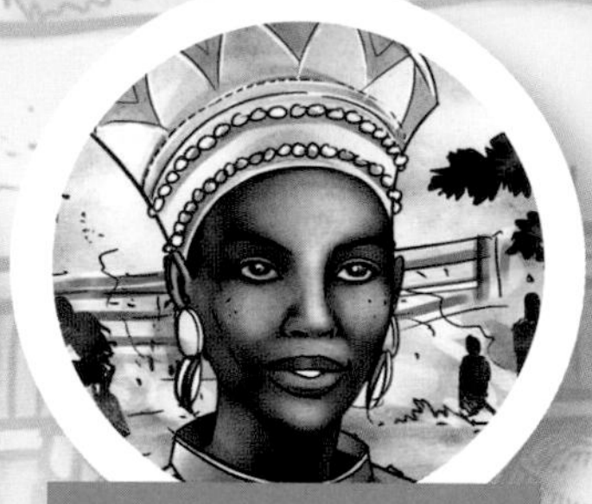

NOMCOBA
Princess of the Zulu and
King Shaka's sister

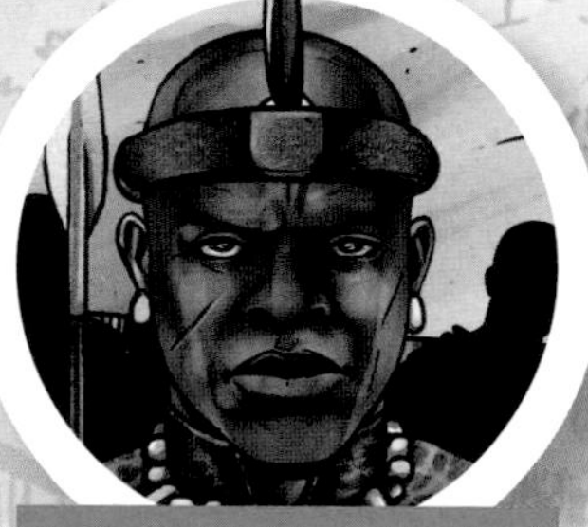

KING SHAKA
King of the Zulu and the
southern chiefdoms

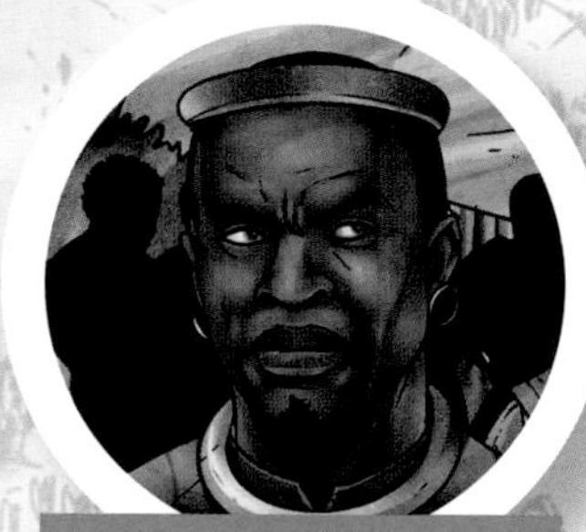

DINGANE
Prince of the Zulu and King
Shaka's half-brother

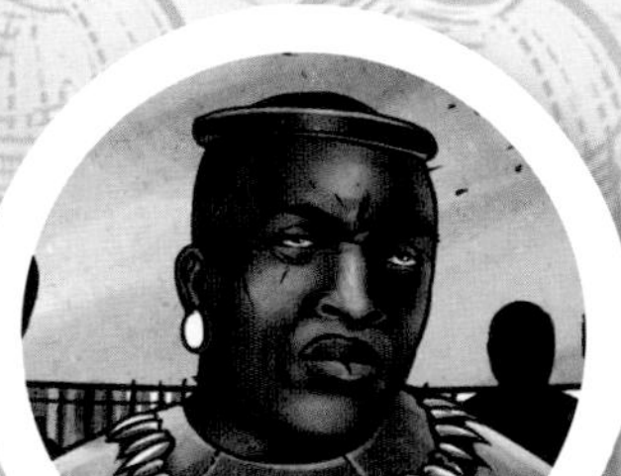

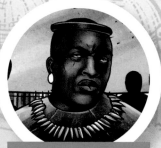

MHLANGANA
Prince of the Zulu and King
Shaka's half-brother

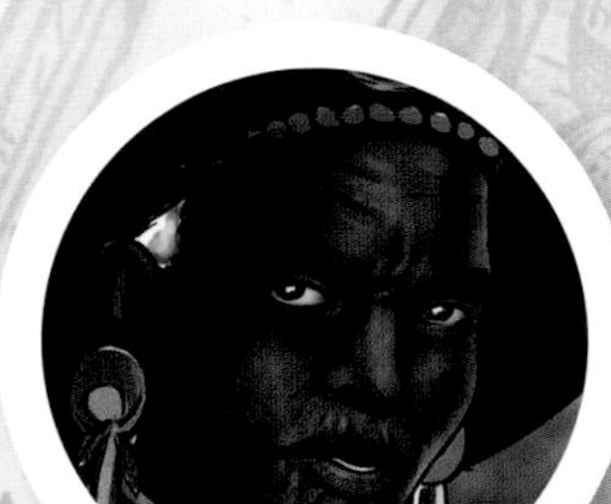

MNKABAYI
("The Kingmaker") King
Shaka's aunt and high-
ranking *inkosikazi*

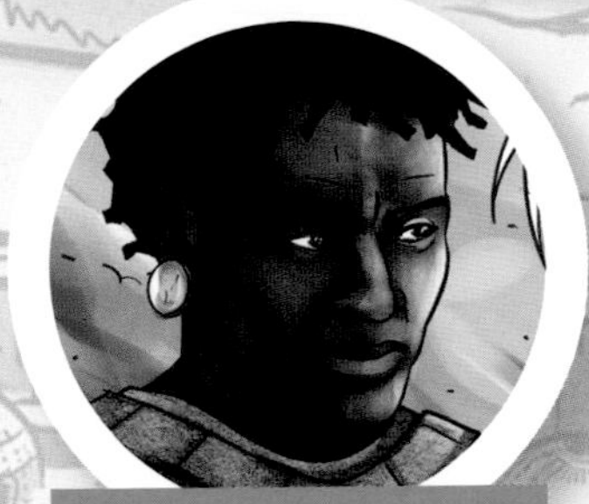

NDENGEZI
King Shaka's closest friend and trusted advisor

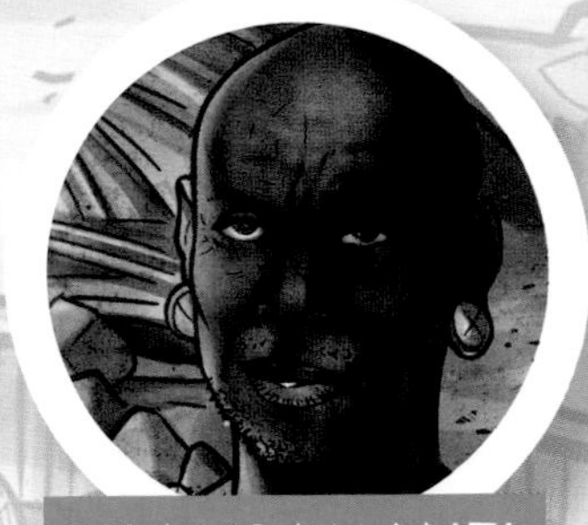

HLAMBAMANZI
Former slave and King Shaka's interpreter

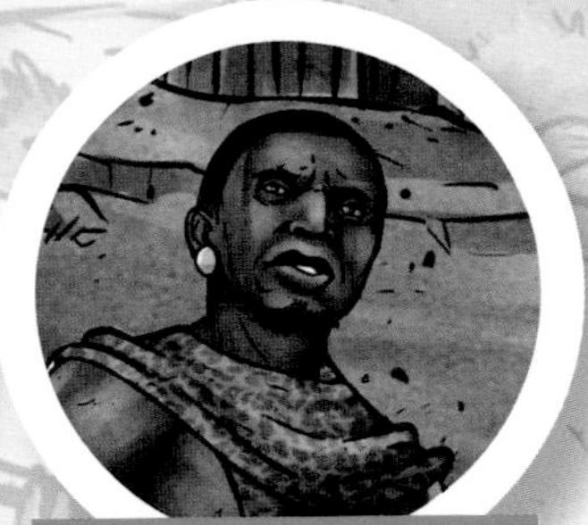

MANANGA
High-ranking general in King Shaka's army

"King Shaka: Zulu Legend"

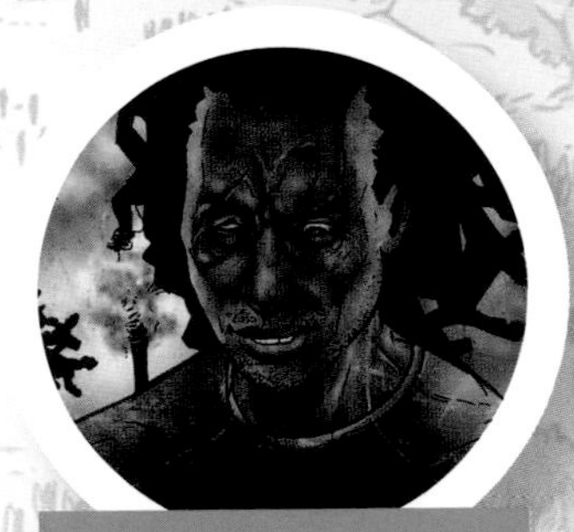

NONZAMA
Commander of the iziYendane *ibutho*

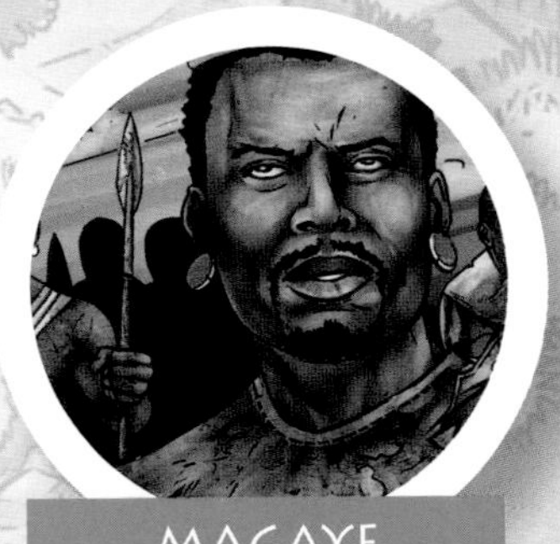

MAGAYE
Chief of the Cele, allies to the Zulu

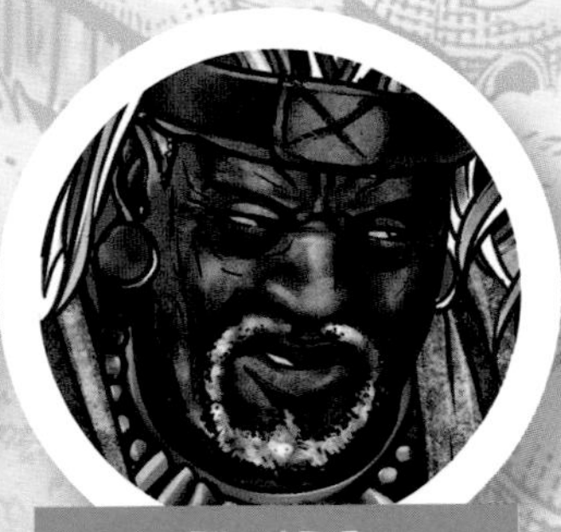

ZWIDE
King of the Ndwandwe, a northern slaver clan

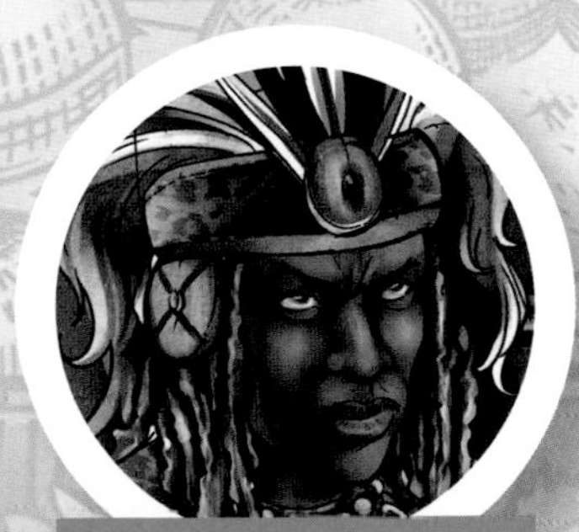

SIKHUNYANE
Prince of the Ndwandwe and Zwide's son and heir

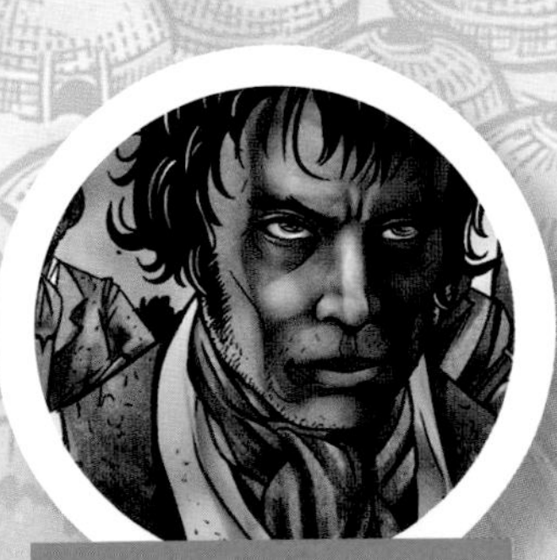

HENRY FYNN
("Mbulazi") Port Natal settler, hunter and mercenary

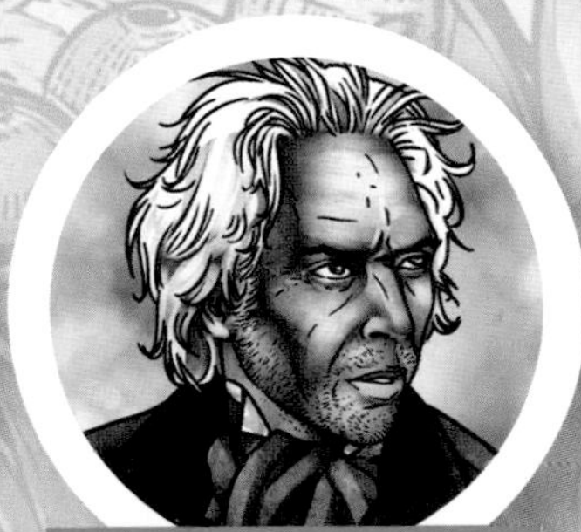

FRANCIS FAREWELL
Port Natal settler, hunter

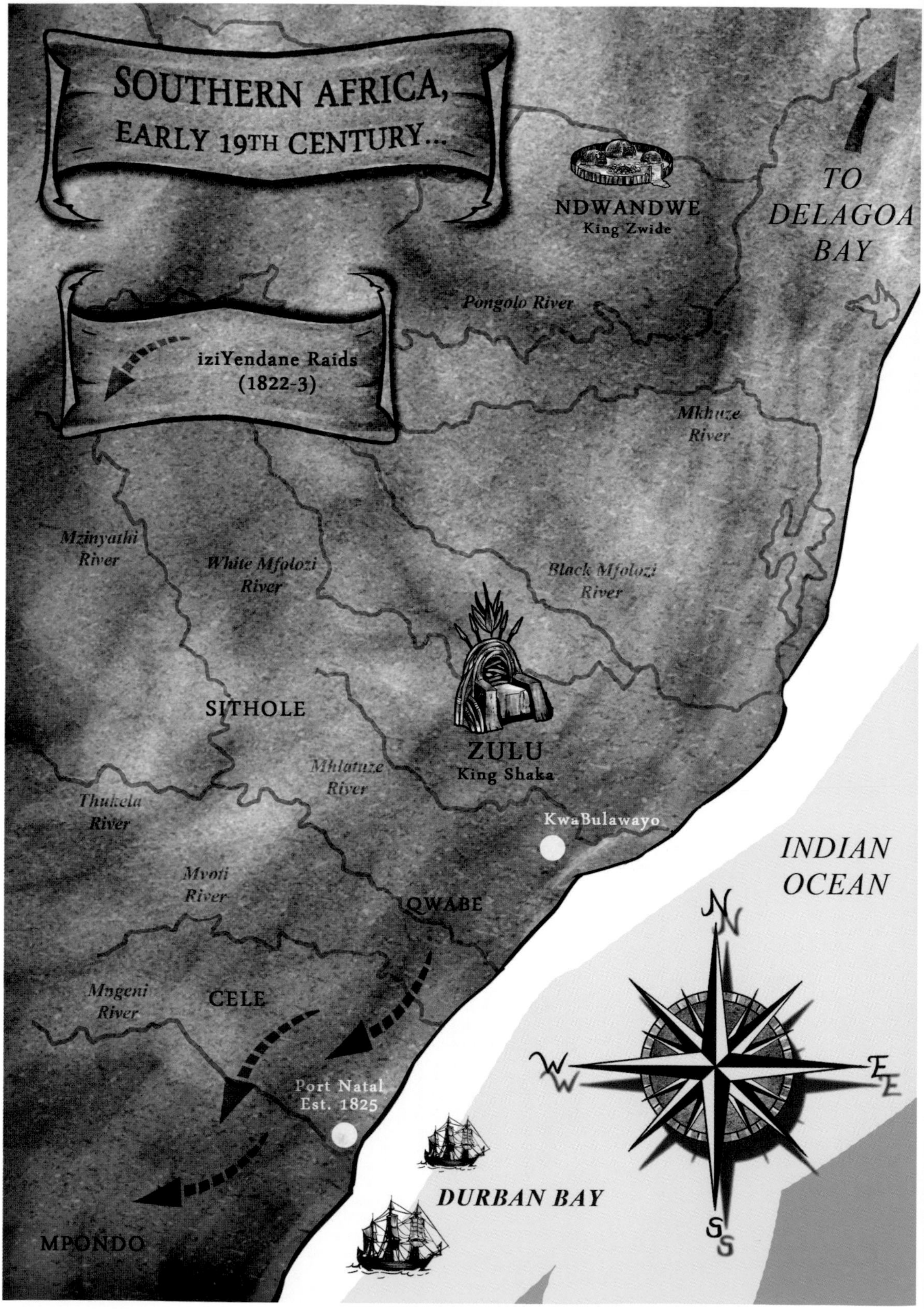

SOUTHERN AFRICA,
EARLY 19TH CENTURY...
iziYendane Raids
(1822-3)
NDWANDWE
King Zwide
TO
DELAGOA
BAY
Pongolo River
Mkhuze
River
Mzinyathi
River
White Mfolozi
River
Black Mfolozi
River
SITHOLE
ZULU
King Shaka
Mhlatuze
River
Thukela
River
KwaBulawayo
INDIAN
OCEAN
Mvoti
River
QWABE
Mngeni
River
CELE
Port Natal
Est. 1825
DURBAN BAY
MPONDO
N
W
E
S

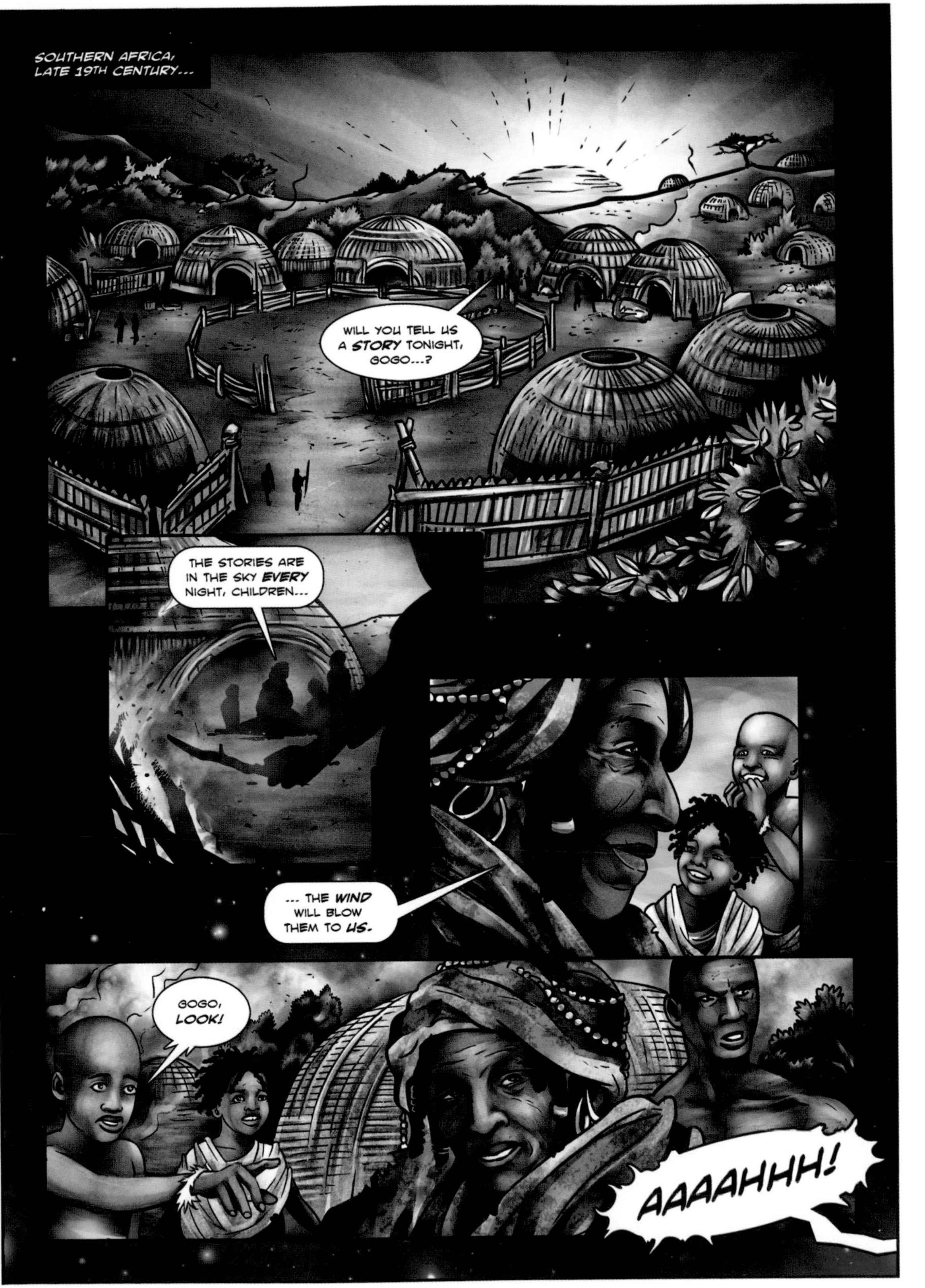
SOUTHERN AFRICA, LATE 19TH CENTURY...
WILL YOU TELL US A STORY TONIGHT, GOGO...?
THE STORIES ARE IN THE SKY EVERY NIGHT, CHILDREN...
... THE WIND WILL BLOW THEM TO US.
GOGO, LOOK!
AAAAHHH!

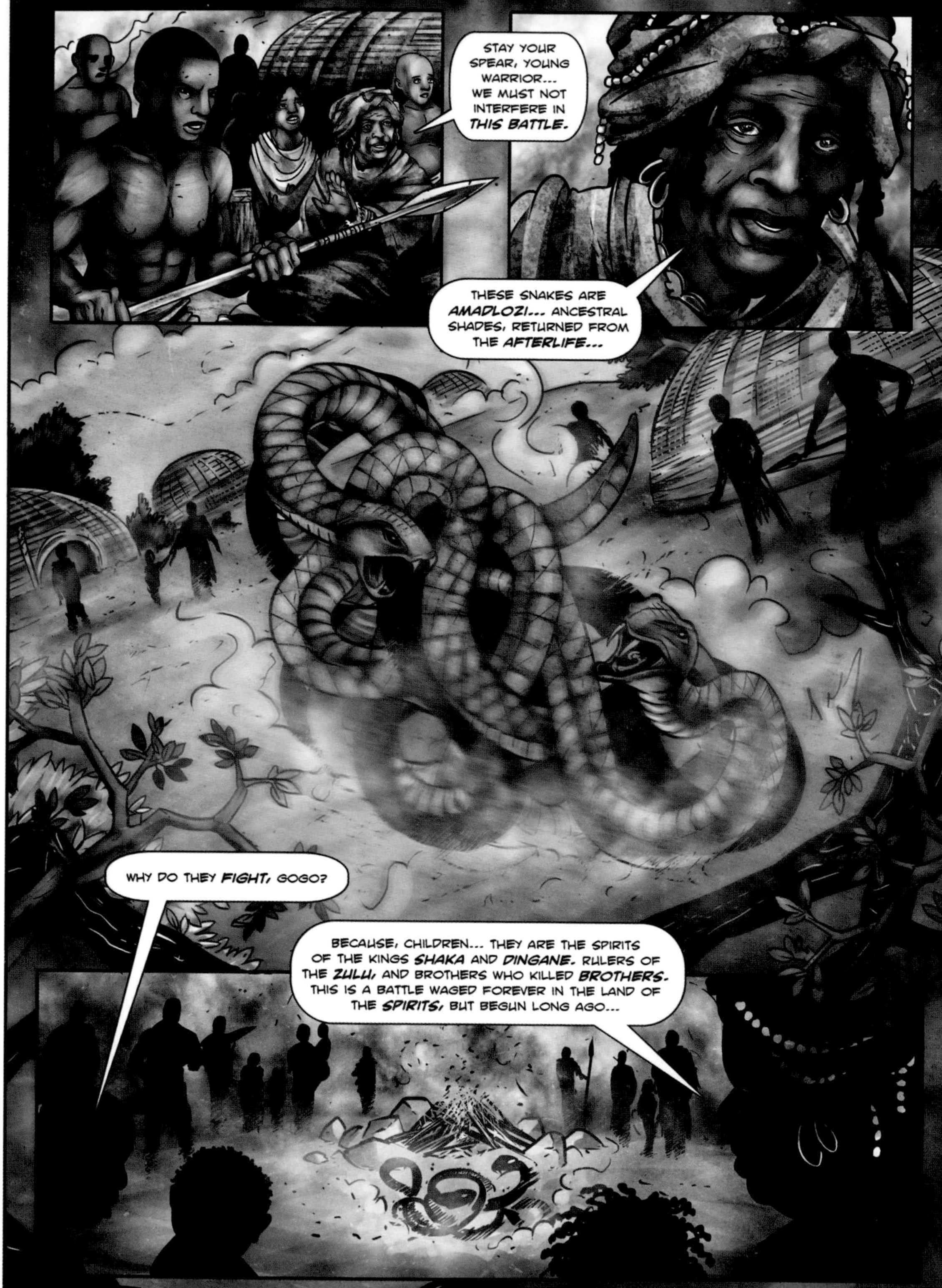
STAY YOUR SPEAR, YOUNG WARRIOR... WE MUST NOT INTERFERE IN THIS BATTLE.
THESE SNAKES ARE AMADLOZI... ANCESTRAL SHADES, RETURNED FROM THE AFTERLIFE...
WHY DO THEY FIGHT, GOGO?
BECAUSE, CHILDREN... THEY ARE THE SPIRITS OF THE KINGS SHAKA AND DINGANE. RULERS OF THE ZULU, AND BROTHERS WHO KILLED BROTHERS. THIS IS A BATTLE WAGED FOREVER IN THE LAND OF THE SPIRITS, BUT BEGUN LONG AGO...

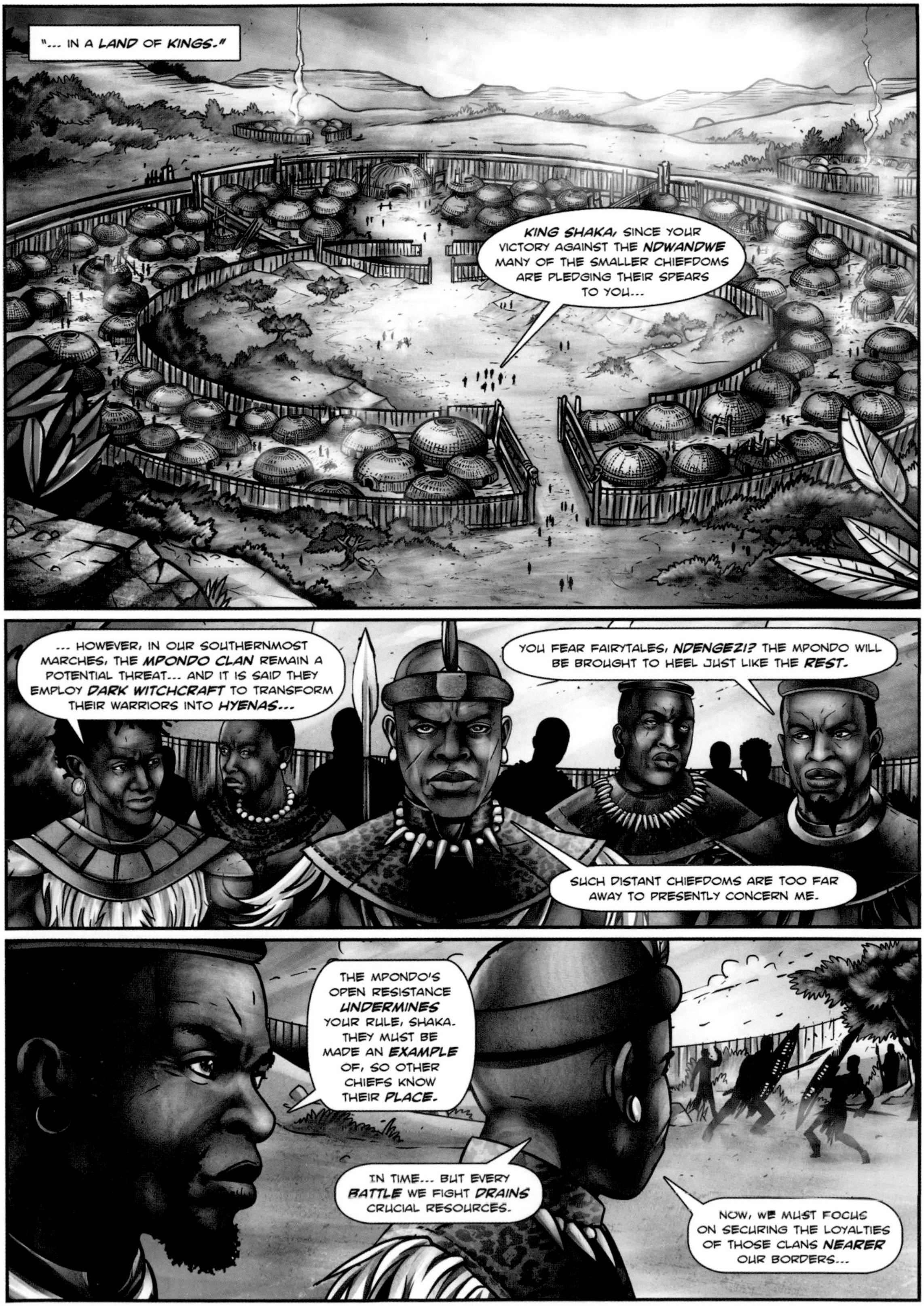
"... IN A LAND OF KINGS."
KING SHAKA, SINCE YOUR VICTORY AGAINST THE NDWANDWE MANY OF THE SMALLER CHIEFDOMS ARE PLEDGING THEIR SPEARS TO YOU...
... HOWEVER, IN OUR SOUTHERNMOST MARCHES, THE MPONDO CLAN REMAIN A POTENTIAL THREAT... AND IT IS SAID THEY EMPLOY DARK WITCHCRAFT TO TRANSFORM THEIR WARRIORS INTO HYENAS...
YOU FEAR FAIRYTALES, NDENGEZI? THE MPONDO WILL BE BROUGHT TO HEEL JUST LIKE THE REST.
SUCH DISTANT CHIEFDOMS ARE TOO FAR AWAY TO PRESENTLY CONCERN ME.
THE MPONDO'S OPEN RESISTANCE UNDERMINES YOUR RULE, SHAKA. THEY MUST BE MADE AN EXAMPLE OF, SO OTHER CHIEFS KNOW THEIR PLACE.
IN TIME... BUT EVERY BATTLE WE FIGHT DRAINS CRUCIAL RESOURCES.
NOW, WE MUST FOCUS ON SECURING THE LOYALTIES OF THOSE CLANS NEARER OUR BORDERS...

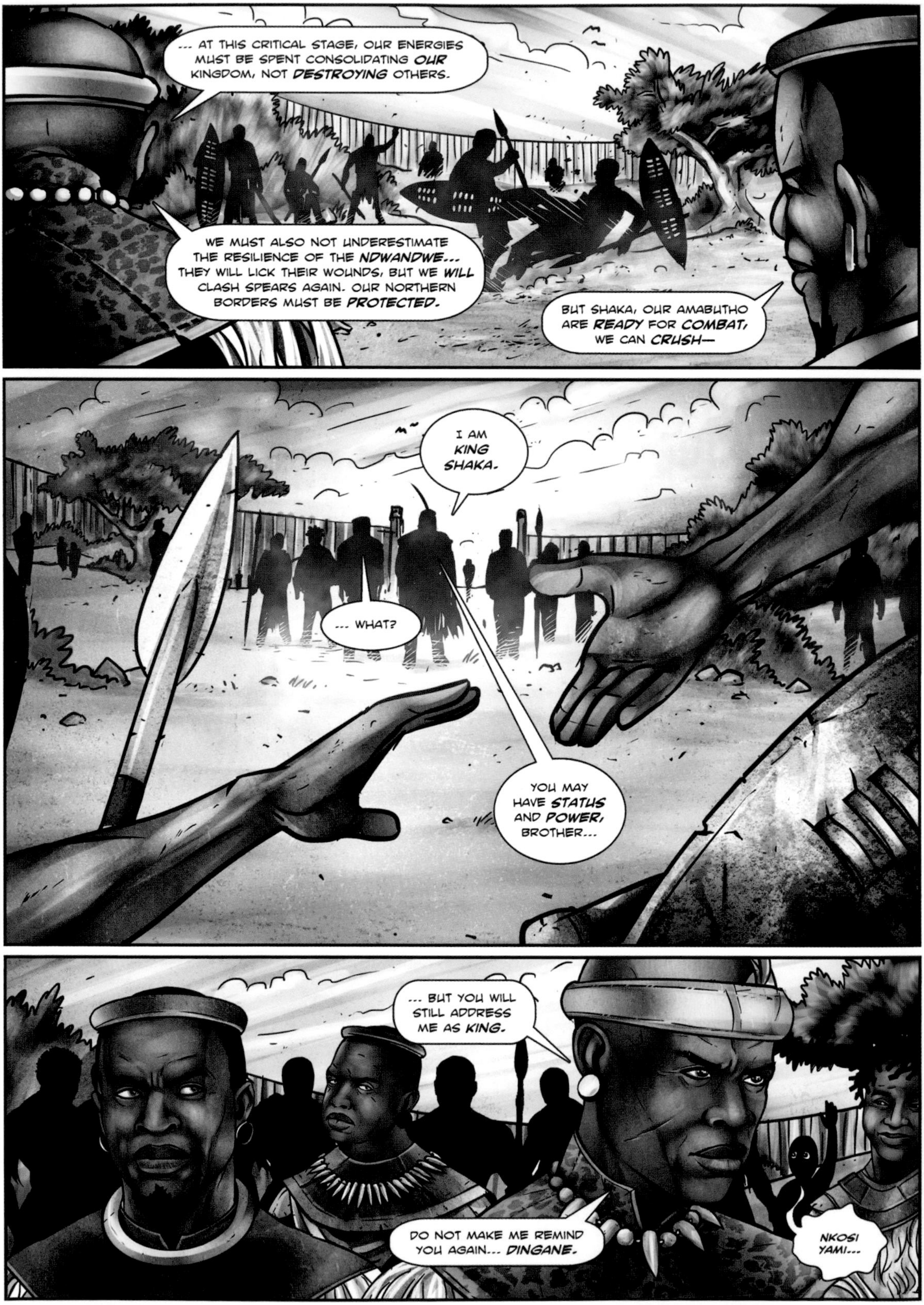
... AT THIS CRITICAL STAGE, OUR ENERGIES MUST BE SPENT CONSOLIDATING OUR KINGDOM, NOT DESTROYING OTHERS.
WE MUST ALSO NOT UNDERESTIMATE THE RESILIENCE OF THE NDWANDWE... THEY WILL LICK THEIR WOUNDS, BUT WE WILL CLASH SPEARS AGAIN. OUR NORTHERN BORDERS MUST BE PROTECTED.
BUT SHAKA, OUR AMABUTHO ARE READY FOR COMBAT, WE CAN CRUSH—
I AM KING SHAKA.
... WHAT?
YOU MAY HAVE STATUS AND POWER, BROTHER...
... BUT YOU WILL STILL ADDRESS ME AS KING.
DO NOT MAKE ME REMIND YOU AGAIN... DINGANE.
NKOSI YAMI...

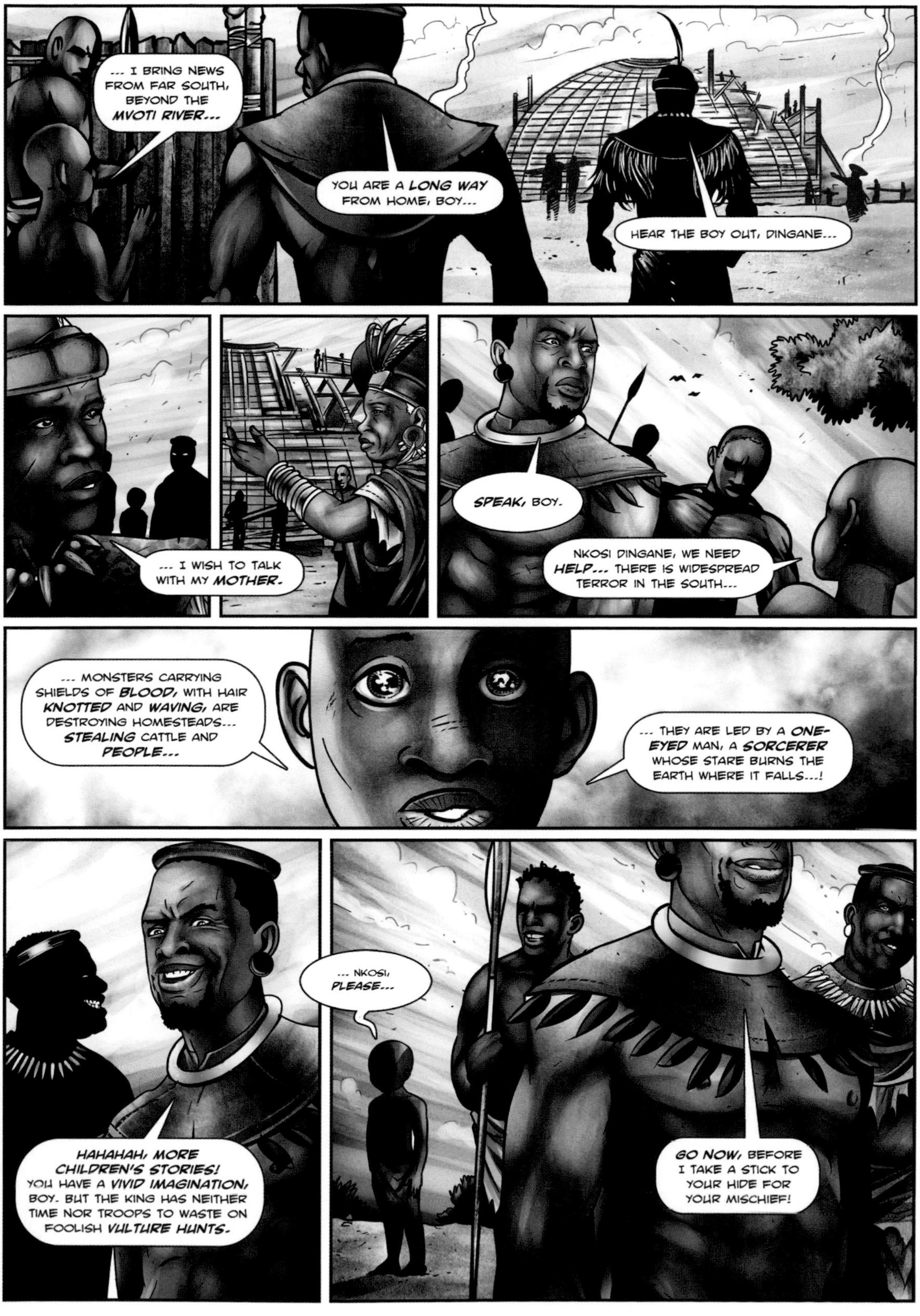
... I BRING NEWS FROM FAR SOUTH, BEYOND THE MVOTI RIVER...
YOU ARE A LONG WAY FROM HOME, BOY...
HEAR THE BOY OUT, DINGANE...
... I WISH TO TALK WITH MY MOTHER.
SPEAK, BOY.
NKOSI DINGANE, WE NEED HELP... THERE IS WIDESPREAD TERROR IN THE SOUTH...
... MONSTERS CARRYING SHIELDS OF BLOOD, WITH HAIR KNOTTED AND WAVING, ARE DESTROYING HOMESTEADS... STEALING CATTLE AND PEOPLE...
... THEY ARE LED BY A ONE-EYED MAN, A SORCERER WHOSE STARE BURNS THE EARTH WHERE IT FALLS...!
HAHAHAH, MORE CHILDREN'S STORIES! YOU HAVE A VIVID IMAGINATION, BOY. BUT THE KING HAS NEITHER TIME NOR TROOPS TO WASTE ON FOOLISH VULTURE HUNTS.
... NKOSI, PLEASE...
GO NOW, BEFORE I TAKE A STICK TO YOUR HIDE FOR YOUR MISCHIEF!

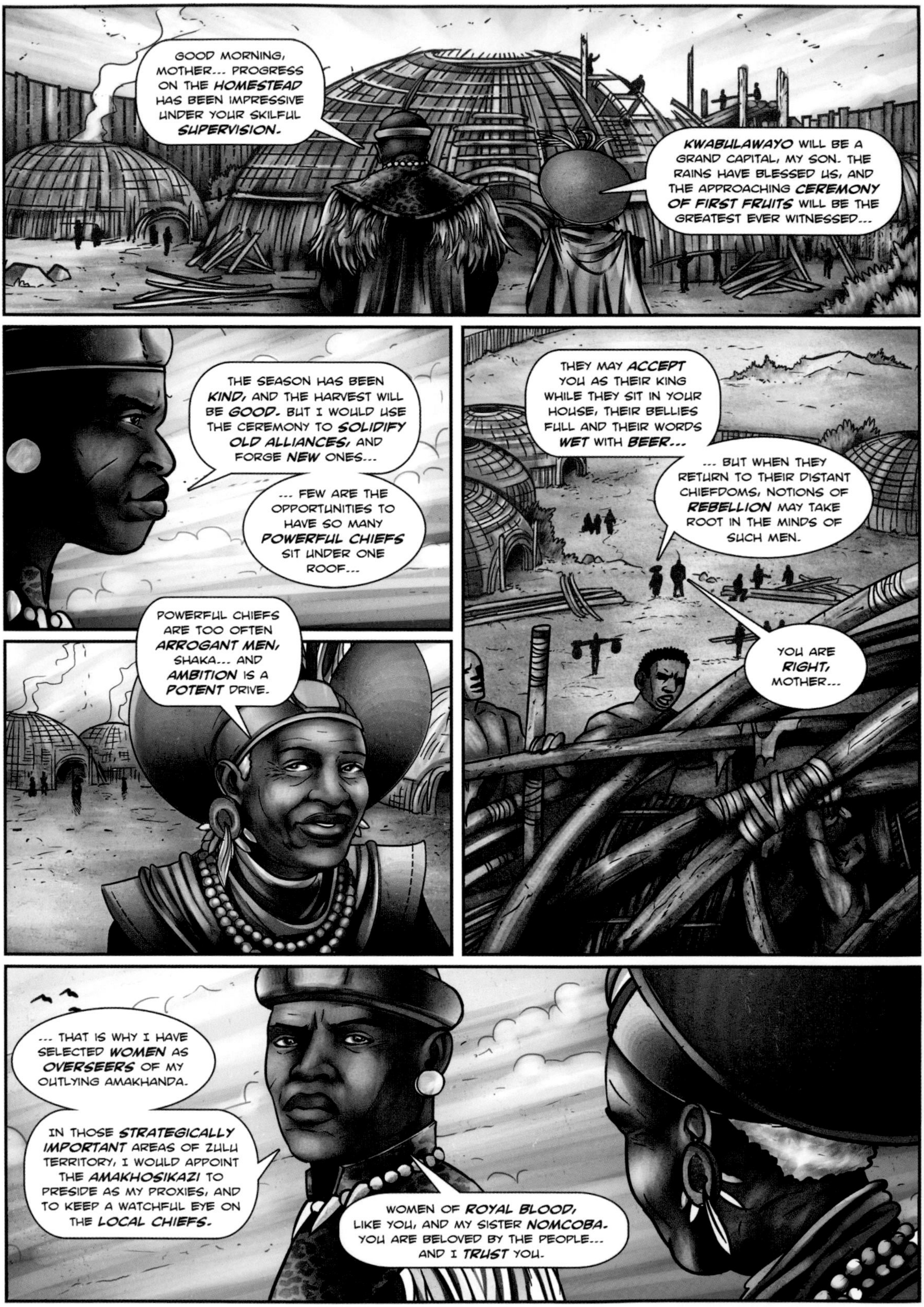
GOOD MORNING, MOTHER... PROGRESS ON THE HOMESTEAD HAS BEEN IMPRESSIVE UNDER YOUR SKILFUL SUPERVISION.
KWABULAWAYO WILL BE A GRAND CAPITAL, MY SON. THE RAINS HAVE BLESSED US, AND THE APPROACHING CEREMONY OF FIRST FRUITS WILL BE THE GREATEST EVER WITNESSED...
THE SEASON HAS BEEN KIND, AND THE HARVEST WILL BE GOOD. BUT I WOULD USE THE CEREMONY TO SOLIDIFY OLD ALLIANCES, AND FORGE NEW ONES...
... FEW ARE THE OPPORTUNITIES TO HAVE SO MANY POWERFUL CHIEFS SIT UNDER ONE ROOF...
POWERFUL CHIEFS ARE TOO OFTEN ARROGANT MEN, SHAKA... AND AMBITION IS A POTENT DRIVE.
THEY MAY ACCEPT YOU AS THEIR KING WHILE THEY SIT IN YOUR HOUSE, THEIR BELLIES FULL AND THEIR WORDS WET WITH BEER...
... BUT WHEN THEY RETURN TO THEIR DISTANT CHIEFDOMS, NOTIONS OF REBELLION MAY TAKE ROOT IN THE MINDS OF SUCH MEN.
YOU ARE RIGHT, MOTHER...
... THAT IS WHY I HAVE SELECTED WOMEN AS OVERSEERS OF MY OUTLYING AMAKHANDA.
IN THOSE STRATEGICALLY IMPORTANT AREAS OF ZULU TERRITORY, I WOULD APPOINT THE AMAKHOSIKAZI TO PRESIDE AS MY PROXIES, AND TO KEEP A WATCHFUL EYE ON THE LOCAL CHIEFS.
WOMEN OF ROYAL BLOOD, LIKE YOU, AND MY SISTER NOMCOBA. YOU ARE BELOVED BY THE PEOPLE... AND I TRUST YOU.

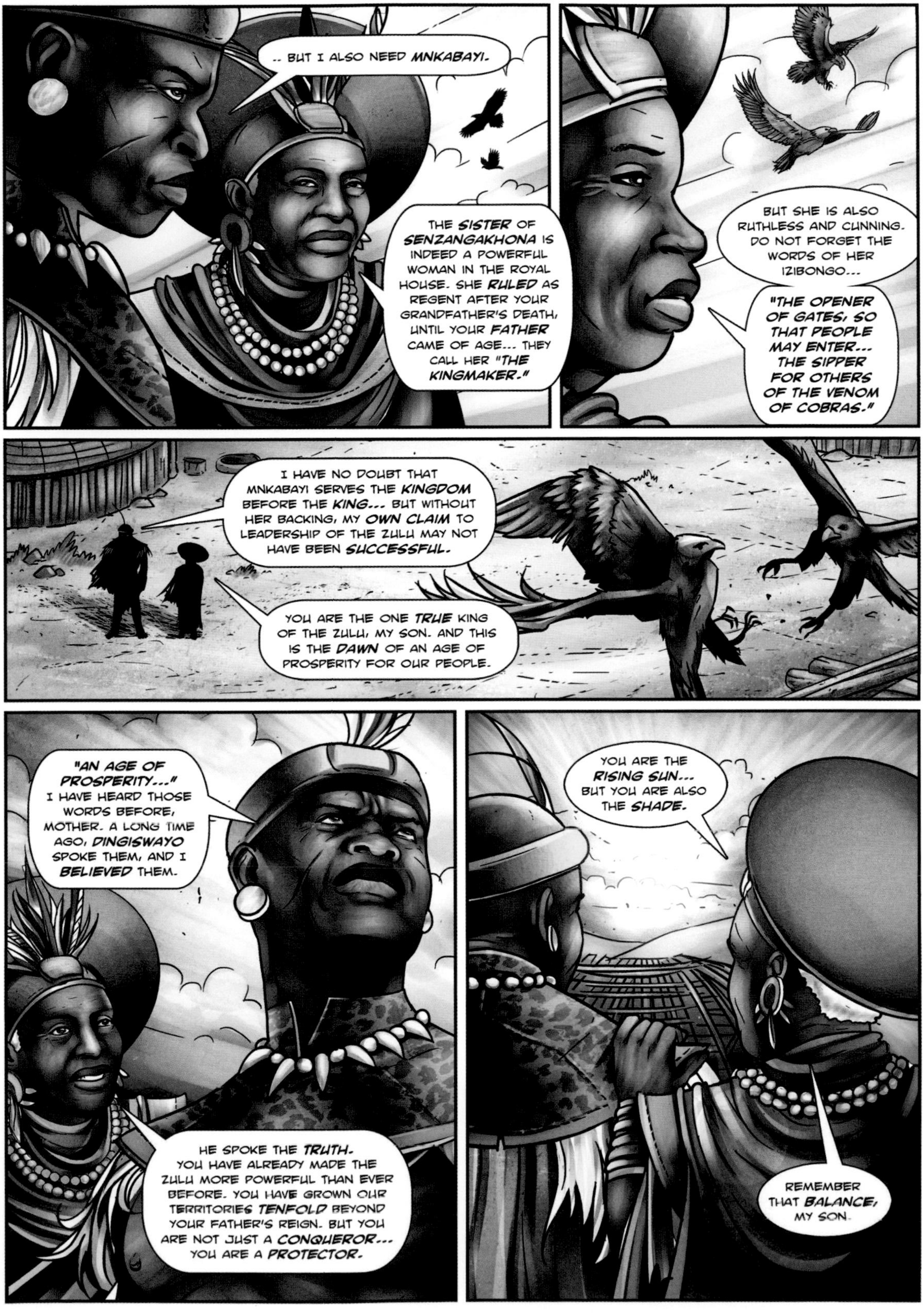
.. BUT I ALSO NEED MNKABAYI.
THE SISTER OF SENZANGAKHONA IS INDEED A POWERFUL WOMAN IN THE ROYAL HOUSE. SHE RULED AS REGENT AFTER YOUR GRANDFATHER'S DEATH, UNTIL YOUR FATHER CAME OF AGE... THEY CALL HER "THE KINGMAKER."
BUT SHE IS ALSO RUTHLESS AND CUNNING. DO NOT FORGET THE WORDS OF HER IZIBONGO...
"THE OPENER OF GATES, SO THAT PEOPLE MAY ENTER... THE SIPPER FOR OTHERS OF THE VENOM OF COBRAS."
I HAVE NO DOUBT THAT MNKABAYI SERVES THE KINGDOM BEFORE THE KING... BUT WITHOUT HER BACKING, MY OWN CLAIM TO LEADERSHIP OF THE ZULU MAY NOT HAVE BEEN SUCCESSFUL.
YOU ARE THE ONE TRUE KING OF THE ZULU, MY SON. AND THIS IS THE DAWN OF AN AGE OF PROSPERITY FOR OUR PEOPLE.
"AN AGE OF PROSPERITY..." I HAVE HEARD THOSE WORDS BEFORE, MOTHER. A LONG TIME AGO, DINGISWAYO SPOKE THEM, AND I BELIEVED THEM.
HE SPOKE THE TRUTH. YOU HAVE ALREADY MADE THE ZULU MORE POWERFUL THAN EVER BEFORE. YOU HAVE GROWN OUR TERRITORIES TENFOLD BEYOND YOUR FATHER'S REIGN. BUT YOU ARE NOT JUST A CONQUEROR... YOU ARE A PROTECTOR.
YOU ARE THE RISING SUN... BUT YOU ARE ALSO THE SHADE.
REMEMBER THAT BALANCE, MY SON.

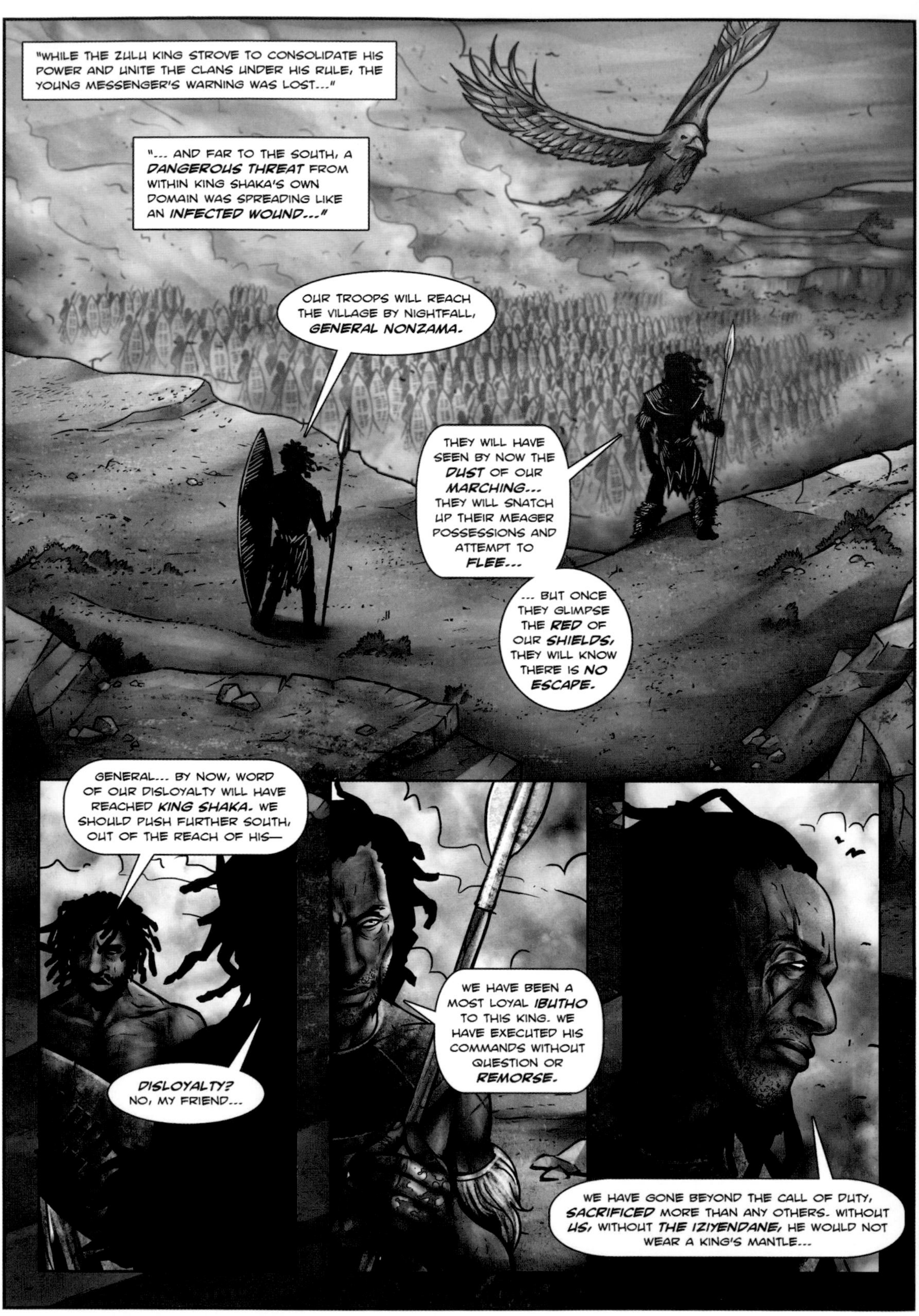
"WHILE THE ZULU KING STROVE TO CONSOLIDATE HIS POWER AND UNITE THE CLANS UNDER HIS RULE, THE YOUNG MESSENGER'S WARNING WAS LOST..."
"... AND FAR TO THE SOUTH, A DANGEROUS THREAT FROM WITHIN KING SHAKA'S OWN DOMAIN WAS SPREADING LIKE AN INFECTED WOUND..."
OUR TROOPS WILL REACH THE VILLAGE BY NIGHTFALL, GENERAL NONZAMA.
THEY WILL HAVE SEEN BY NOW THE DUST OF OUR MARCHING... THEY WILL SNATCH UP THEIR MEAGER POSSESSIONS AND ATTEMPT TO FLEE...
... BUT ONCE THEY GLIMPSE THE RED OF OUR SHIELDS, THEY WILL KNOW THERE IS NO ESCAPE.
GENERAL... BY NOW, WORD OF OUR DISLOYALTY WILL HAVE REACHED KING SHAKA. WE SHOULD PUSH FURTHER SOUTH, OUT OF THE REACH OF HIS—
DISLOYALTY? NO, MY FRIEND...
WE HAVE BEEN A MOST LOYAL IBUTHO TO THIS KING. WE HAVE EXECUTED HIS COMMANDS WITHOUT QUESTION OR REMORSE.
WE HAVE GONE BEYOND THE CALL OF DUTY, SACRIFICED MORE THAN ANY OTHERS. WITHOUT US, WITHOUT THE IZIYENDANE, HE WOULD NOT WEAR A KING'S MANTLE...

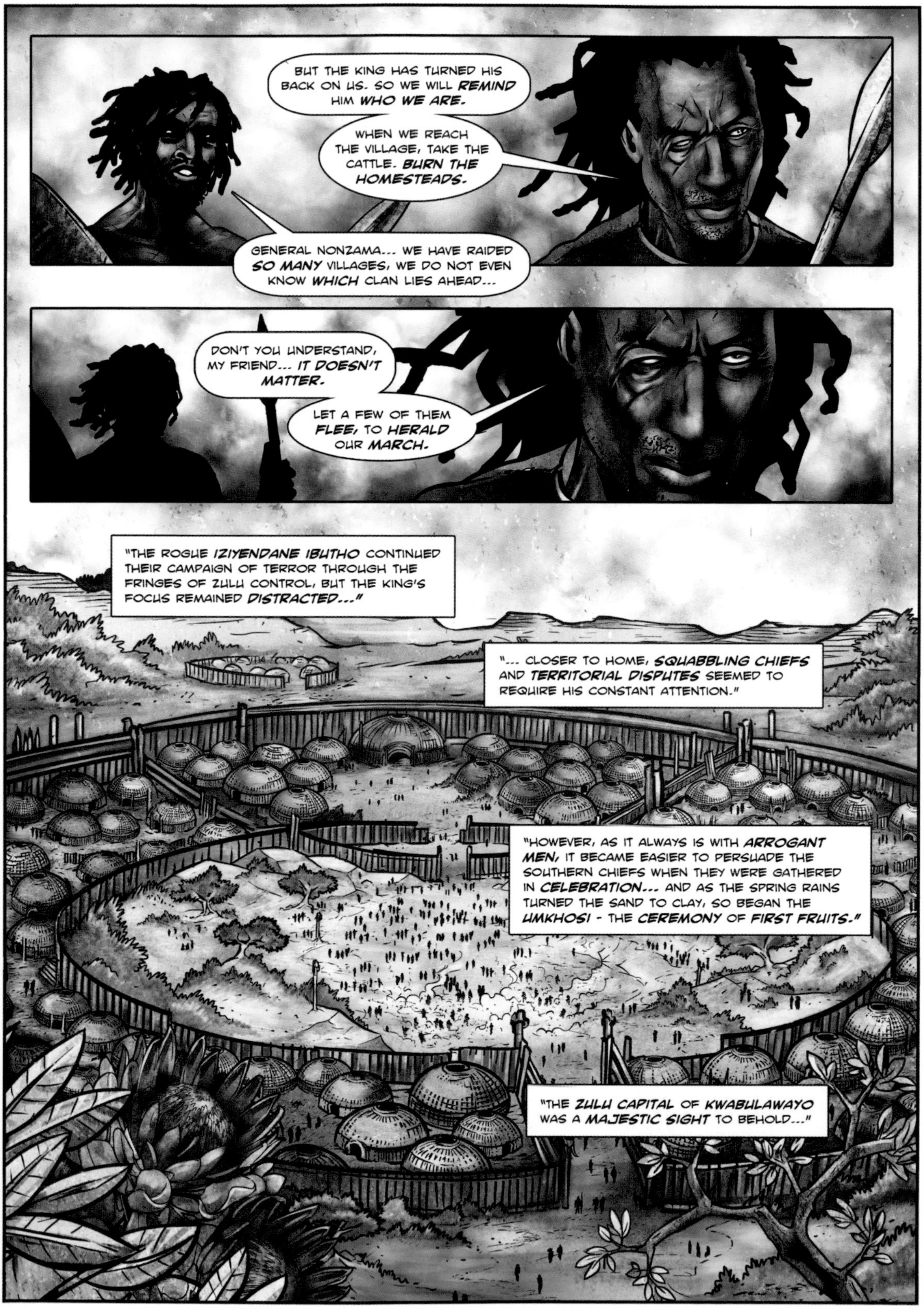
GENERAL NONZAMA... WE HAVE RAIDED SO MANY VILLAGES, WE DO NOT EVEN KNOW WHICH CLAN LIES AHEAD...
BUT THE KING HAS TURNED HIS BACK ON US. SO WE WILL REMIND HIM WHO WE ARE.
WHEN WE REACH THE VILLAGE, TAKE THE CATTLE. BURN THE HOMESTEADS.
DON'T YOU UNDERSTAND, MY FRIEND... IT DOESN'T MATTER.
LET A FEW OF THEM FLEE, TO HERALD OUR MARCH.
"THE ROGUE IZIYENDANE IBUTHO CONTINUED THEIR CAMPAIGN OF TERROR THROUGH THE FRINGES OF ZULU CONTROL, BUT THE KING'S FOCUS REMAINED DISTRACTED..."
"... CLOSER TO HOME, SQUABBLING CHIEFS AND TERRITORIAL DISPUTES SEEMED TO REQUIRE HIS CONSTANT ATTENTION."
"HOWEVER, AS IT ALWAYS IS WITH ARROGANT MEN, IT BECAME EASIER TO PERSUADE THE SOUTHERN CHIEFS WHEN THEY WERE GATHERED IN CELEBRATION... AND AS THE SPRING RAINS TURNED THE SAND TO CLAY, SO BEGAN THE UMKHOSI - THE CEREMONY OF FIRST FRUITS."
"THE ZULU CAPITAL OF KWABULAWAYO WAS A MAJESTIC SIGHT TO BEHOLD..."

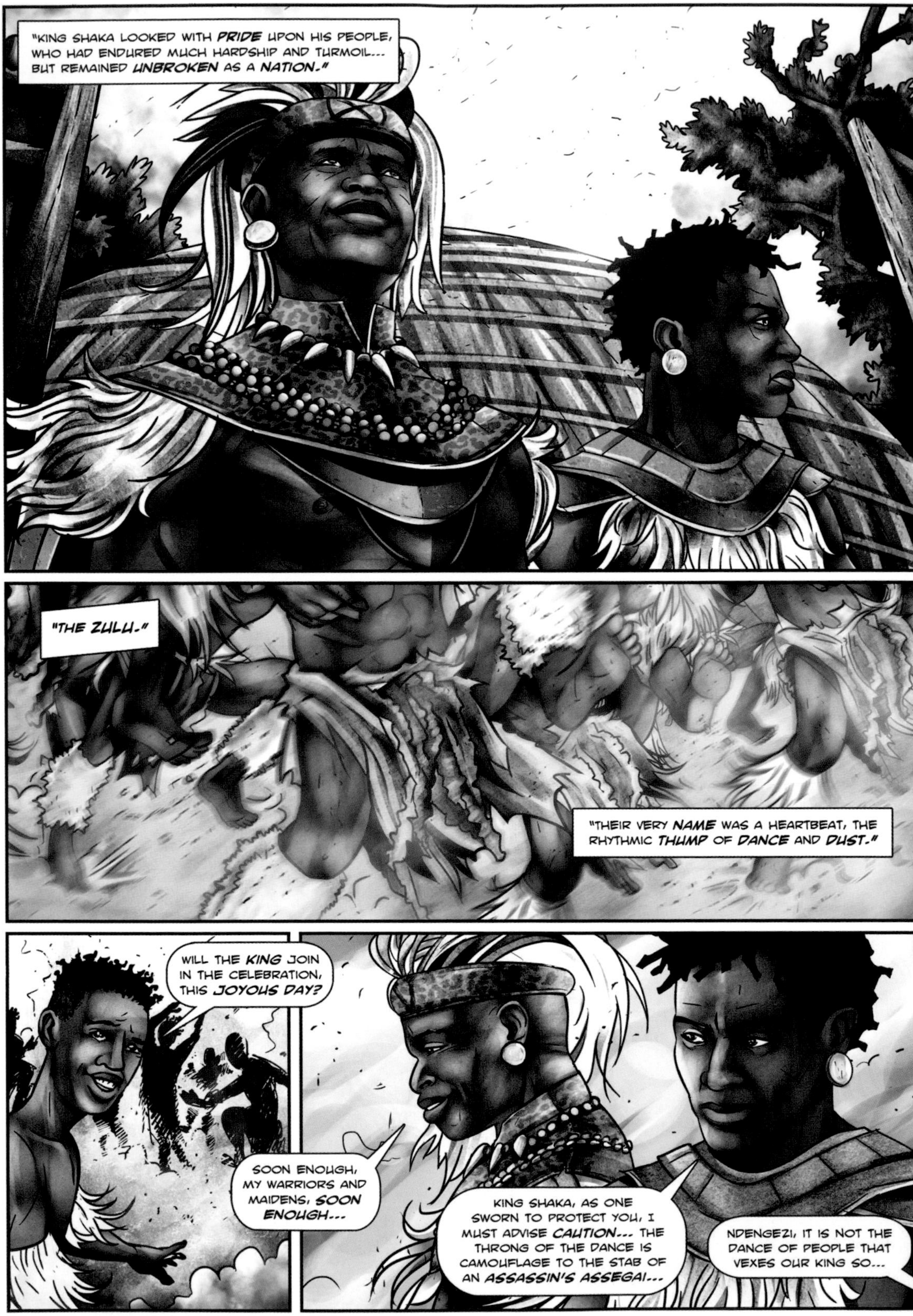

"KING SHAKA LOOKED WITH PRIDE UPON HIS PEOPLE, WHO HAD ENDURED MUCH HARDSHIP AND TURMOIL... BUT REMAINED UNBROKEN AS A NATION."
"THE ZULU."
"THEIR VERY NAME WAS A HEARTBEAT, THE RHYTHMIC THUMP OF DANCE AND DUST."
WILL THE KING JOIN IN THE CELEBRATION, THIS JOYOUS DAY?
SOON ENOUGH, MY WARRIORS AND MAIDENS, SOON ENOUGH...
KING SHAKA, AS ONE SWORN TO PROTECT YOU, I MUST ADVISE CAUTION... THE THRONG OF THE DANCE IS CAMOUFLAGE TO THE STAB OF AN ASSASSIN'S ASSEGAI...
NDENGEZI, IT IS NOT THE DANCE OF PEOPLE THAT VEXES OUR KING SO...

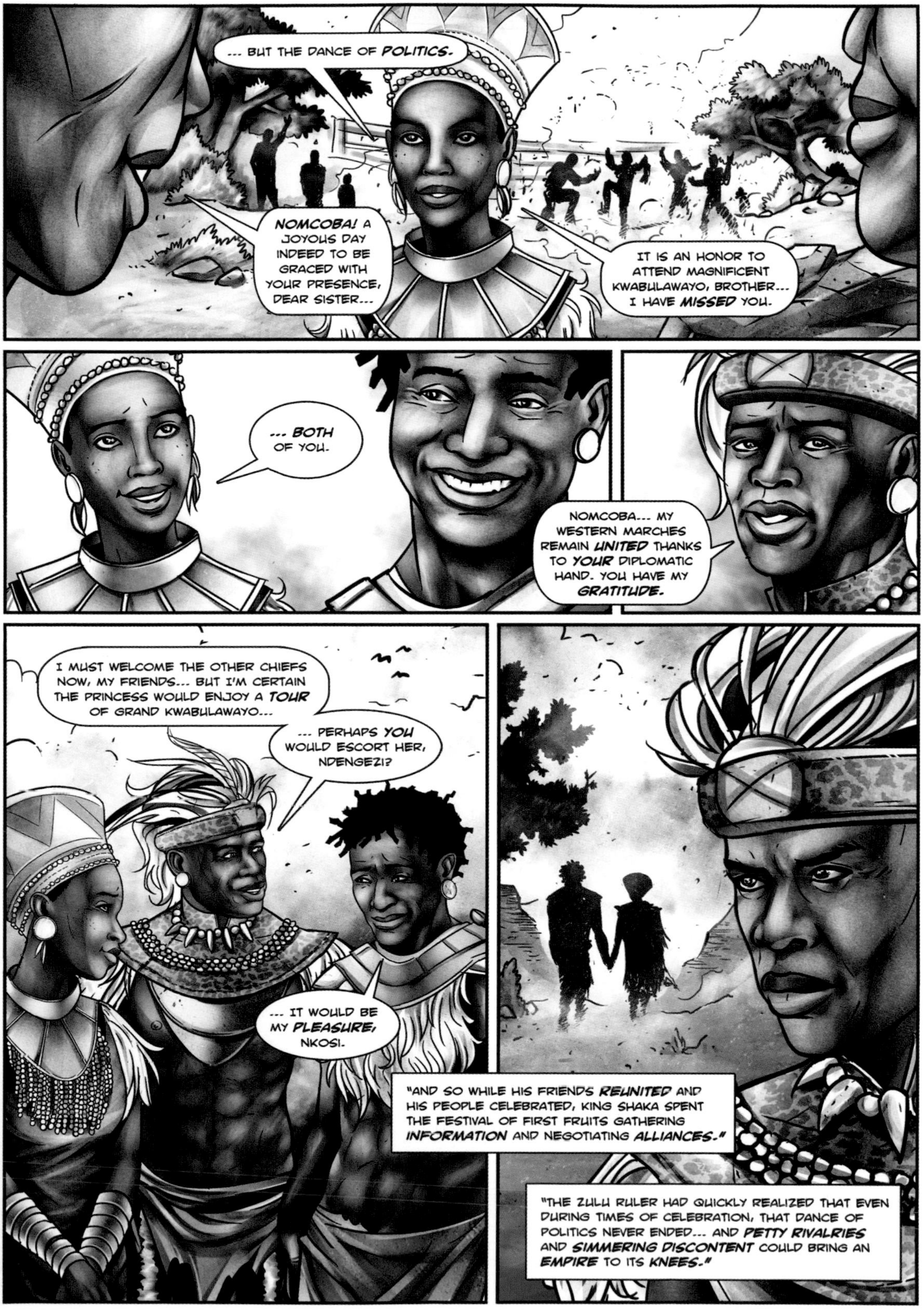

... BUT THE DANCE OF POLITICS.
NOMCOBA! A JOYOUS DAY INDEED TO BE GRACED WITH YOUR PRESENCE, DEAR SISTER...
IT IS AN HONOR TO ATTEND MAGNIFICENT KWABULAWAYO, BROTHER... I HAVE MISSED YOU.
... BOTH OF YOU.
NOMCOBA... MY WESTERN MARCHES REMAIN UNITED THANKS TO YOUR DIPLOMATIC HAND. YOU HAVE MY GRATITUDE.
I MUST WELCOME THE OTHER CHIEFS NOW, MY FRIENDS... BUT I'M CERTAIN THE PRINCESS WOULD ENJOY A TOUR OF GRAND KWABULAWAYO...
... PERHAPS YOU WOULD ESCORT HER, NDENGEZI?
... IT WOULD BE MY PLEASURE, NKOSI.
"AND SO WHILE HIS FRIENDS REUNITED AND HIS PEOPLE CELEBRATED, KING SHAKA SPENT THE FESTIVAL OF FIRST FRUITS GATHERING INFORMATION AND NEGOTIATING ALLIANCES."
"THE ZULU RULER HAD QUICKLY REALIZED THAT EVEN DURING TIMES OF CELEBRATION, THAT DANCE OF POLITICS NEVER ENDED... AND PETTY RIVALRIES AND SIMMERING DISCONTENT COULD BRING AN EMPIRE TO ITS KNEES."

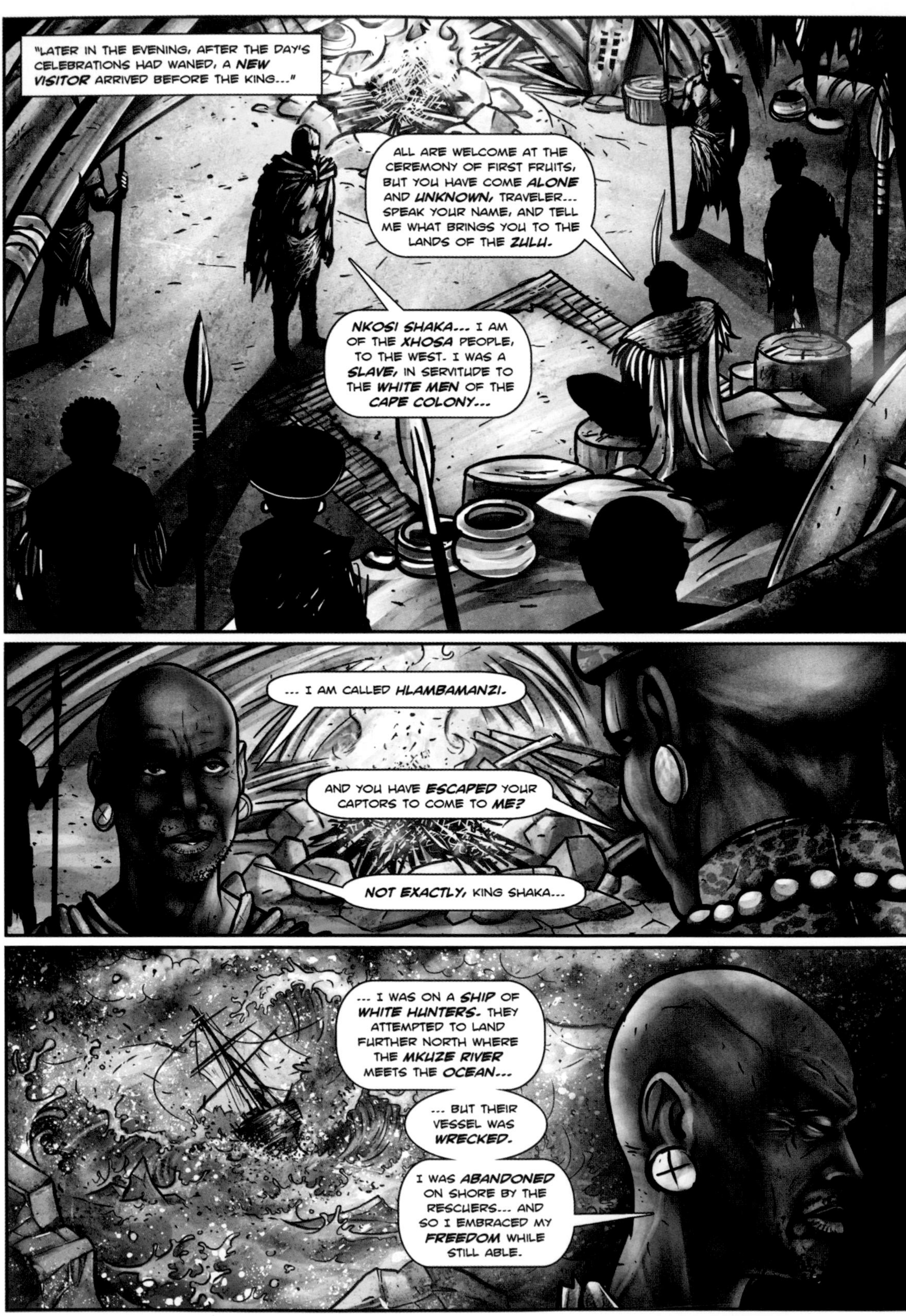
"LATER IN THE EVENING, AFTER THE DAY'S CELEBRATIONS HAD WANED, A NEW VISITOR ARRIVED BEFORE THE KING..."
ALL ARE WELCOME AT THE CEREMONY OF FIRST FRUITS, BUT YOU HAVE COME ALONE AND UNKNOWN, TRAVELER... SPEAK YOUR NAME, AND TELL ME WHAT BRINGS YOU TO THE LANDS OF THE ZULU.
NKOSI SHAKA... I AM OF THE XHOSA PEOPLE, TO THE WEST. I WAS A SLAVE, IN SERVITUDE TO THE WHITE MEN OF THE CAPE COLONY...
... I AM CALLED HLAMBAMANZI.
AND YOU HAVE ESCAPED YOUR CAPTORS TO COME TO ME?
NOT EXACTLY, KING SHAKA...
... I WAS ON A SHIP OF WHITE HUNTERS. THEY ATTEMPTED TO LAND FURTHER NORTH WHERE THE MKUZE RIVER MEETS THE OCEAN...
... BUT THEIR VESSEL WAS WRECKED.
I WAS ABANDONED ON SHORE BY THE RESCUERS... AND SO I EMBRACED MY FREEDOM WHILE STILL ABLE.

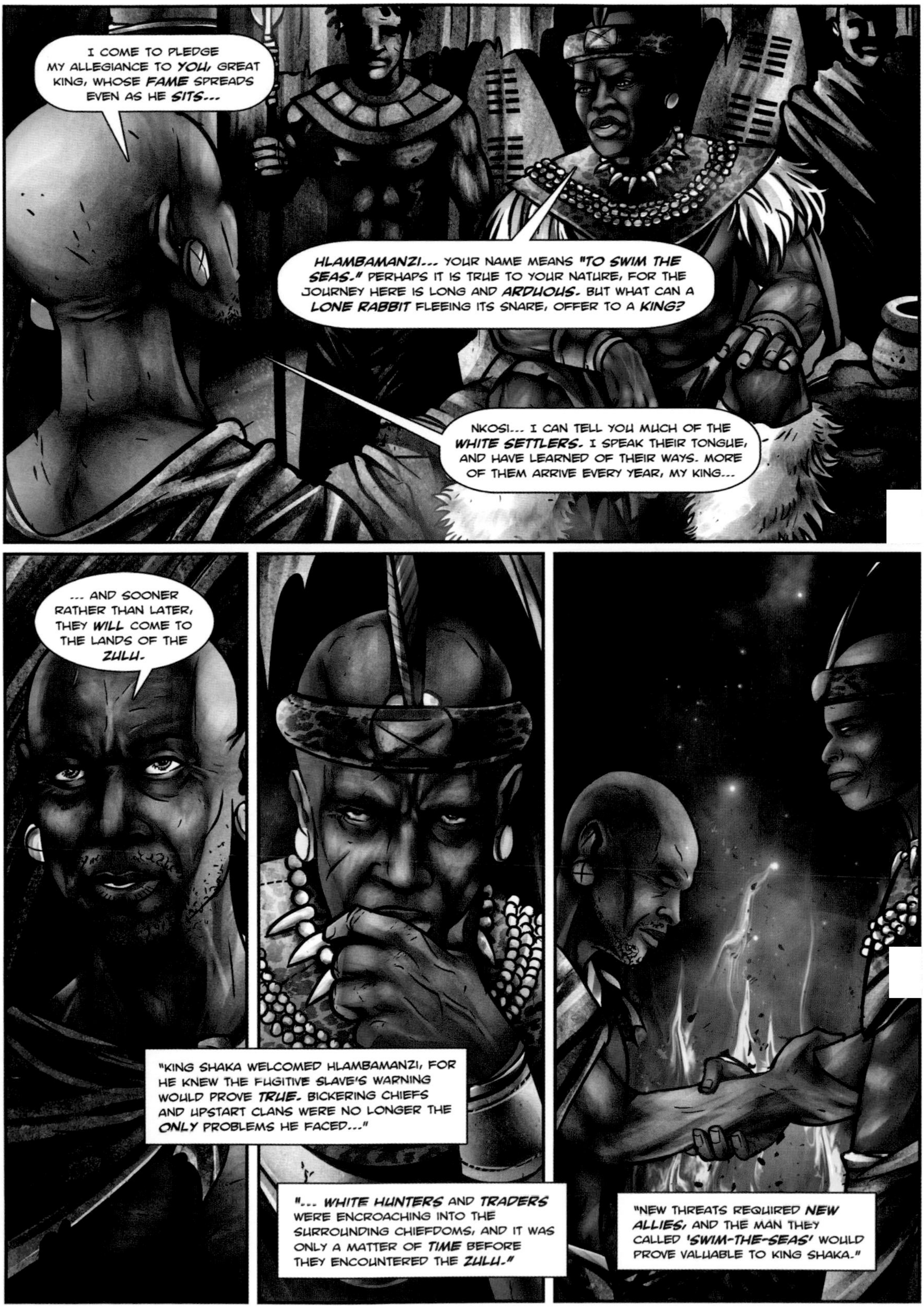
I COME TO PLEDGE MY ALLEGIANCE TO YOU, GREAT KING, WHOSE FAME SPREADS EVEN AS HE SITS...
HLAMBAMANZI... YOUR NAME MEANS "TO SWIM THE SEAS." PERHAPS IT IS TRUE TO YOUR NATURE, FOR THE JOURNEY HERE IS LONG AND ARDUOUS. BUT WHAT CAN A LONE RABBIT FLEEING ITS SNARE, OFFER TO A KING?
NKOSI... I CAN TELL YOU MUCH OF THE WHITE SETTLERS. I SPEAK THEIR TONGUE, AND HAVE LEARNED OF THEIR WAYS. MORE OF THEM ARRIVE EVERY YEAR, MY KING...
... AND SOONER RATHER THAN LATER, THEY WILL COME TO THE LANDS OF THE ZULU.
"KING SHAKA WELCOMED HLAMBAMANZI, FOR HE KNEW THE FUGITIVE SLAVE'S WARNING WOULD PROVE TRUE. BICKERING CHIEFS AND UPSTART CLANS WERE NO LONGER THE ONLY PROBLEMS HE FACED..."
"... WHITE HUNTERS AND TRADERS WERE ENCROACHING INTO THE SURROUNDING CHIEFDOMS, AND IT WAS ONLY A MATTER OF TIME BEFORE THEY ENCOUNTERED THE ZULU."
"NEW THREATS REQUIRED NEW ALLIES, AND THE MAN THEY CALLED 'SWIM-THE-SEAS' WOULD PROVE VALUABLE TO KING SHAKA."

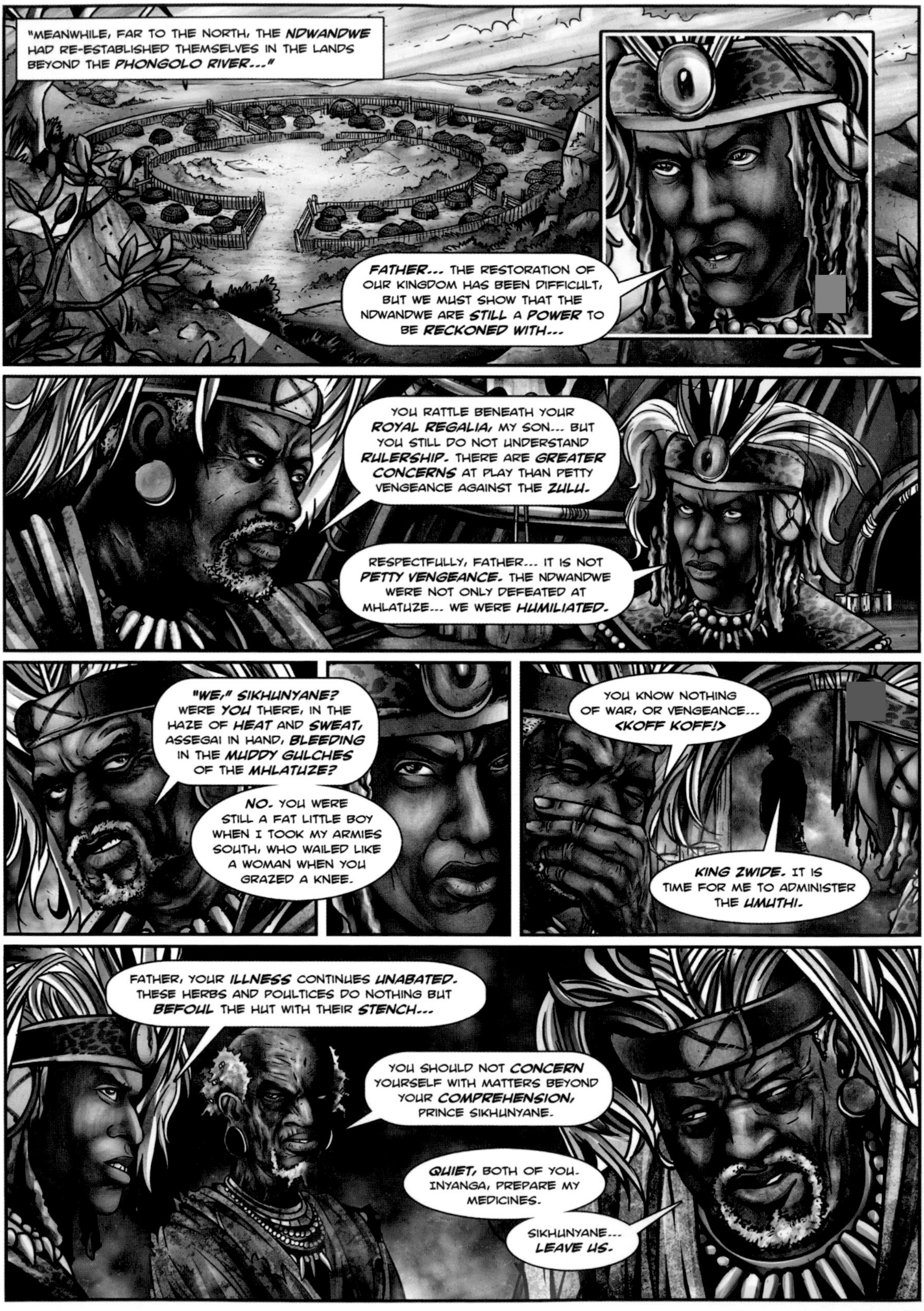

"MEANWHILE, FAR TO THE NORTH, THE NDWANDWE HAD RE-ESTABLISHED THEMSELVES IN THE LANDS BEYOND THE PHONGOLO RIVER..."
FATHER... THE RESTORATION OF OUR KINGDOM HAS BEEN DIFFICULT, BUT WE MUST SHOW THAT THE NDWANDWE ARE STILL A POWER TO BE RECKONED WITH...
YOU RATTLE BENEATH YOUR ROYAL REGALIA, MY SON... BUT YOU STILL DO NOT UNDERSTAND RULERSHIP. THERE ARE GREATER CONCERNS AT PLAY THAN PETTY VENGEANCE AGAINST THE ZULU.
RESPECTFULLY, FATHER... IT IS NOT PETTY VENGEANCE. THE NDWANDWE WERE NOT ONLY DEFEATED AT MHLATUZE... WE WERE HUMILIATED.
"WE," SIKHUNYANE? WERE YOU THERE, IN THE HAZE OF HEAT AND SWEAT, ASSEGAI IN HAND, BLEEDING IN THE MUDDY GULCHES OF THE MHLATUZE?
NO. YOU WERE STILL A FAT LITTLE BOY WHEN I TOOK MY ARMIES SOUTH, WHO WAILED LIKE A WOMAN WHEN YOU GRAZED A KNEE.
YOU KNOW NOTHING OF WAR, OR VENGEANCE... <KOFF KOFF!>
KING ZWIDE. IT IS TIME FOR ME TO ADMINISTER THE UMUTHI.
FATHER, YOUR ILLNESS CONTINUES UNABATED. THESE HERBS AND POULTICES DO NOTHING BUT BEFOUL THE HUT WITH THEIR STENCH...
YOU SHOULD NOT CONCERN YOURSELF WITH MATTERS BEYOND YOUR COMPREHENSION, PRINCE SIKHUNYANE.
QUIET, BOTH OF YOU. INYANGA, PREPARE MY MEDICINES.
SIKHUNYANE... LEAVE US.

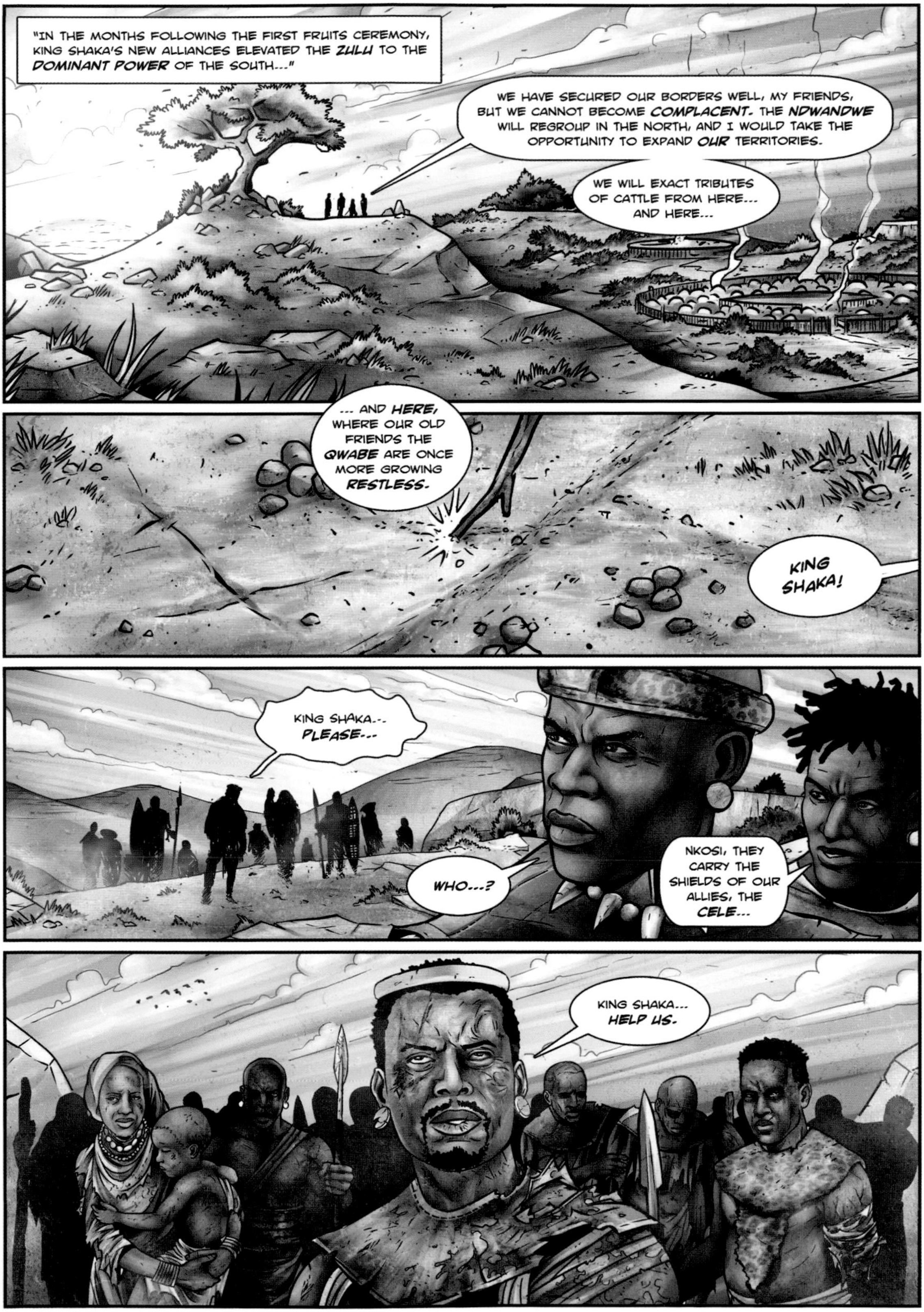
"IN THE MONTHS FOLLOWING THE FIRST FRUITS CEREMONY, KING SHAKA'S NEW ALLIANCES ELEVATED THE ZULU TO THE DOMINANT POWER OF THE SOUTH..."
WE HAVE SECURED OUR BORDERS WELL, MY FRIENDS, BUT WE CANNOT BECOME COMPLACENT. THE NDWANDWE WILL REGROUP IN THE NORTH, AND I WOULD TAKE THE OPPORTUNITY TO EXPAND OUR TERRITORIES.
WE WILL EXACT TRIBUTES OF CATTLE FROM HERE... AND HERE...
... AND HERE, WHERE OUR OLD FRIENDS THE QWABE ARE ONCE MORE GROWING RESTLESS.
KING SHAKA!
KING SHAKA... PLEASE...
WHO...?
NKOSI, THEY CARRY THE SHIELDS OF OUR ALLIES, THE CELE...
KING SHAKA... HELP US.

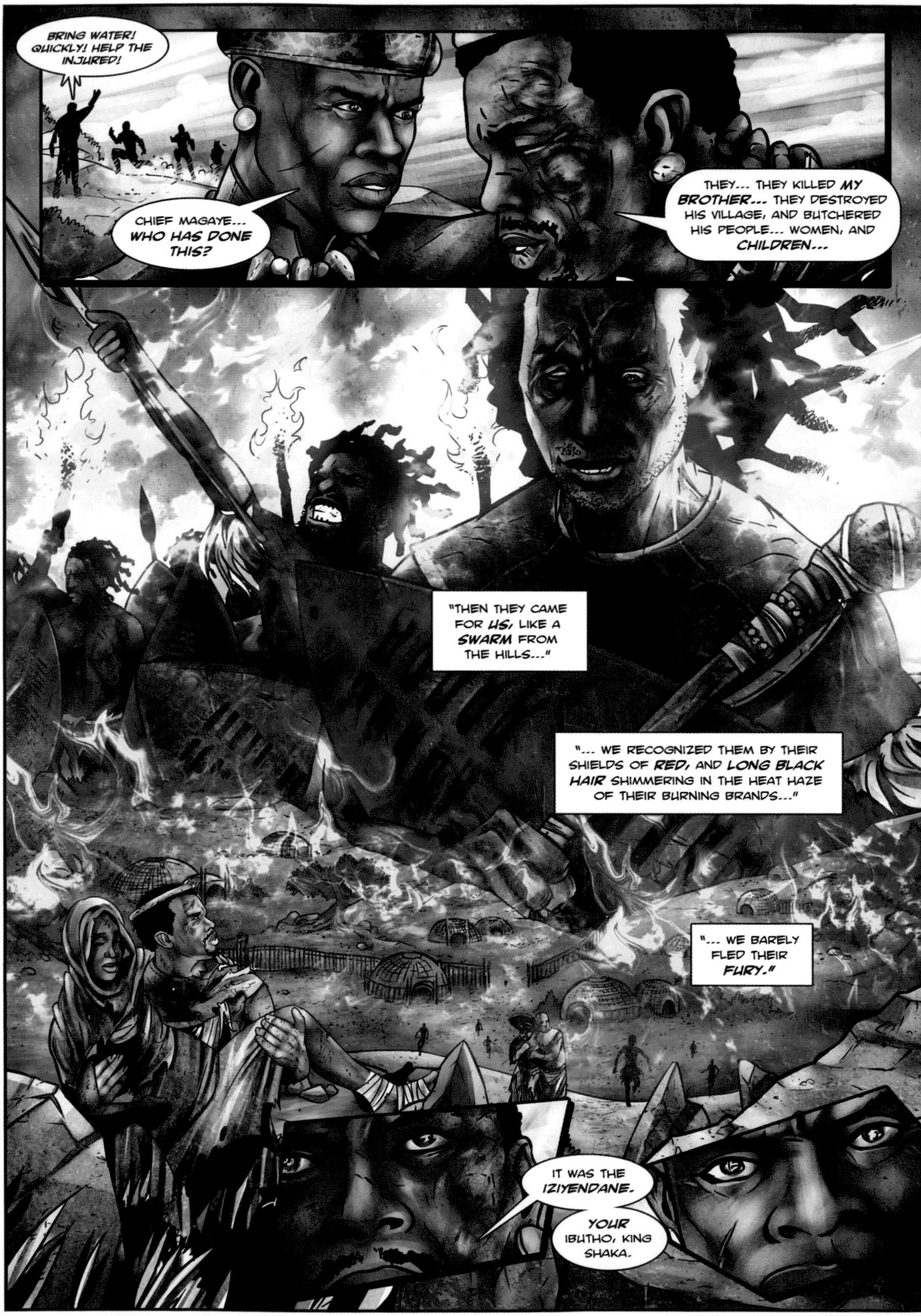
BRING WATER! QUICKLY! HELP THE INJURED!
CHIEF MAGAYE... WHO HAS DONE THIS?
THEY... THEY KILLED MY BROTHER... THEY DESTROYED HIS VILLAGE, AND BUTCHERED HIS PEOPLE... WOMEN, AND CHILDREN...
"THEN THEY CAME FOR US, LIKE A SWARM FROM THE HILLS..."
"... WE RECOGNIZED THEM BY THEIR SHIELDS OF RED, AND LONG BLACK HAIR SHIMMERING IN THE HEAT HAZE OF THEIR BURNING BRANDS..."
"... WE BARELY FLED THEIR FURY."
IT WAS THE IZIYENDANE.
YOUR IBUTHO, KING SHAKA.

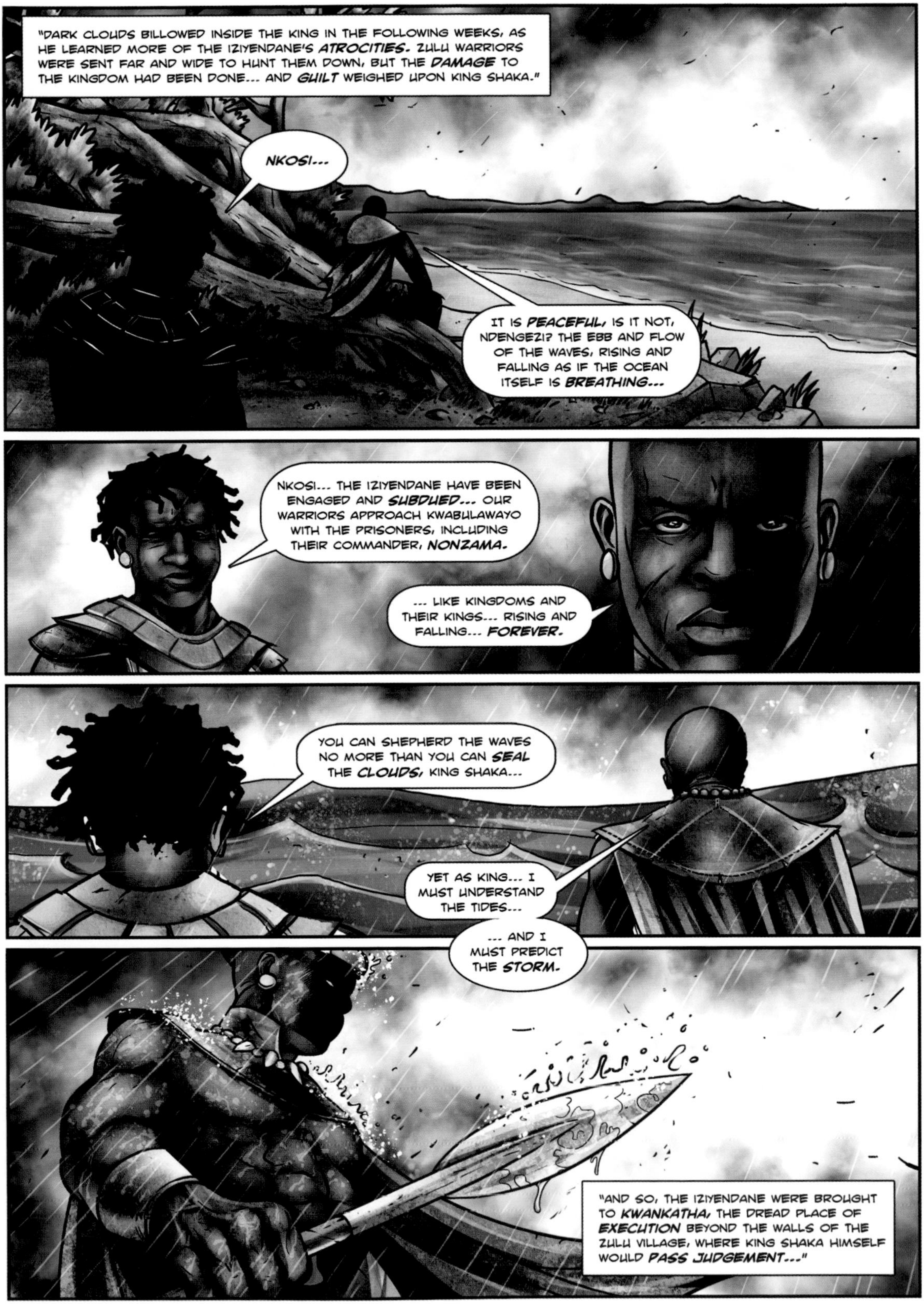
"DARK CLOUDS BILLOWED INSIDE THE KING IN THE FOLLOWING WEEKS, AS HE LEARNED MORE OF THE IZIYENDANE'S ATROCITIES. ZULU WARRIORS WERE SENT FAR AND WIDE TO HUNT THEM DOWN, BUT THE DAMAGE TO THE KINGDOM HAD BEEN DONE... AND GUILT WEIGHED UPON KING SHAKA."
NKOSI...
IT IS PEACEFUL, IS IT NOT, NDENGEZI? THE EBB AND FLOW OF THE WAVES, RISING AND FALLING AS IF THE OCEAN ITSELF IS BREATHING...
NKOSI... THE IZIYENDANE HAVE BEEN ENGAGED AND SUBDUED... OUR WARRIORS APPROACH KWABULAWAYO WITH THE PRISONERS, INCLUDING THEIR COMMANDER, NONZAMA.
... LIKE KINGDOMS AND THEIR KINGS... RISING AND FALLING... FOREVER.
YOU CAN SHEPHERD THE WAVES NO MORE THAN YOU CAN SEAL THE CLOUDS, KING SHAKA...
YET AS KING... I MUST UNDERSTAND THE TIDES...
... AND I MUST PREDICT THE STORM.
"AND SO, THE IZIYENDANE WERE BROUGHT TO KWANKATHA, THE DREAD PLACE OF EXECUTION BEYOND THE WALLS OF THE ZULU VILLAGE, WHERE KING SHAKA HIMSELF WOULD PASS JUDGEMENT..."

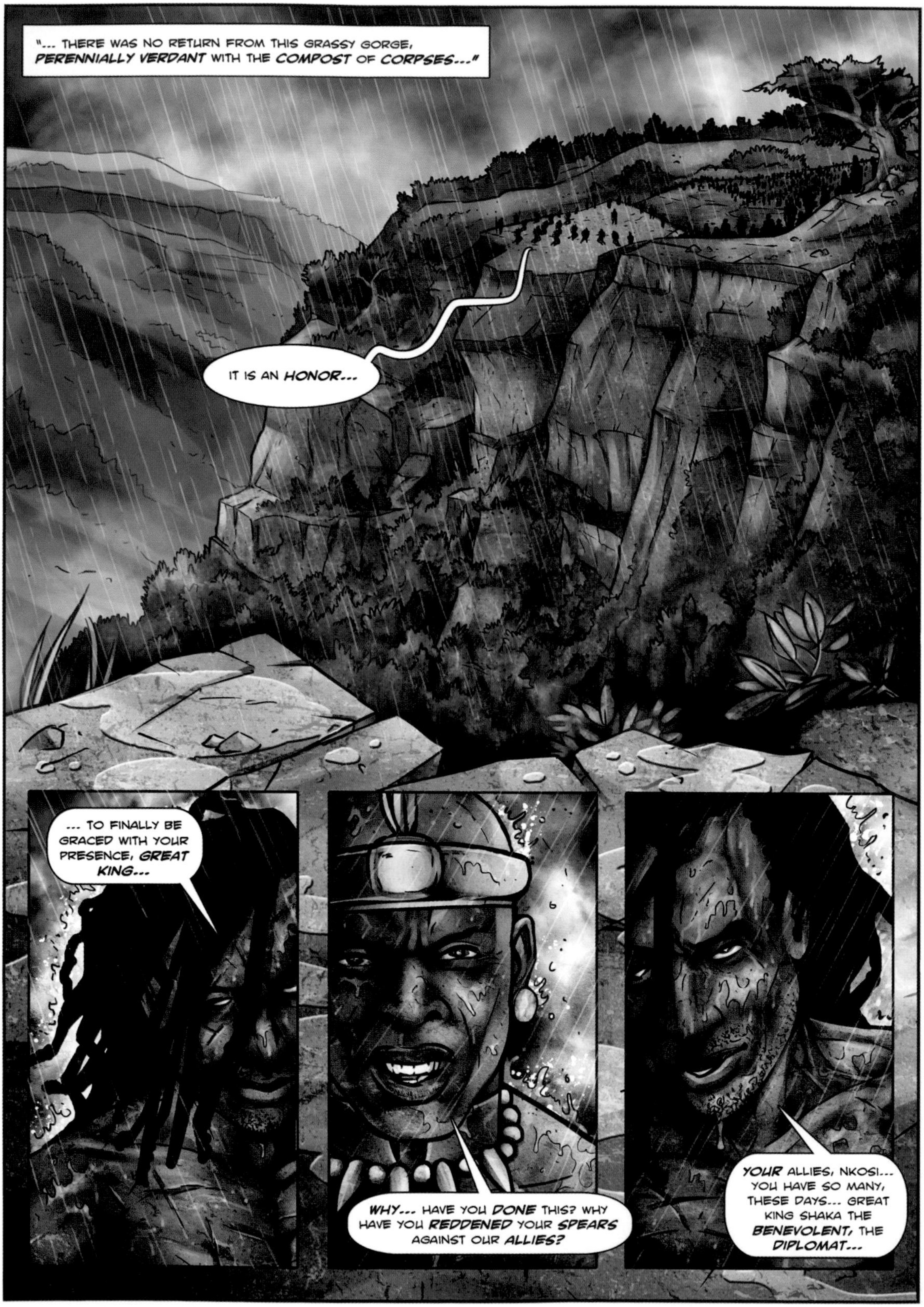
"... THERE WAS NO RETURN FROM THIS GRASSY GORGE, PERENNIALLY VERDANT WITH THE COMPOST OF CORPSES..."
IT IS AN HONOR...
... TO FINALLY BE GRACED WITH YOUR PRESENCE, GREAT KING...
WHY... HAVE YOU DONE THIS? WHY HAVE YOU REDDENED YOUR SPEARS AGAINST OUR ALLIES?
YOUR ALLIES, NKOSI... YOU HAVE SO MANY, THESE DAYS... GREAT KING SHAKA THE BENEVOLENT, THE DIPLOMAT...

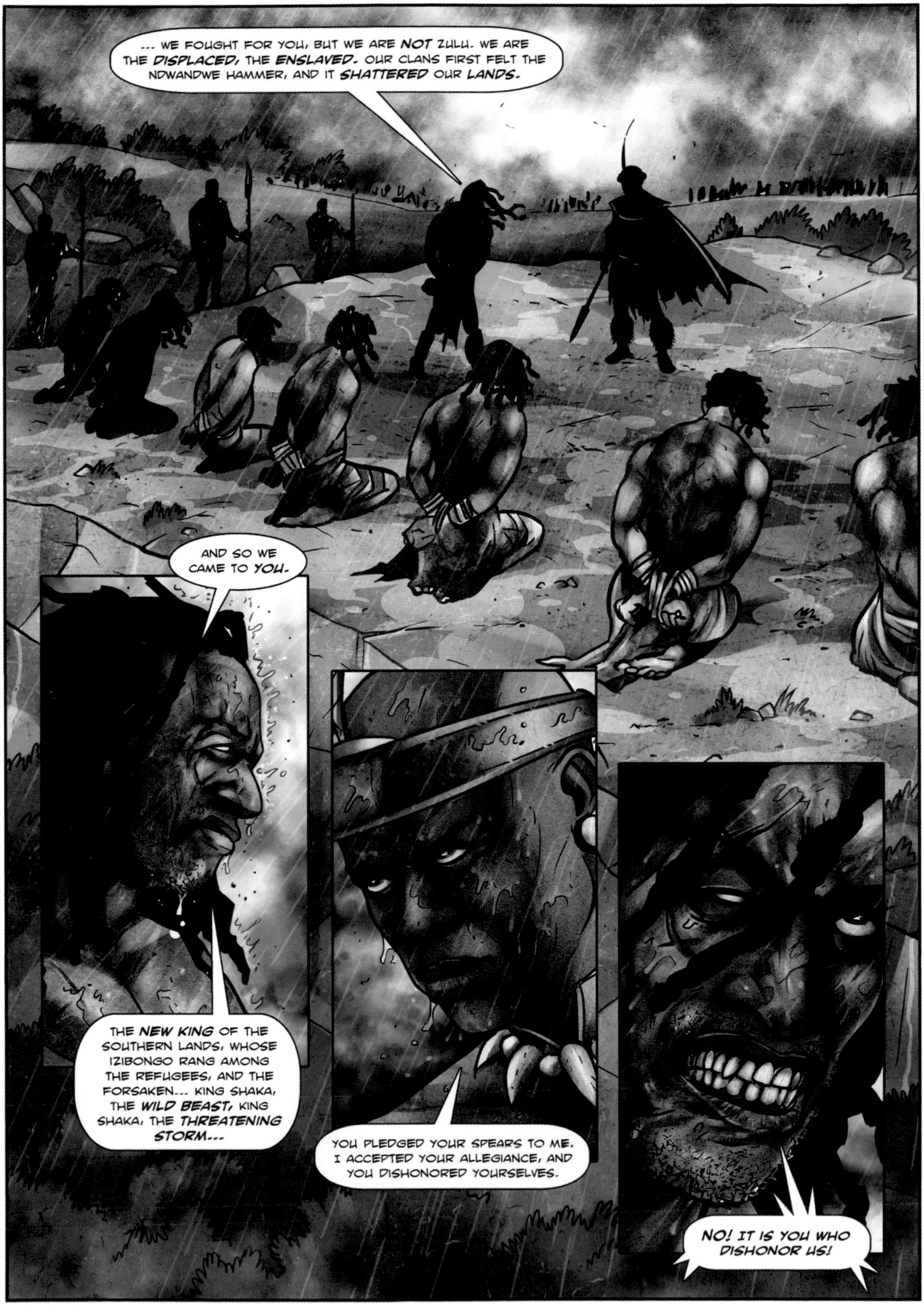
... WE FOUGHT FOR YOU, BUT WE ARE NOT ZULU. WE ARE THE DISPLACED, THE ENSLAVED. OUR CLANS FIRST FELT THE NDWANDWE HAMMER, AND IT SHATTERED OUR LANDS.
AND SO WE CAME TO YOU.
THE NEW KING OF THE SOUTHERN LANDS, WHOSE IZIBONGO RANG AMONG THE REFUGEES, AND THE FORSAKEN... KING SHAKA, THE WILD BEAST, KING SHAKA, THE THREATENING STORM...
YOU PLEDGED YOUR SPEARS TO ME. I ACCEPTED YOUR ALLEGIANCE, AND YOU DISHONORED YOURSELVES.
NO! IT IS YOU WHO DISHONOR US!

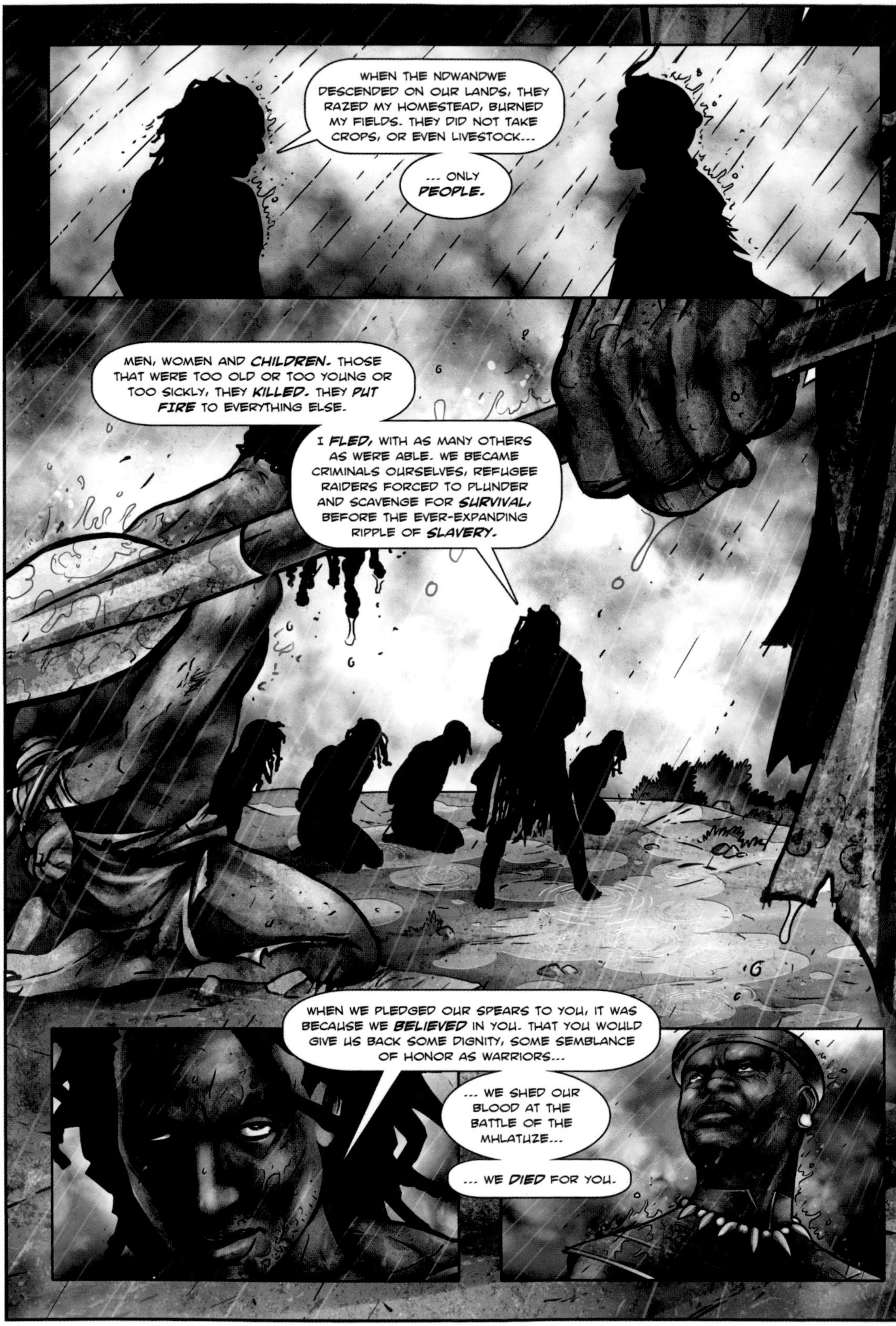
WHEN THE NDWANDWE DESCENDED ON OUR LANDS, THEY RAZED MY HOMESTEAD, BURNED MY FIELDS. THEY DID NOT TAKE CROPS, OR EVEN LIVESTOCK...
... ONLY PEOPLE.
MEN, WOMEN AND CHILDREN. THOSE THAT WERE TOO OLD OR TOO YOUNG OR TOO SICKLY, THEY KILLED. THEY PUT FIRE TO EVERYTHING ELSE.
I FLED, WITH AS MANY OTHERS AS WERE ABLE. WE BECAME CRIMINALS OURSELVES, REFUGEE RAIDERS FORCED TO PLUNDER AND SCAVENGE FOR SURVIVAL, BEFORE THE EVER-EXPANDING RIPPLE OF SLAVERY.
WHEN WE PLEDGED OUR SPEARS TO YOU, IT WAS BECAUSE WE BELIEVED IN YOU. THAT YOU WOULD GIVE US BACK SOME DIGNITY, SOME SEMBLANCE OF HONOR AS WARRIORS...
... WE SHED OUR BLOOD AT THE BATTLE OF THE MHLATUZE...
... WE DIED FOR YOU.

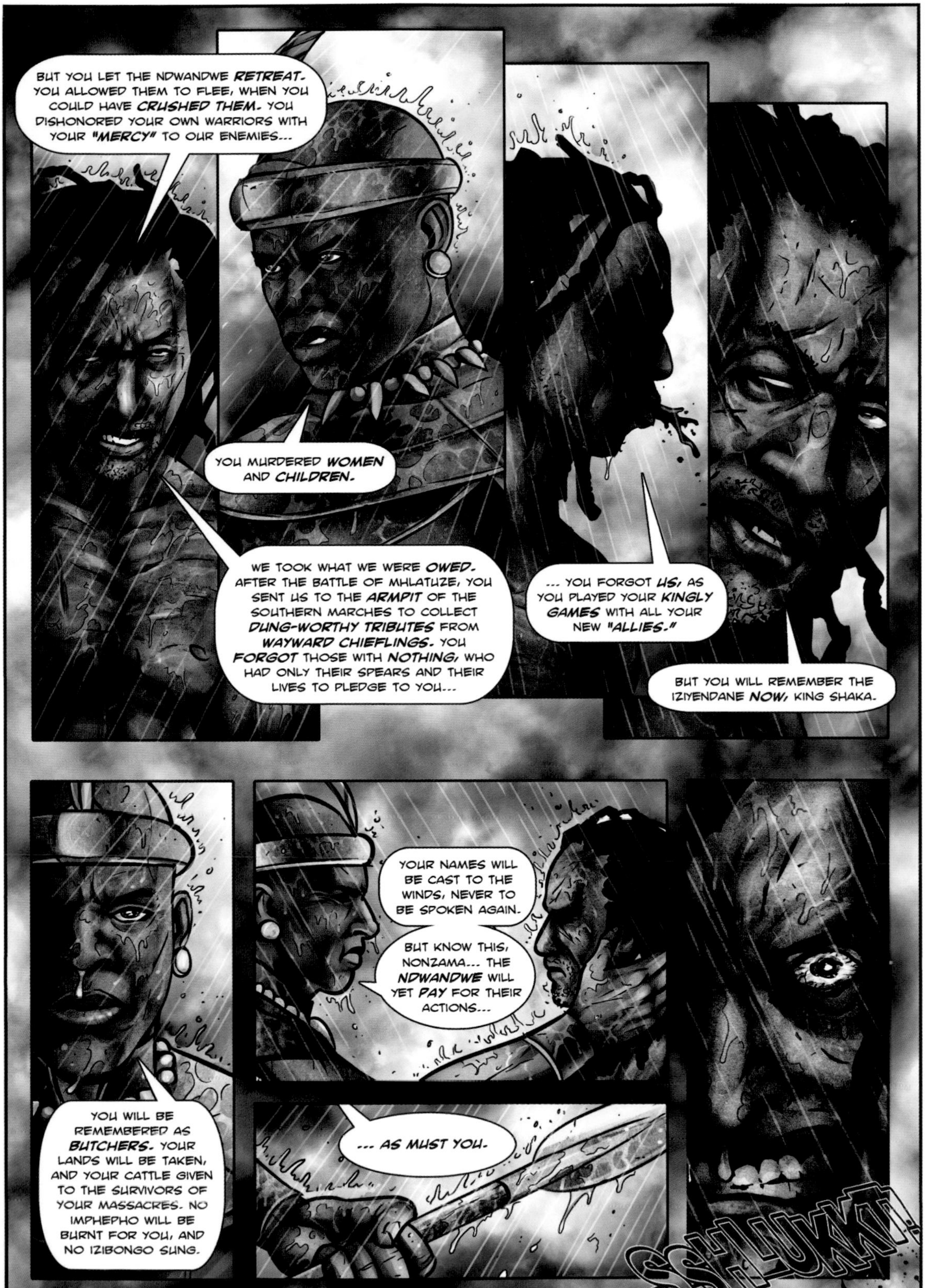
BUT YOU LET THE NDWANDWE RETREAT. YOU ALLOWED THEM TO FLEE, WHEN YOU COULD HAVE CRUSHED THEM. YOU DISHONORED YOUR OWN WARRIORS WITH YOUR "MERCY" TO OUR ENEMIES...
YOU MURDERED WOMEN AND CHILDREN.
WE TOOK WHAT WE WERE OWED. AFTER THE BATTLE OF MHLATUZE, YOU SENT US TO THE ARMPIT OF THE SOUTHERN MARCHES TO COLLECT DUNG-WORTHY TRIBUTES FROM WAYWARD CHIEFLINGS. YOU FORGOT THOSE WITH NOTHING, WHO HAD ONLY THEIR SPEARS AND THEIR LIVES TO PLEDGE TO YOU...
... YOU FORGOT US, AS YOU PLAYED YOUR KINGLY GAMES WITH ALL YOUR NEW "ALLIES."
BUT YOU WILL REMEMBER THE IZIYENDANE NOW, KING SHAKA.
YOUR NAMES WILL BE CAST TO THE WINDS, NEVER TO BE SPOKEN AGAIN.
BUT KNOW THIS, NONZAMA... THE NDWANDWE WILL YET PAY FOR THEIR ACTIONS...
YOU WILL BE REMEMBERED AS BUTCHERS. YOUR LANDS WILL BE TAKEN, AND YOUR CATTLE GIVEN TO THE SURVIVORS OF YOUR MASSACRES. NO IMPHEPHO WILL BE BURNT FOR YOU, AND NO IZIBONGO SUNG.
... AS MUST YOU.
SSHLUKK!

THE CENTER CANNOT HOLD, KING SHAKA. YOUR GRIP WILL TIGHTEN AND YOUR SPEAR WILL BREAK...

... WE ARE ONLY... THE FIRST... SPLINTER.

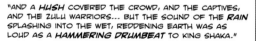

"AND A HUSH COVERED THE CROWD, AND THE CAPTIVES, AND THE ZULU WARRIORS... BUT THE SOUND OF THE RAIN SPLASHING INTO THE WET, REDDENING EARTH WAS AS LOUD AS A HAMMERING DRUMBEAT TO KING SHAKA."

"MANY OF THE IZIYENDANE WERE PUT TO DEATH IN THE DAYS THAT FOLLOWED, AND MANY MORE FLED TO ESCAPE KING SHAKA'S WRATH... BUT NONZAMA'S ACCUSATIONS HAD TAKEN INSIDIOUS ROOT IN THE KING'S MIND, TO SPROUT DARK WEEDS AND TANGLE HIS THOUGHTS IN DOUBT."

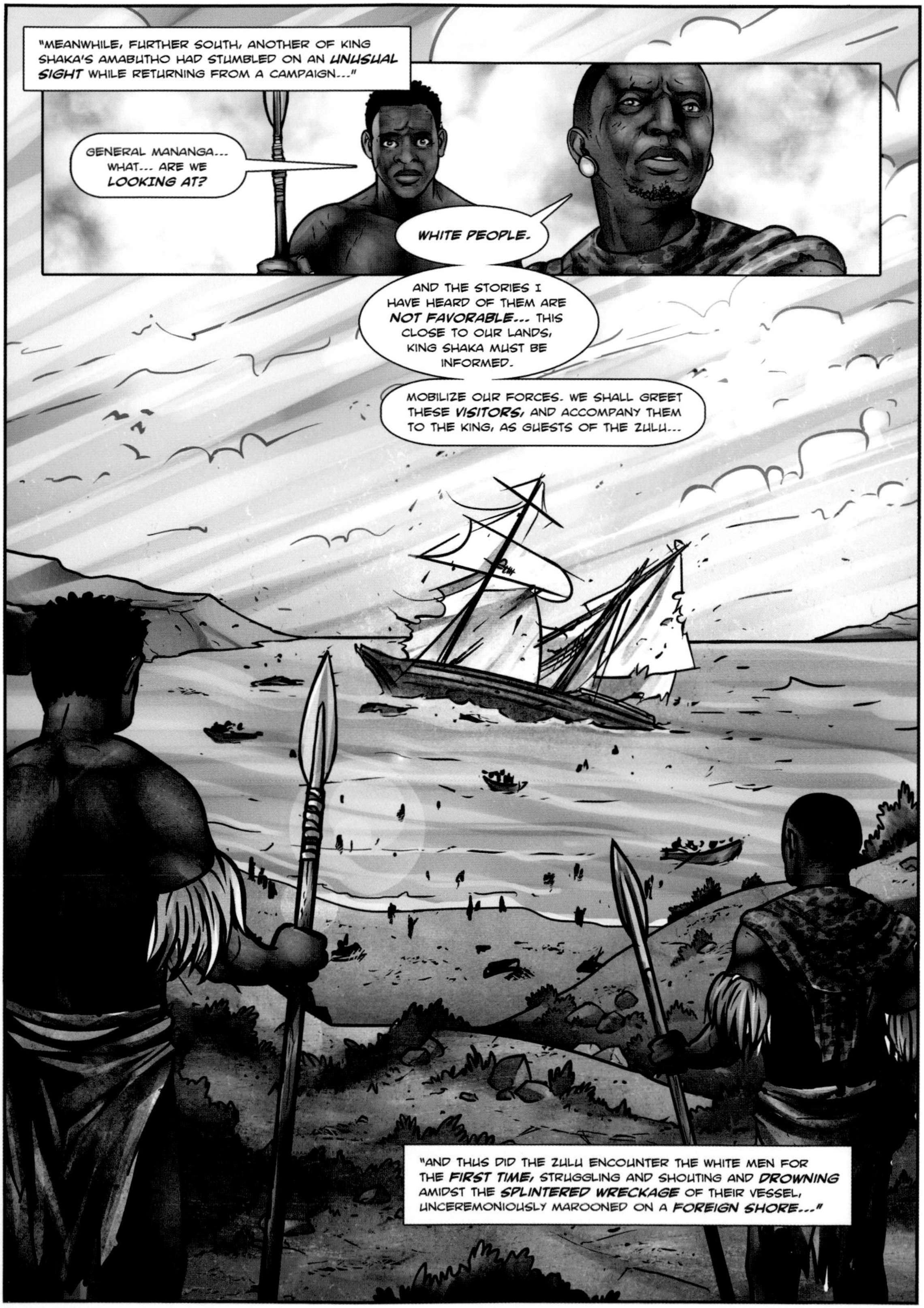
"MEANWHILE, FURTHER SOUTH, ANOTHER OF KING SHAKA'S AMABUTHO HAD STUMBLED ON AN UNUSUAL SIGHT WHILE RETURNING FROM A CAMPAIGN..."
GENERAL MANANGA... WHAT... ARE WE LOOKING AT?
WHITE PEOPLE.
AND THE STORIES I HAVE HEARD OF THEM ARE NOT FAVORABLE... THIS CLOSE TO OUR LANDS, KING SHAKA MUST BE INFORMED.
MOBILIZE OUR FORCES. WE SHALL GREET THESE VISITORS, AND ACCOMPANY THEM TO THE KING, AS GUESTS OF THE ZULU...
"AND THUS DID THE ZULU ENCOUNTER THE WHITE MEN FOR THE FIRST TIME, STRUGGLING AND SHOUTING AND DROWNING AMIDST THE SPLINTERED WRECKAGE OF THEIR VESSEL, UNCEREMONIOUSLY MAROONED ON A FOREIGN SHORE..."

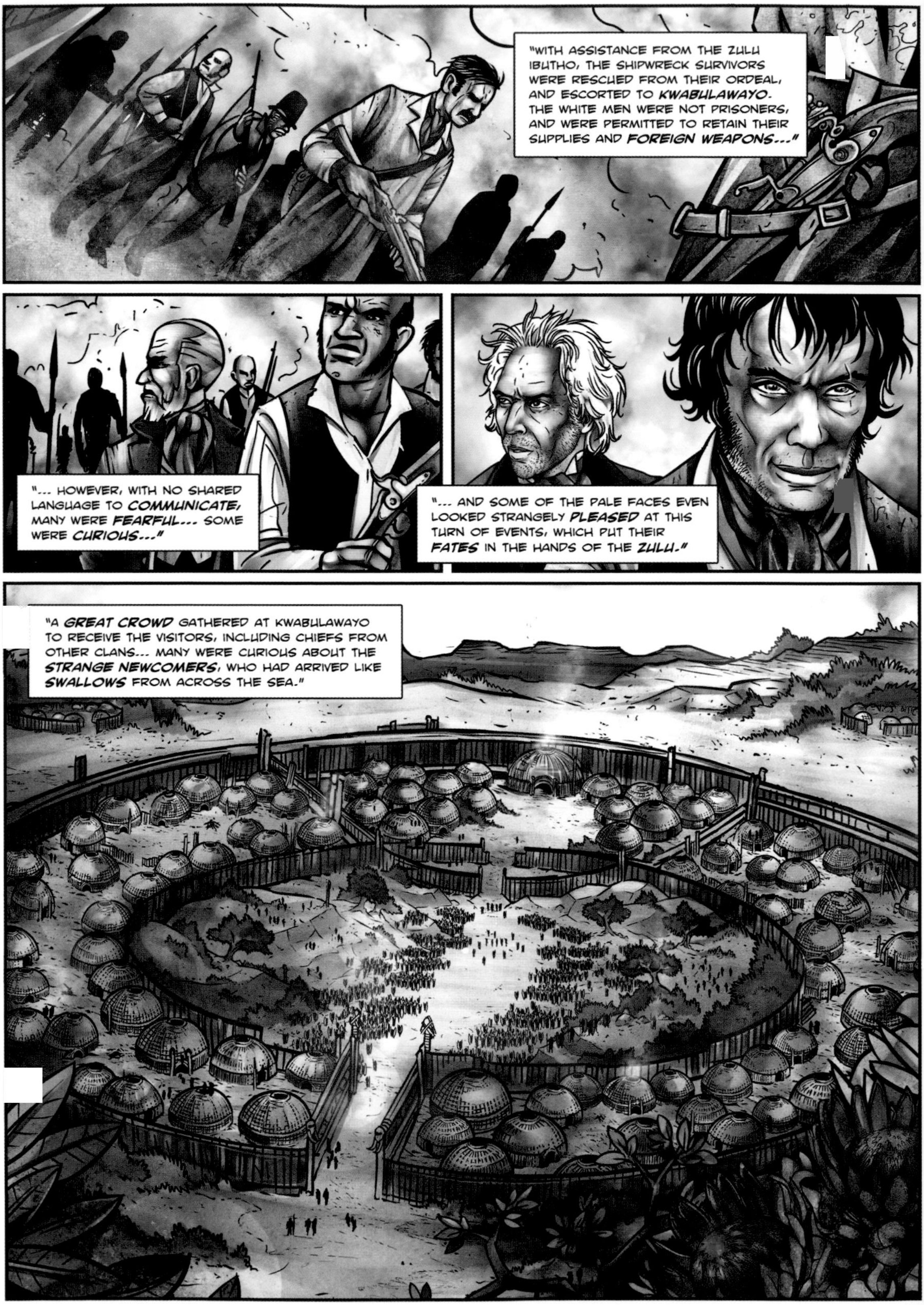
"WITH ASSISTANCE FROM THE ZULU IBUTHO, THE SHIPWRECK SURVIVORS WERE RESCUED FROM THEIR ORDEAL, AND ESCORTED TO KWABULAWAYO. THE WHITE MEN WERE NOT PRISONERS, AND WERE PERMITTED TO RETAIN THEIR SUPPLIES AND FOREIGN WEAPONS..."
"... HOWEVER, WITH NO SHARED LANGUAGE TO COMMUNICATE, MANY WERE FEARFUL... SOME WERE CURIOUS..."
"... AND SOME OF THE PALE FACES EVEN LOOKED STRANGELY PLEASED AT THIS TURN OF EVENTS, WHICH PUT THEIR FATES IN THE HANDS OF THE ZULU."
"A GREAT CROWD GATHERED AT KWABULAWAYO TO RECEIVE THE VISITORS, INCLUDING CHIEFS FROM OTHER CLANS... MANY WERE CURIOUS ABOUT THE STRANGE NEWCOMERS, WHO HAD ARRIVED LIKE SWALLOWS FROM ACROSS THE SEA."

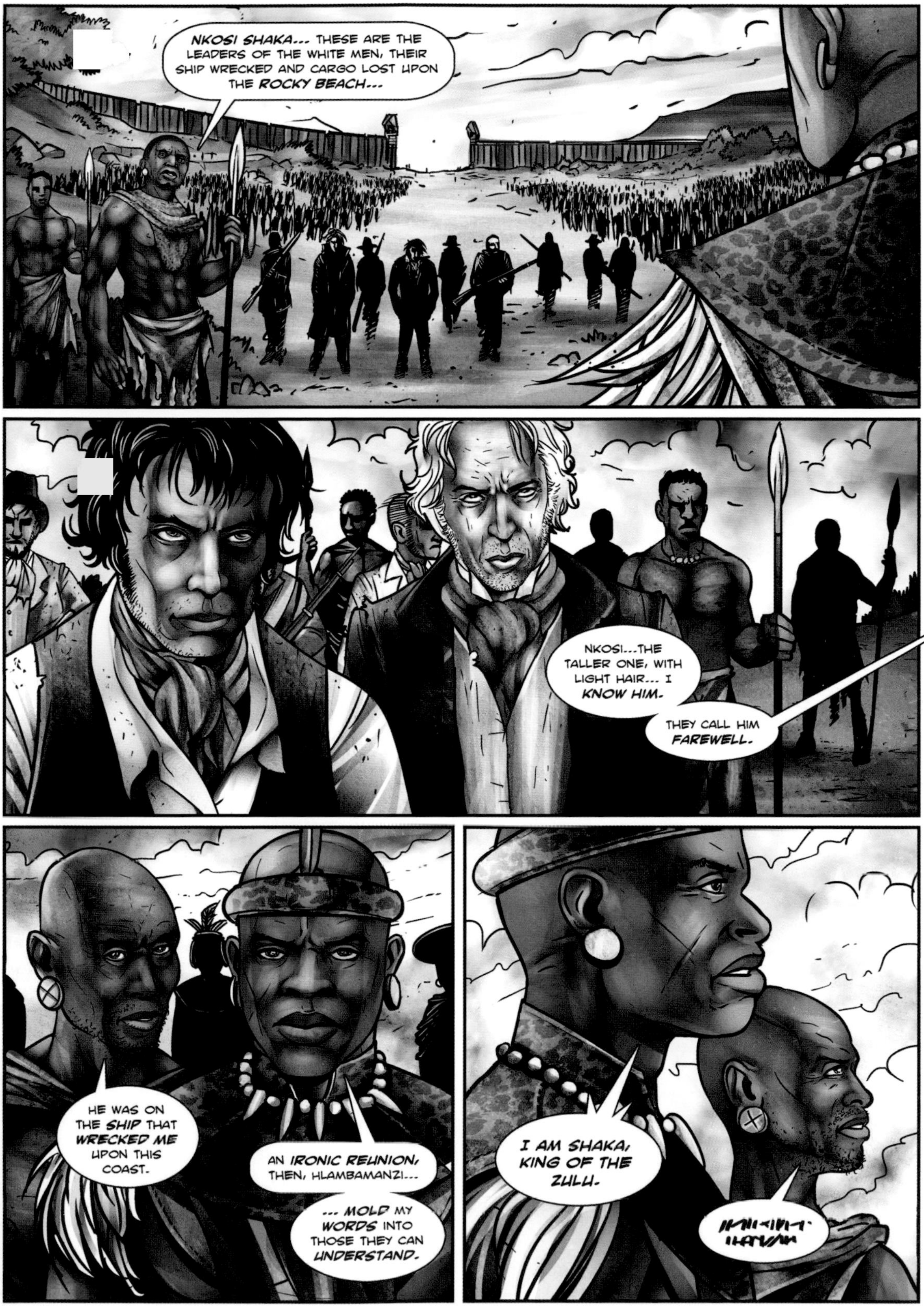

NKOSI SHAKA... THESE ARE THE LEADERS OF THE WHITE MEN, THEIR SHIP WRECKED AND CARGO LOST UPON THE ROCKY BEACH...
NKOSI...THE TALLER ONE, WITH LIGHT HAIR... I KNOW HIM.
THEY CALL HIM FAREWELL.
HE WAS ON THE SHIP THAT WRECKED ME UPON THIS COAST.
AN IRONIC REUNION, THEN, HLAMBAMANZI...
... MOLD MY WORDS INTO THOSE THEY CAN UNDERSTAND.
I AM SHAKA, KING OF THE ZULU.

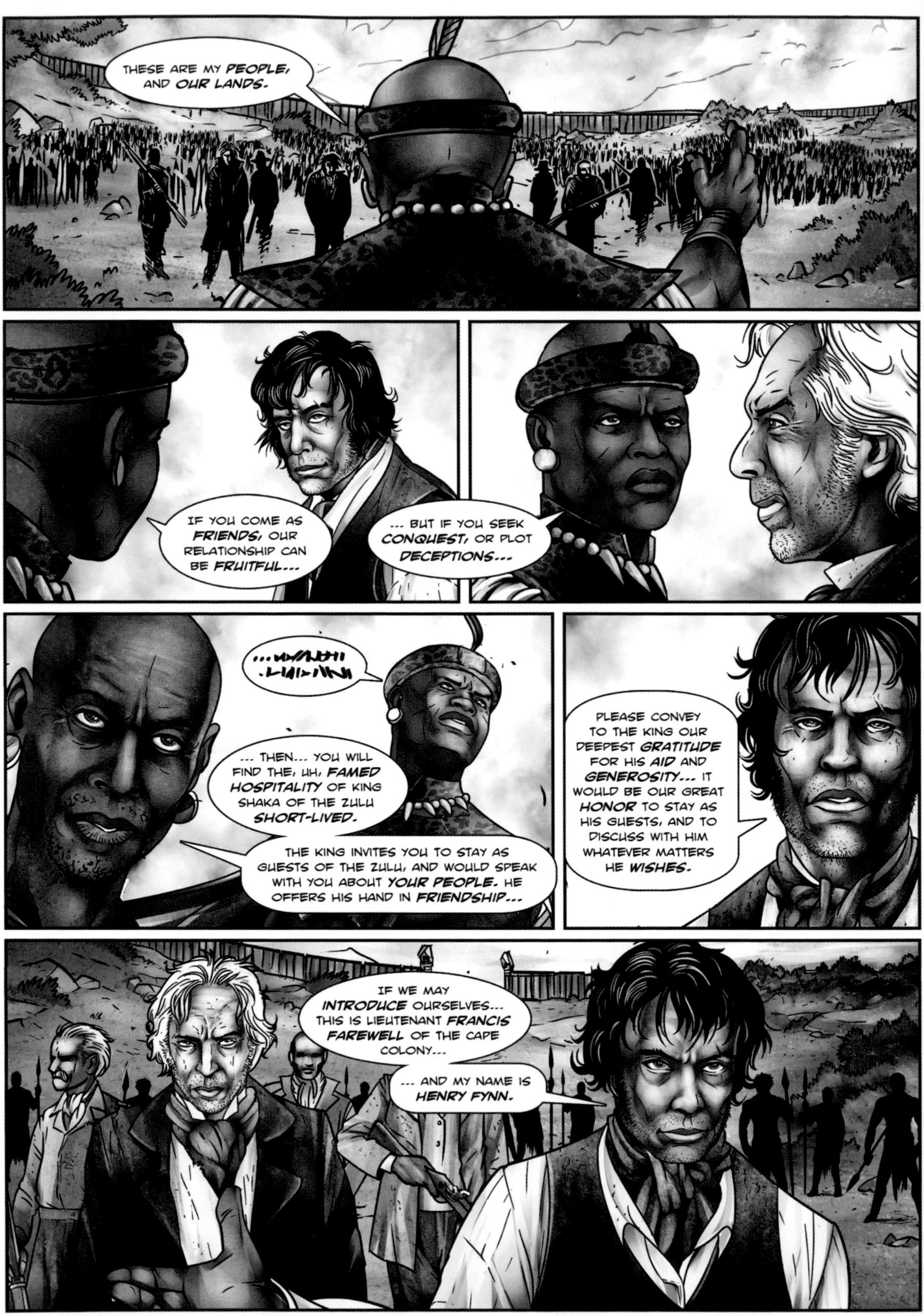
THESE ARE MY PEOPLE, AND OUR LANDS.
IF YOU COME AS FRIENDS, OUR RELATIONSHIP CAN BE FRUITFUL...
... BUT IF YOU SEEK CONQUEST, OR PLOT DECEPTIONS...
... THEN... YOU WILL FIND THE, UH, FAMED HOSPITALITY OF KING SHAKA OF THE ZULU SHORT-LIVED.
THE KING INVITES YOU TO STAY AS GUESTS OF THE ZULU, AND WOULD SPEAK WITH YOU ABOUT YOUR PEOPLE. HE OFFERS HIS HAND IN FRIENDSHIP...
PLEASE CONVEY TO THE KING OUR DEEPEST GRATITUDE FOR HIS AID AND GENEROSITY... IT WOULD BE OUR GREAT HONOR TO STAY AS HIS GUESTS, AND TO DISCUSS WITH HIM WHATEVER MATTERS HE WISHES.
IF WE MAY INTRODUCE OURSELVES... THIS IS LIEUTENANT FRANCIS FAREWELL OF THE CAPE COLONY...
... AND MY NAME IS HENRY FYNN.

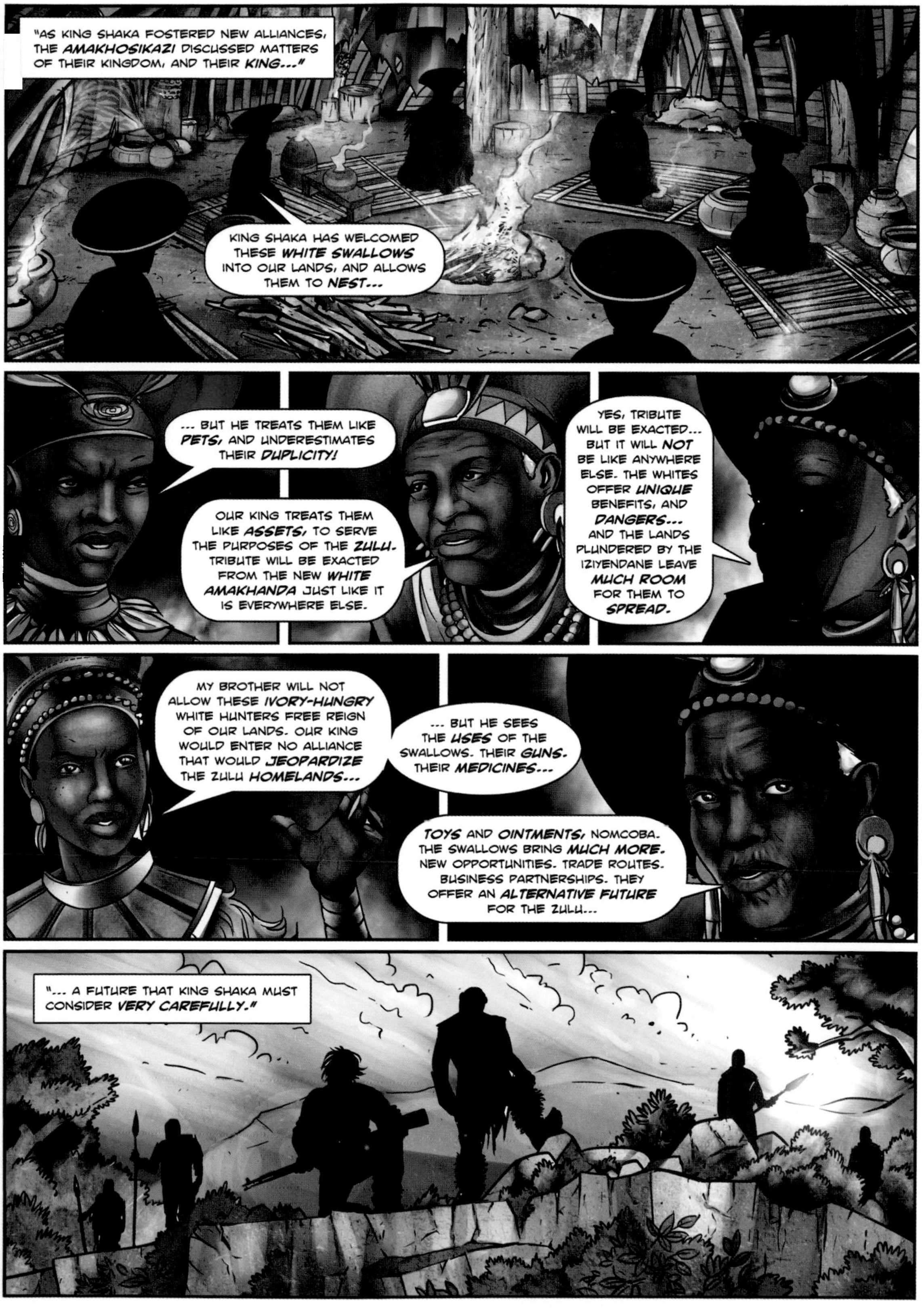
"AS KING SHAKA FOSTERED NEW ALLIANCES, THE AMAKHOSIKAZI DISCUSSED MATTERS OF THEIR KINGDOM, AND THEIR KING..."
KING SHAKA HAS WELCOMED THESE WHITE SWALLOWS INTO OUR LANDS, AND ALLOWS THEM TO NEST...
... BUT HE TREATS THEM LIKE PETS, AND UNDERESTIMATES THEIR DUPLICITY!
OUR KING TREATS THEM LIKE ASSETS, TO SERVE THE PURPOSES OF THE ZULU. TRIBUTE WILL BE EXACTED FROM THE NEW WHITE AMAKHANDA JUST LIKE IT IS EVERYWHERE ELSE.
YES, TRIBUTE WILL BE EXACTED... BUT IT WILL NOT BE LIKE ANYWHERE ELSE. THE WHITES OFFER UNIQUE BENEFITS, AND DANGERS... AND THE LANDS PLUNDERED BY THE IZIYENDANE LEAVE MUCH ROOM FOR THEM TO SPREAD.
MY BROTHER WILL NOT ALLOW THESE IVORY-HUNGRY WHITE HUNTERS FREE REIGN OF OUR LANDS. OUR KING WOULD ENTER NO ALLIANCE THAT WOULD JEOPARDIZE THE ZULU HOMELANDS...
... BUT HE SEES THE USES OF THE SWALLOWS. THEIR GUNS. THEIR MEDICINES...
TOYS AND OINTMENTS, NOMCOBA. THE SWALLOWS BRING MUCH MORE. NEW OPPORTUNITIES. TRADE ROUTES. BUSINESS PARTNERSHIPS. THEY OFFER AN ALTERNATIVE FUTURE FOR THE ZULU...
"... A FUTURE THAT KING SHAKA MUST CONSIDER VERY CAREFULLY."

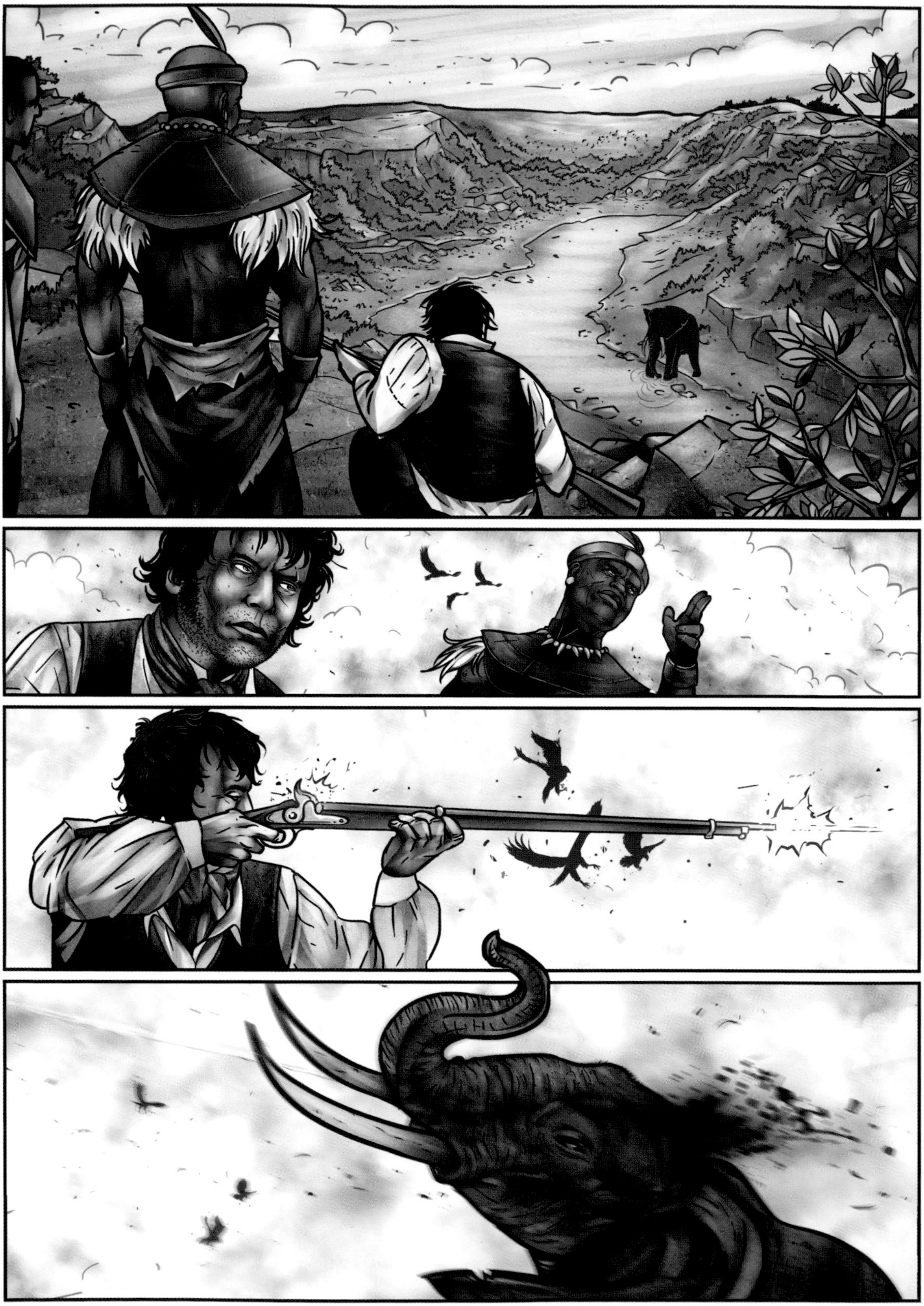

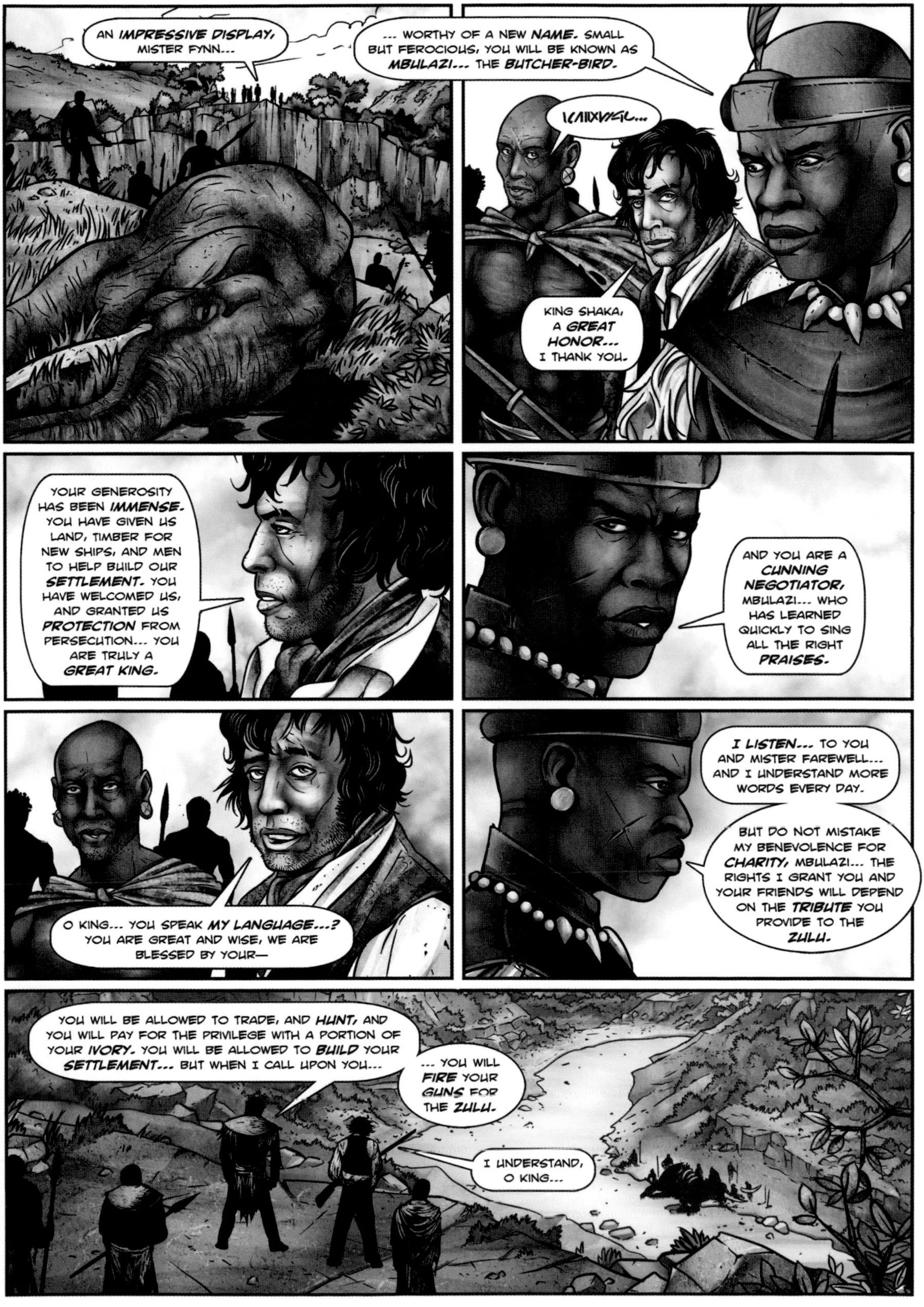
AN IMPRESSIVE DISPLAY, MISTER FYNN...
... WORTHY OF A NEW NAME. SMALL BUT FEROCIOUS, YOU WILL BE KNOWN AS MBULAZI... THE BUTCHER-BIRD.
KING SHAKA, A GREAT HONOR... I THANK YOU.
YOUR GENEROSITY HAS BEEN IMMENSE. YOU HAVE GIVEN US LAND, TIMBER FOR NEW SHIPS, AND MEN TO HELP BUILD OUR SETTLEMENT. YOU HAVE WELCOMED US, AND GRANTED US PROTECTION FROM PERSECUTION... YOU ARE TRULY A GREAT KING.
AND YOU ARE A CUNNING NEGOTIATOR, MBULAZI... WHO HAS LEARNED QUICKLY TO SING ALL THE RIGHT PRAISES.
O KING... YOU SPEAK MY LANGUAGE...? YOU ARE GREAT AND WISE, WE ARE BLESSED BY YOUR—
I LISTEN... TO YOU AND MISTER FAREWELL... AND I UNDERSTAND MORE WORDS EVERY DAY.
BUT DO NOT MISTAKE MY BENEVOLENCE FOR CHARITY, MBULAZI... THE RIGHTS I GRANT YOU AND YOUR FRIENDS WILL DEPEND ON THE TRIBUTE YOU PROVIDE TO THE ZULU.
YOU WILL BE ALLOWED TO TRADE, AND HUNT, AND YOU WILL PAY FOR THE PRIVILEGE WITH A PORTION OF YOUR IVORY. YOU WILL BE ALLOWED TO BUILD YOUR SETTLEMENT... BUT WHEN I CALL UPON YOU...
... YOU WILL FIRE YOUR GUNS FOR THE ZULU.
I UNDERSTAND, O KING...

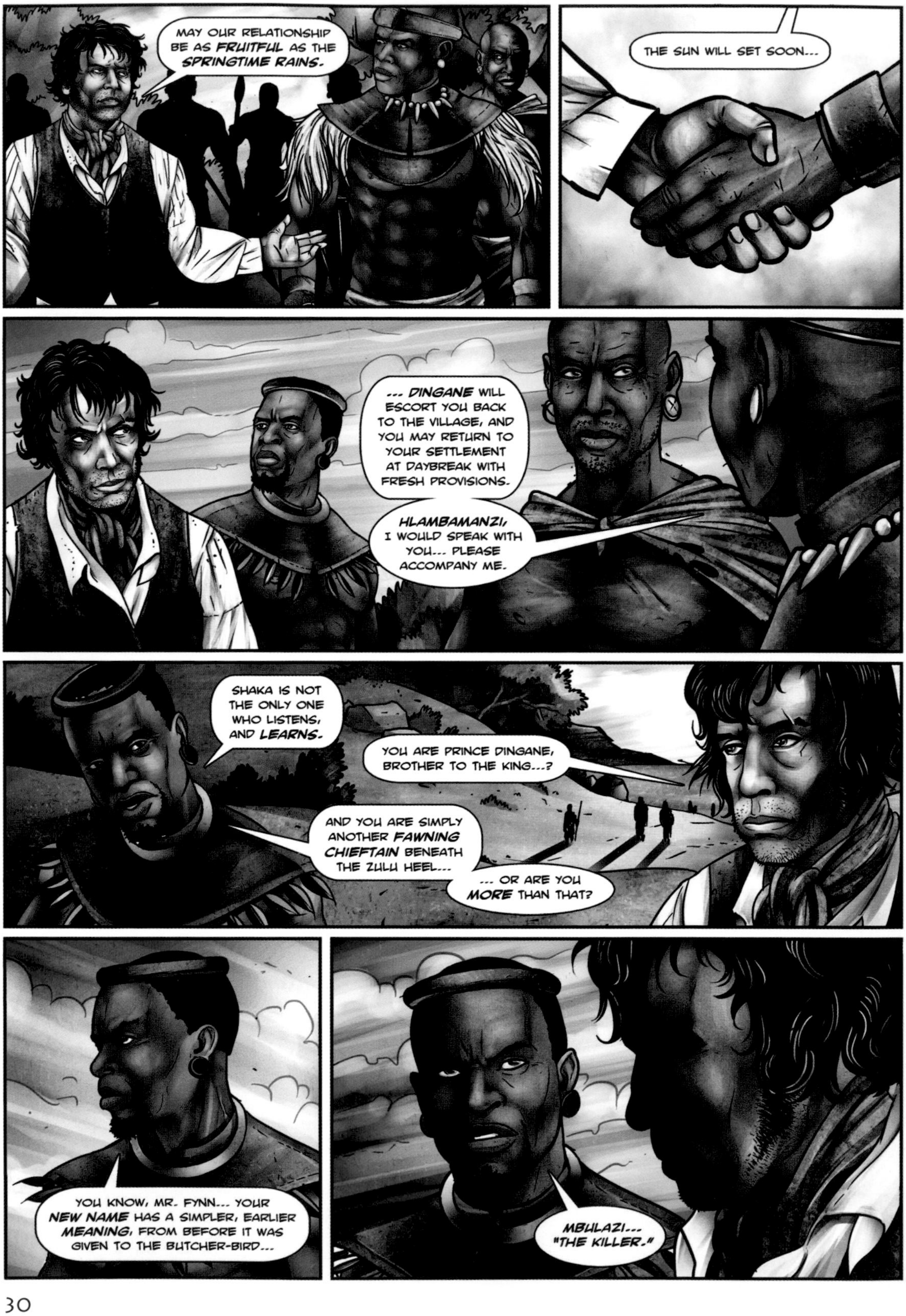
MAY OUR RELATIONSHIP BE AS FRUITFUL AS THE SPRINGTIME RAINS.
THE SUN WILL SET SOON...
... DINGANE WILL ESCORT YOU BACK TO THE VILLAGE, AND YOU MAY RETURN TO YOUR SETTLEMENT AT DAYBREAK WITH FRESH PROVISIONS.
HLAMBAMANZI, I WOULD SPEAK WITH YOU... PLEASE ACCOMPANY ME.
SHAKA IS NOT THE ONLY ONE WHO LISTENS, AND LEARNS.
YOU ARE PRINCE DINGANE, BROTHER TO THE KING...?
AND YOU ARE SIMPLY ANOTHER FAWNING CHIEFTAIN BENEATH THE ZULU HEEL...
... OR ARE YOU MORE THAN THAT?
YOU KNOW, MR. FYNN... YOUR NEW NAME HAS A SIMPLER, EARLIER MEANING, FROM BEFORE IT WAS GIVEN TO THE BUTCHER-BIRD...
MBULAZI... "THE KILLER."

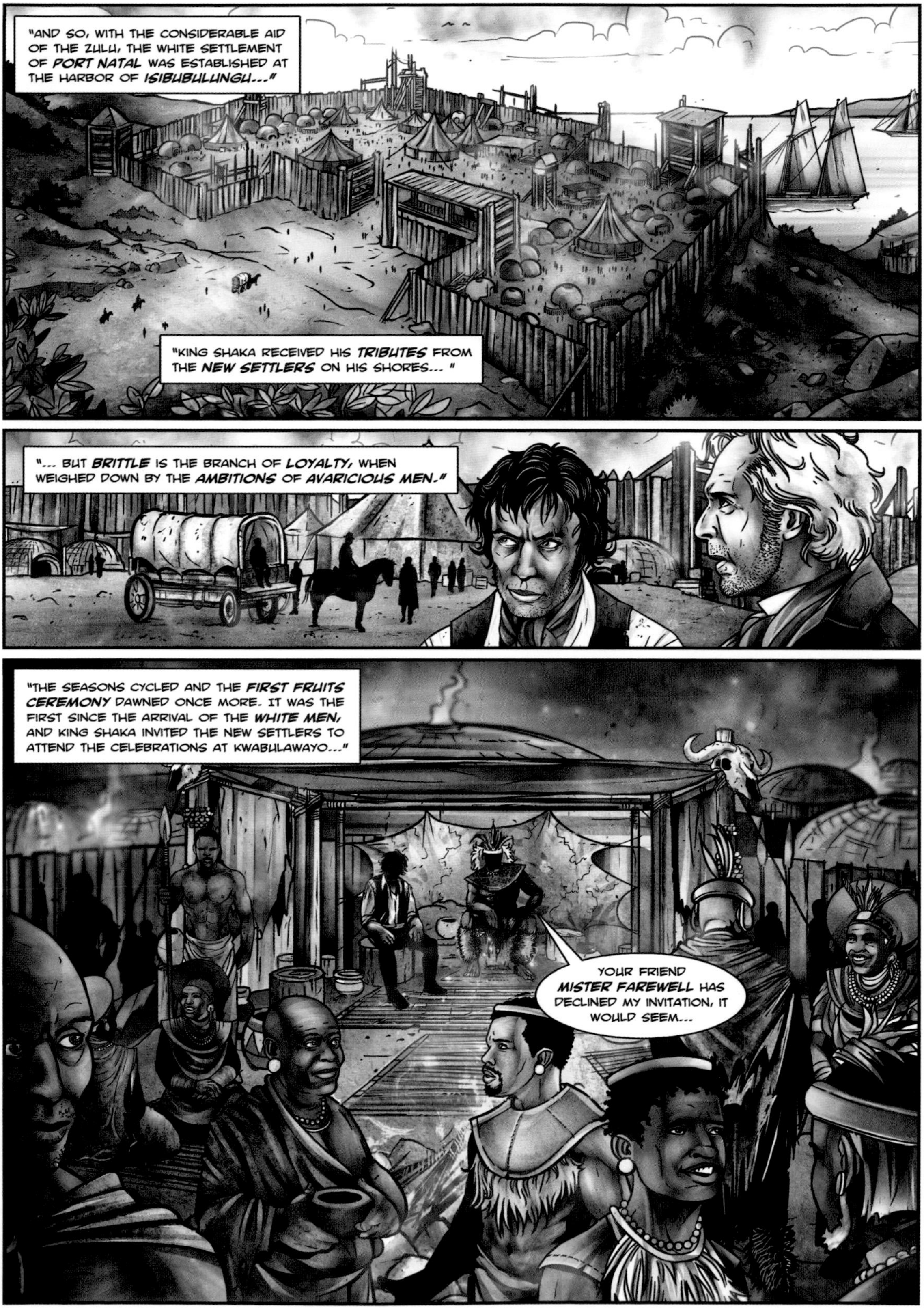
"AND SO, WITH THE CONSIDERABLE AID OF THE ZULU, THE WHITE SETTLEMENT OF PORT NATAL WAS ESTABLISHED AT THE HARBOR OF ISIBUBULUNGU..."
"KING SHAKA RECEIVED HIS TRIBUTES FROM THE NEW SETTLERS ON HIS SHORES..."
"... BUT BRITTLE IS THE BRANCH OF LOYALTY, WHEN WEIGHED DOWN BY THE AMBITIONS OF AVARICIOUS MEN."
"THE SEASONS CYCLED AND THE FIRST FRUITS CEREMONY DAWNED ONCE MORE. IT WAS THE FIRST SINCE THE ARRIVAL OF THE WHITE MEN, AND KING SHAKA INVITED THE NEW SETTLERS TO ATTEND THE CELEBRATIONS AT KWABULAWAYO..."
YOUR FRIEND MISTER FAREWELL HAS DECLINED MY INVITATION, IT WOULD SEEM...

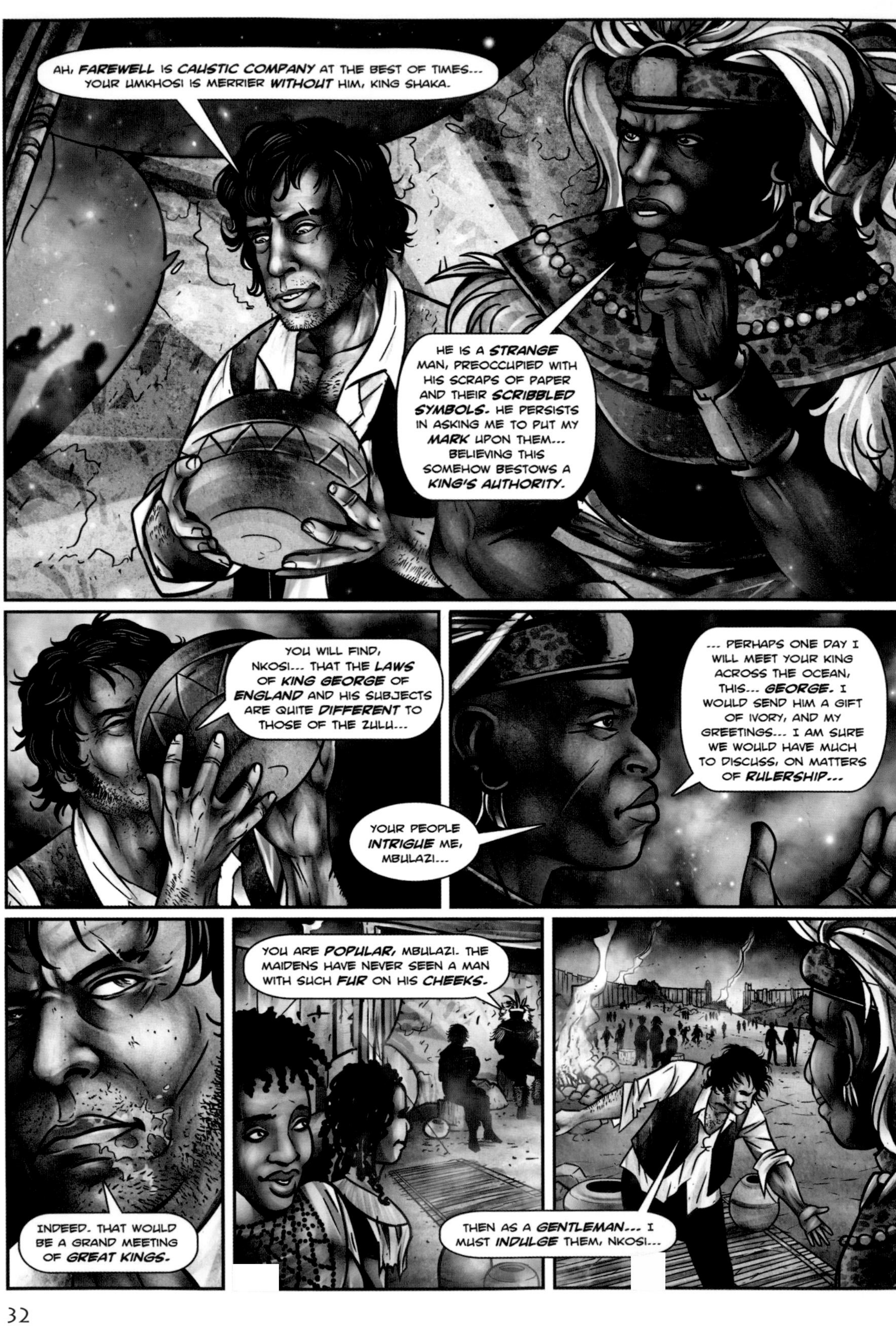

AH, FAREWELL IS CAUSTIC COMPANY AT THE BEST OF TIMES... YOUR UMKHOSI IS MERRIER WITHOUT HIM, KING SHAKA.
HE IS A STRANGE MAN, PREOCCUPIED WITH HIS SCRAPS OF PAPER AND THEIR SCRIBBLED SYMBOLS. HE PERSISTS IN ASKING ME TO PUT MY MARK UPON THEM... BELIEVING THIS SOMEHOW BESTOWS A KING'S AUTHORITY.
YOU WILL FIND, NKOSI... THAT THE LAWS OF KING GEORGE OF ENGLAND AND HIS SUBJECTS ARE QUITE DIFFERENT TO THOSE OF THE ZULU...
YOUR PEOPLE INTRIGUE ME, MBULAZI...
... PERHAPS ONE DAY I WILL MEET YOUR KING ACROSS THE OCEAN, THIS... GEORGE. I WOULD SEND HIM A GIFT OF IVORY, AND MY GREETINGS... I AM SURE WE WOULD HAVE MUCH TO DISCUSS, ON MATTERS OF RULERSHIP...
INDEED. THAT WOULD BE A GRAND MEETING OF GREAT KINGS.
YOU ARE POPULAR, MBULAZI. THE MAIDENS HAVE NEVER SEEN A MAN WITH SUCH FUR ON HIS CHEEKS.
THEN AS A GENTLEMAN... I MUST INDULGE THEM, NKOSI...

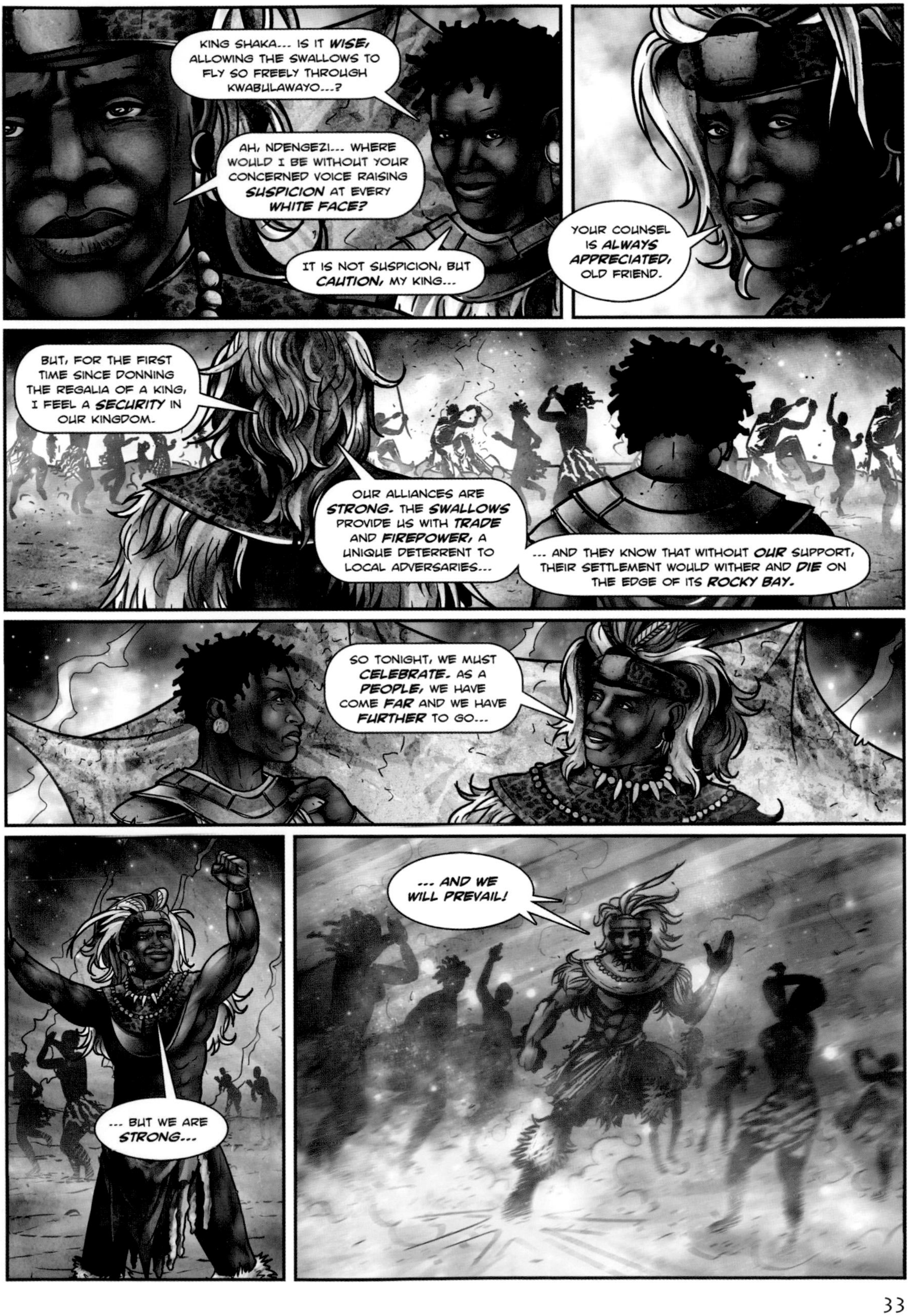
KING SHAKA... IS IT WISE, ALLOWING THE SWALLOWS TO FLY SO FREELY THROUGH KWABULAWAYO...?
AH, NDENGEZI... WHERE WOULD I BE WITHOUT YOUR CONCERNED VOICE RAISING SUSPICION AT EVERY WHITE FACE?
IT IS NOT SUSPICION, BUT CAUTION, MY KING...
YOUR COUNSEL IS ALWAYS APPRECIATED, OLD FRIEND.
BUT, FOR THE FIRST TIME SINCE DONNING THE REGALIA OF A KING, I FEEL A SECURITY IN OUR KINGDOM.
OUR ALLIANCES ARE STRONG. THE SWALLOWS PROVIDE US WITH TRADE AND FIREPOWER, A UNIQUE DETERRENT TO LOCAL ADVERSARIES...
... AND THEY KNOW THAT WITHOUT OUR SUPPORT, THEIR SETTLEMENT WOULD WITHER AND DIE ON THE EDGE OF ITS ROCKY BAY.
SO TONIGHT, WE MUST CELEBRATE. AS A PEOPLE, WE HAVE COME FAR AND WE HAVE FURTHER TO GO...
... BUT WE ARE STRONG...
... AND WE WILL PREVAIL!

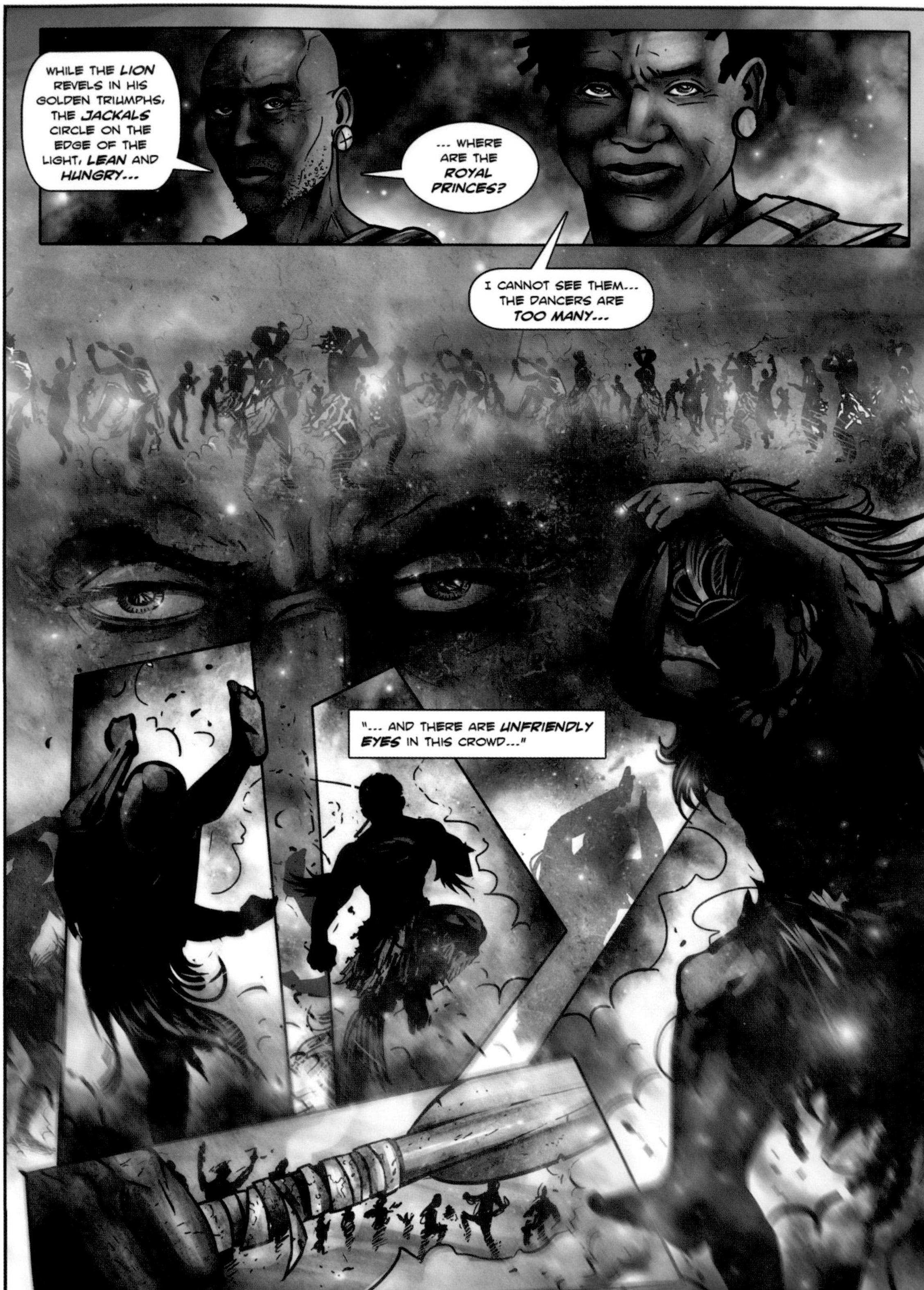
WHILE THE LION REVELS IN HIS GOLDEN TRIUMPHS, THE JACKALS CIRCLE ON THE EDGE OF THE LIGHT, LEAN AND HUNGRY...
... WHERE ARE THE ROYAL PRINCES?
I CANNOT SEE THEM... THE DANCERS ARE TOO MANY...
"... AND THERE ARE UNFRIENDLY EYES IN THIS CROWD..."

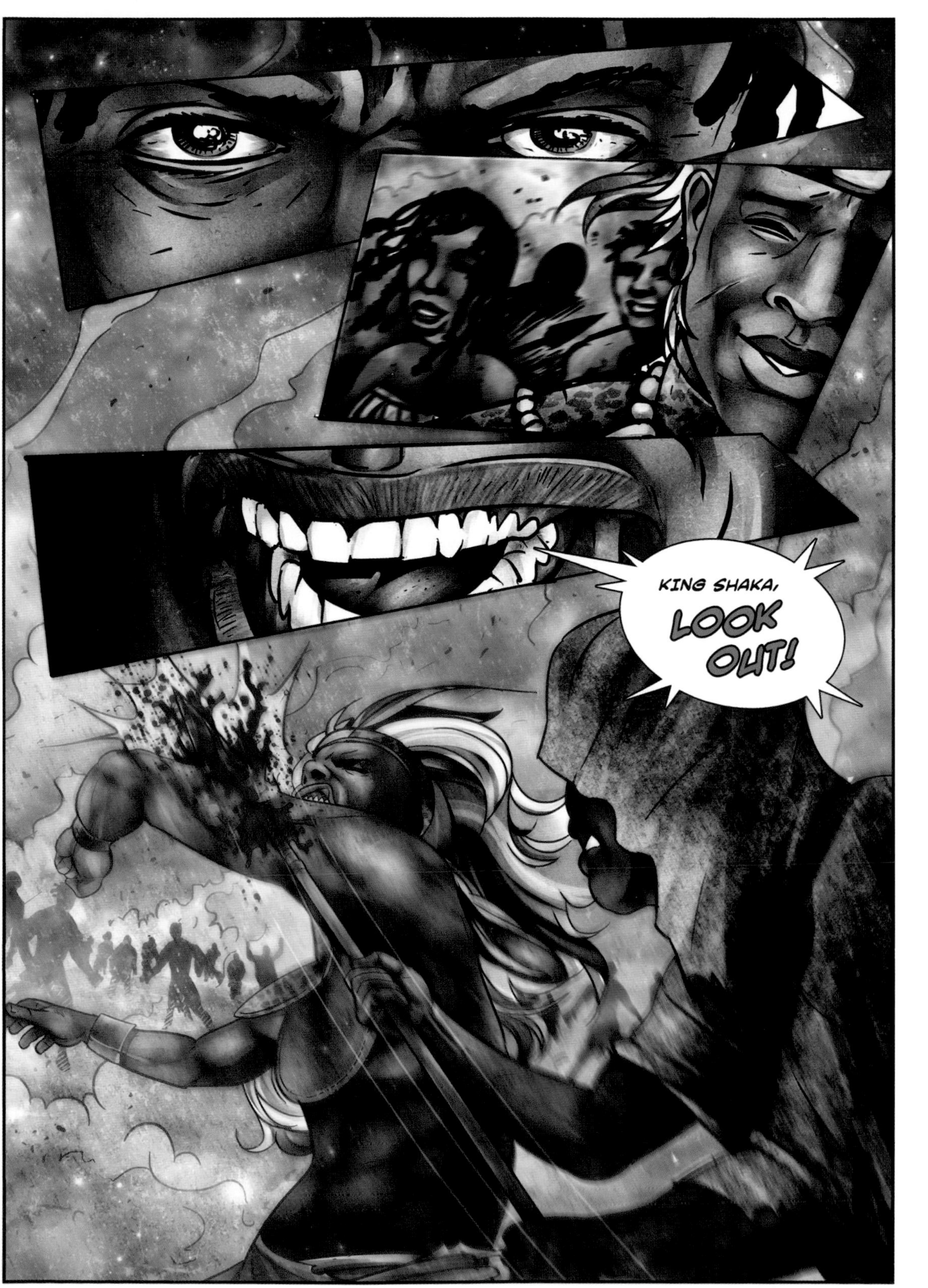
KING SHAKA,
LOOK OUT!

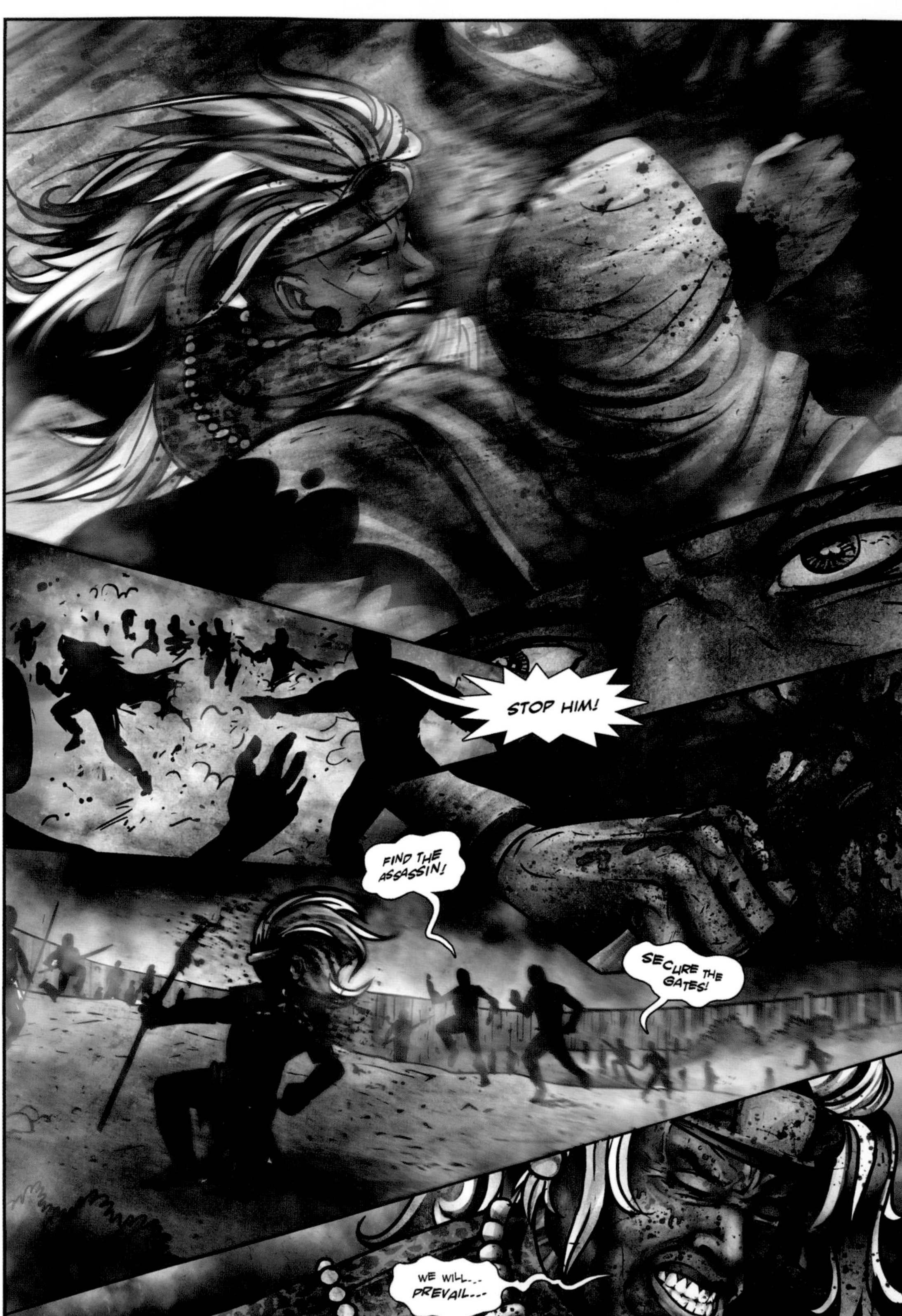
STOP HIM!
FIND THE ASSASSIN!
SECURE THE GATES!
WE WILL... PREVAIL...

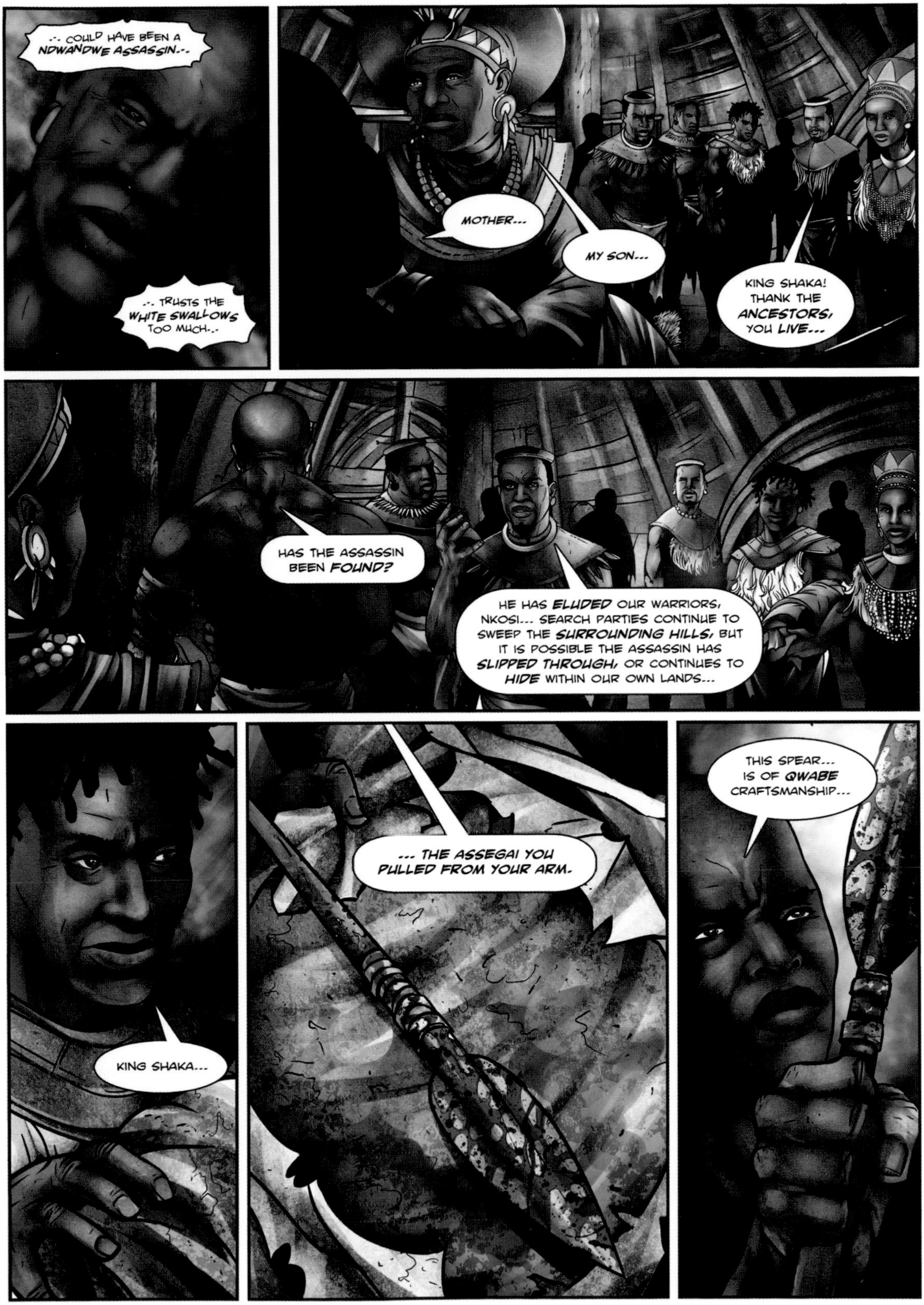

-- COULD HAVE BEEN A NDWANDWE ASSASSIN.--
-- TRUSTS THE WHITE SWALLOWS TOO MUCH.--
MOTHER...
MY SON...
KING SHAKA! THANK THE ANCESTORS, YOU LIVE...
HAS THE ASSASSIN BEEN FOUND?
HE HAS ELUDED OUR WARRIORS, NKOSI... SEARCH PARTIES CONTINUE TO SWEEP THE SURROUNDING HILLS, BUT IT IS POSSIBLE THE ASSASSIN HAS SLIPPED THROUGH, OR CONTINUES TO HIDE WITHIN OUR OWN LANDS...
KING SHAKA...
... THE ASSEGAI YOU PULLED FROM YOUR ARM.
THIS SPEAR... IS OF QWABE CRAFTSMANSHIP...

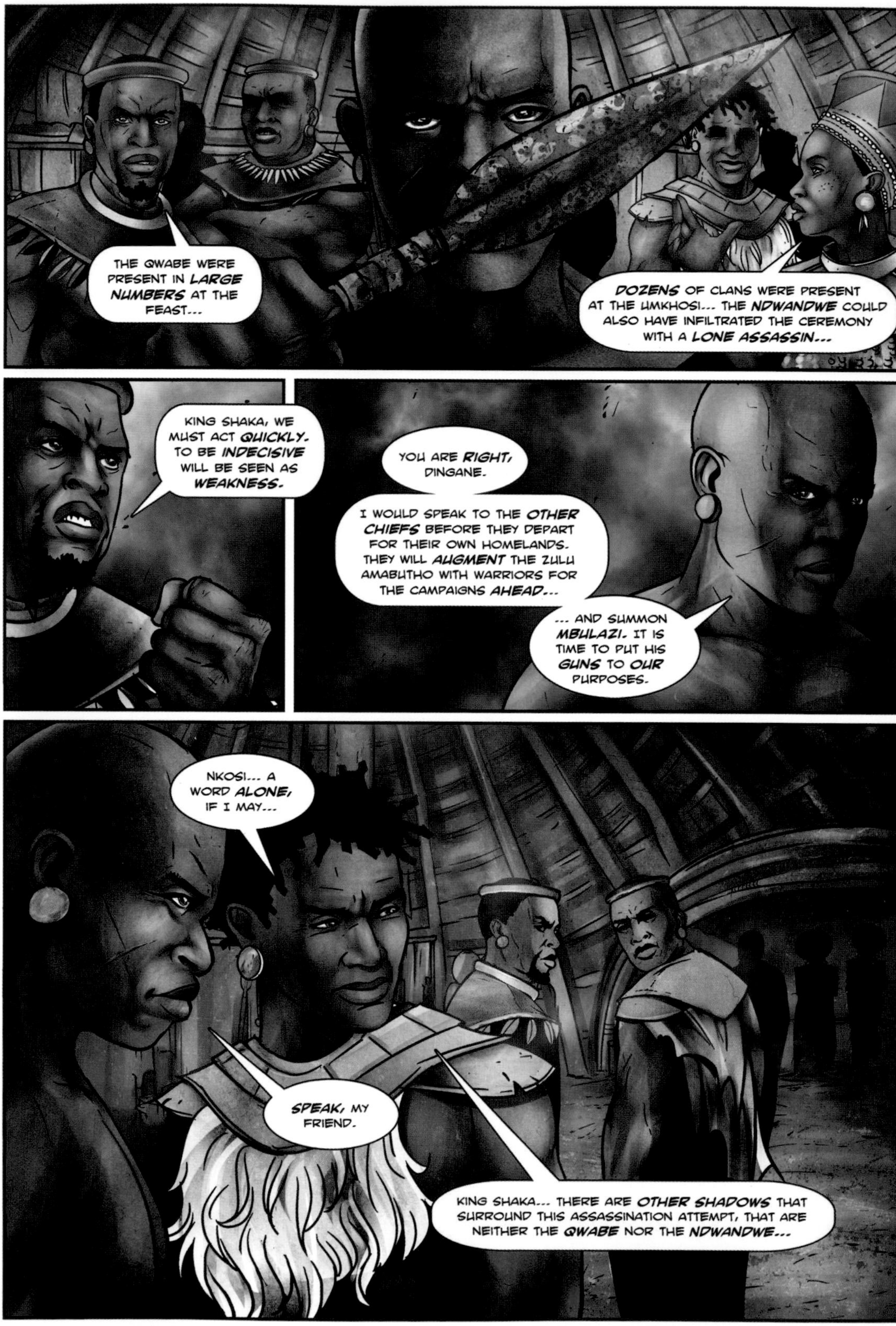
THE QWABE WERE PRESENT IN LARGE NUMBERS AT THE FEAST...
DOZENS OF CLANS WERE PRESENT AT THE UMKHOSI... THE NDWANDWE COULD ALSO HAVE INFILTRATED THE CEREMONY WITH A LONE ASSASSIN...
KING SHAKA, WE MUST ACT QUICKLY. TO BE INDECISIVE WILL BE SEEN AS WEAKNESS.
YOU ARE RIGHT, DINGANE.
I WOULD SPEAK TO THE OTHER CHIEFS BEFORE THEY DEPART FOR THEIR OWN HOMELANDS. THEY WILL AUGMENT THE ZULU AMABUTHO WITH WARRIORS FOR THE CAMPAIGNS AHEAD...
... AND SUMMON MBULAZI. IT IS TIME TO PUT HIS GUNS TO OUR PURPOSES.
NKOSI... A WORD ALONE, IF I MAY...
SPEAK, MY FRIEND.
KING SHAKA... THERE ARE OTHER SHADOWS THAT SURROUND THIS ASSASSINATION ATTEMPT, THAT ARE NEITHER THE QWABE NOR THE NDWANDWE...

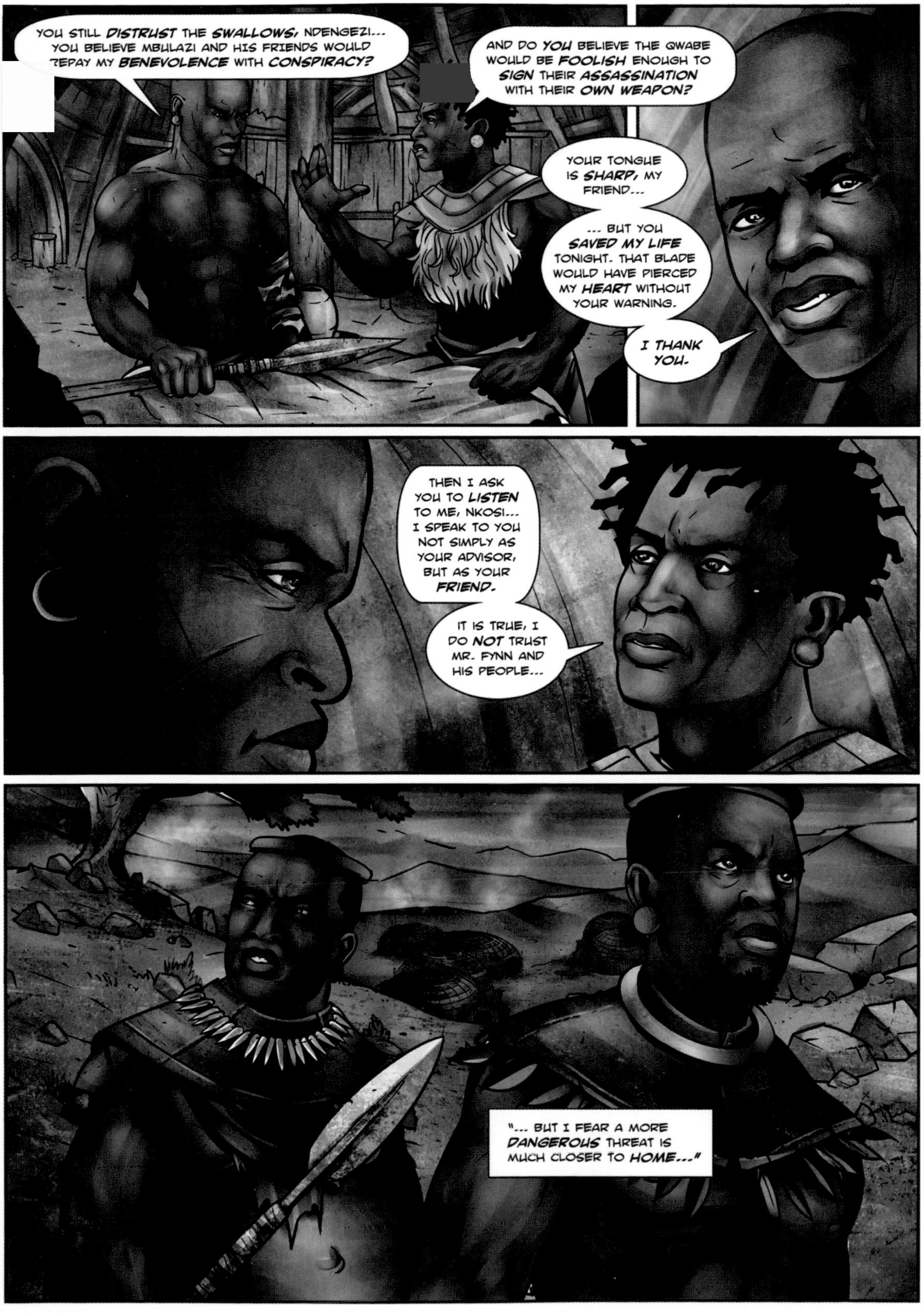
YOU STILL DISTRUST THE SWALLOWS, NDENGEZI... YOU BELIEVE MBULAZI AND HIS FRIENDS WOULD REPAY MY BENEVOLENCE WITH CONSPIRACY?
AND DO YOU BELIEVE THE QWABE WOULD BE FOOLISH ENOUGH TO SIGN THEIR ASSASSINATION WITH THEIR OWN WEAPON?
YOUR TONGUE IS SHARP, MY FRIEND...
... BUT YOU SAVED MY LIFE TONIGHT. THAT BLADE WOULD HAVE PIERCED MY HEART WITHOUT YOUR WARNING.
I THANK YOU.
THEN I ASK YOU TO LISTEN TO ME, NKOSI... I SPEAK TO YOU NOT SIMPLY AS YOUR ADVISOR, BUT AS YOUR FRIEND.
IT IS TRUE, I DO NOT TRUST MR. FYNN AND HIS PEOPLE...
"... BUT I FEAR A MORE DANGEROUS THREAT IS MUCH CLOSER TO HOME..."

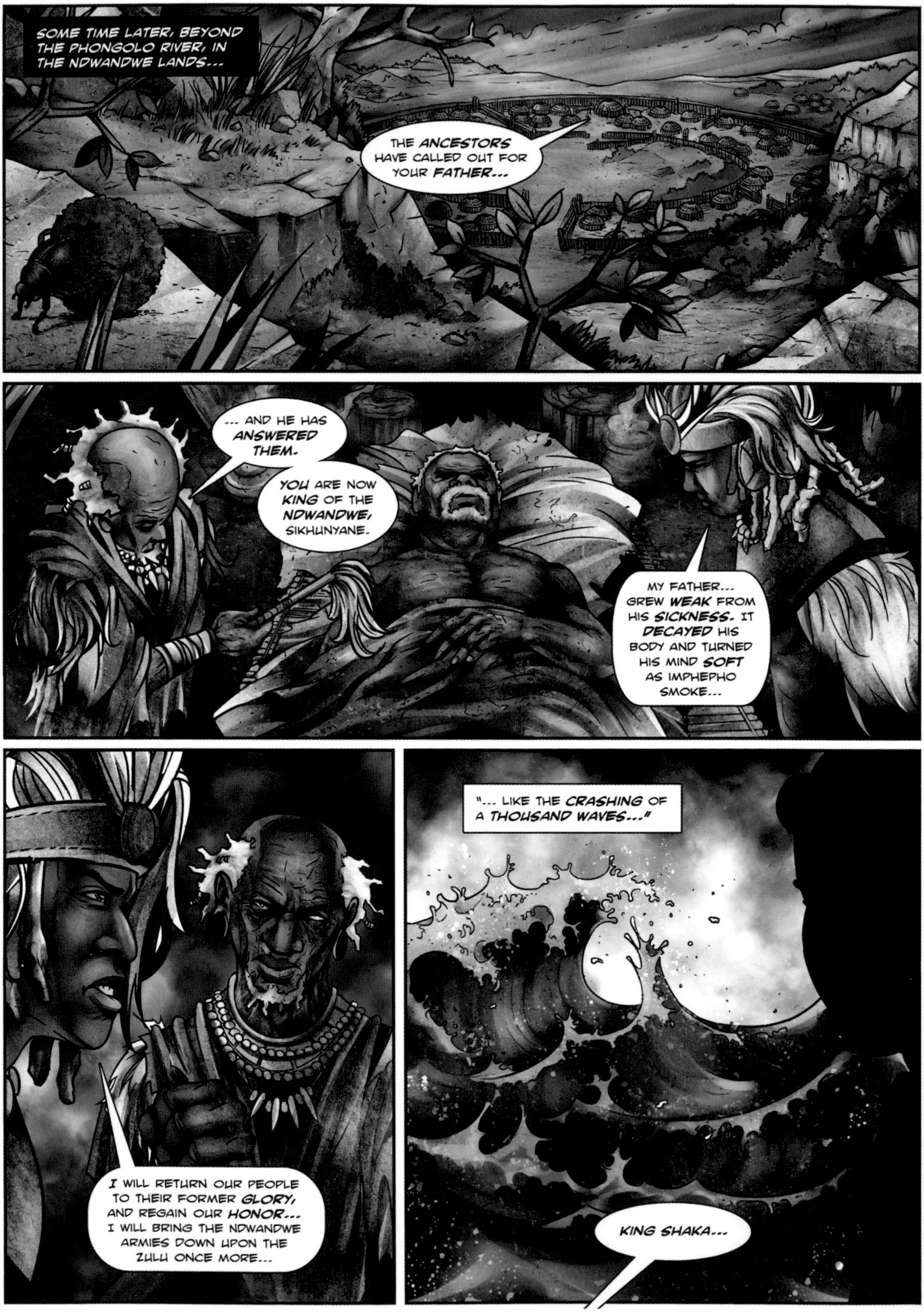

SOME TIME LATER, BEYOND THE PHONGOLO RIVER, IN THE NDWANDWE LANDS...
THE ANCESTORS HAVE CALLED OUT FOR YOUR FATHER...
... AND HE HAS ANSWERED THEM.
YOU ARE NOW KING OF THE NDWANDWE, SIKHUNYANE.
MY FATHER... GREW WEAK FROM HIS SICKNESS. IT DECAYED HIS BODY AND TURNED HIS MIND SOFT AS IMPHEPHO SMOKE...
I WILL RETURN OUR PEOPLE TO THEIR FORMER GLORY, AND REGAIN OUR HONOR... I WILL BRING THE NDWANDWE ARMIES DOWN UPON THE ZULU ONCE MORE...
"... LIKE THE CRASHING OF A THOUSAND WAVES..."
KING SHAKA...

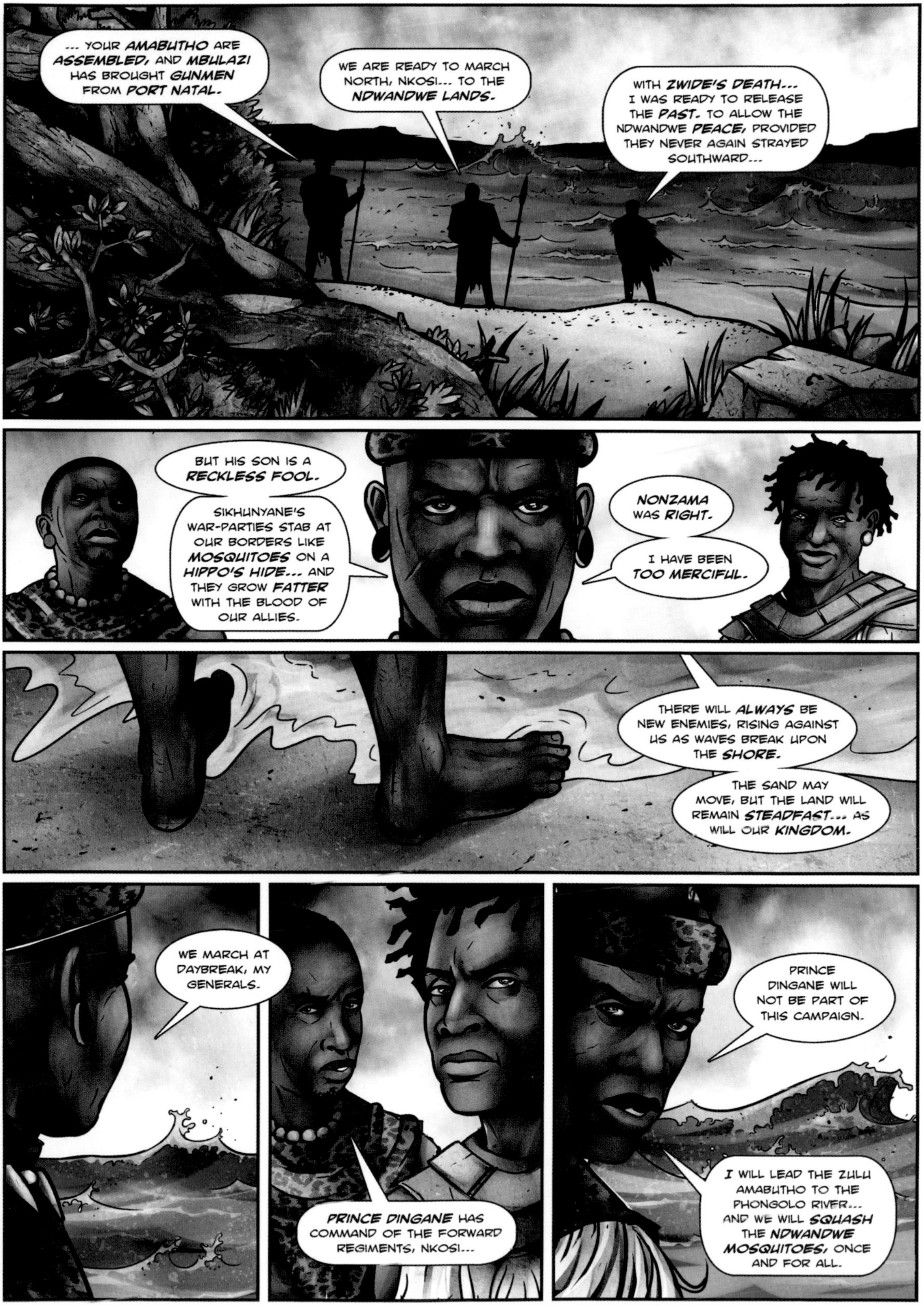
... YOUR AMABUTHO ARE ASSEMBLED, AND MBULAZI HAS BROUGHT GUNMEN FROM PORT NATAL.
WE ARE READY TO MARCH NORTH, NKOSI... TO THE NDWANDWE LANDS.
WITH ZWIDE'S DEATH... I WAS READY TO RELEASE THE PAST. TO ALLOW THE NDWANDWE PEACE, PROVIDED THEY NEVER AGAIN STRAYED SOUTHWARD...
BUT HIS SON IS A RECKLESS FOOL.
SIKHUNYANE'S WAR-PARTIES STAB AT OUR BORDERS LIKE MOSQUITOES ON A HIPPO'S HIDE... AND THEY GROW FATTER WITH THE BLOOD OF OUR ALLIES.
NONZAMA WAS RIGHT.
I HAVE BEEN TOO MERCIFUL.
THERE WILL ALWAYS BE NEW ENEMIES, RISING AGAINST US AS WAVES BREAK UPON THE SHORE.
THE SAND MAY MOVE, BUT THE LAND WILL REMAIN STEADFAST... AS WILL OUR KINGDOM.
WE MARCH AT DAYBREAK, MY GENERALS.
PRINCE DINGANE HAS COMMAND OF THE FORWARD REGIMENTS, NKOSI...
PRINCE DINGANE WILL NOT BE PART OF THIS CAMPAIGN.
I WILL LEAD THE ZULU AMABUTHO TO THE PHONGOLO RIVER... AND WE WILL SQUASH THE NDWANDWE MOSQUITOES, ONCE AND FOR ALL.

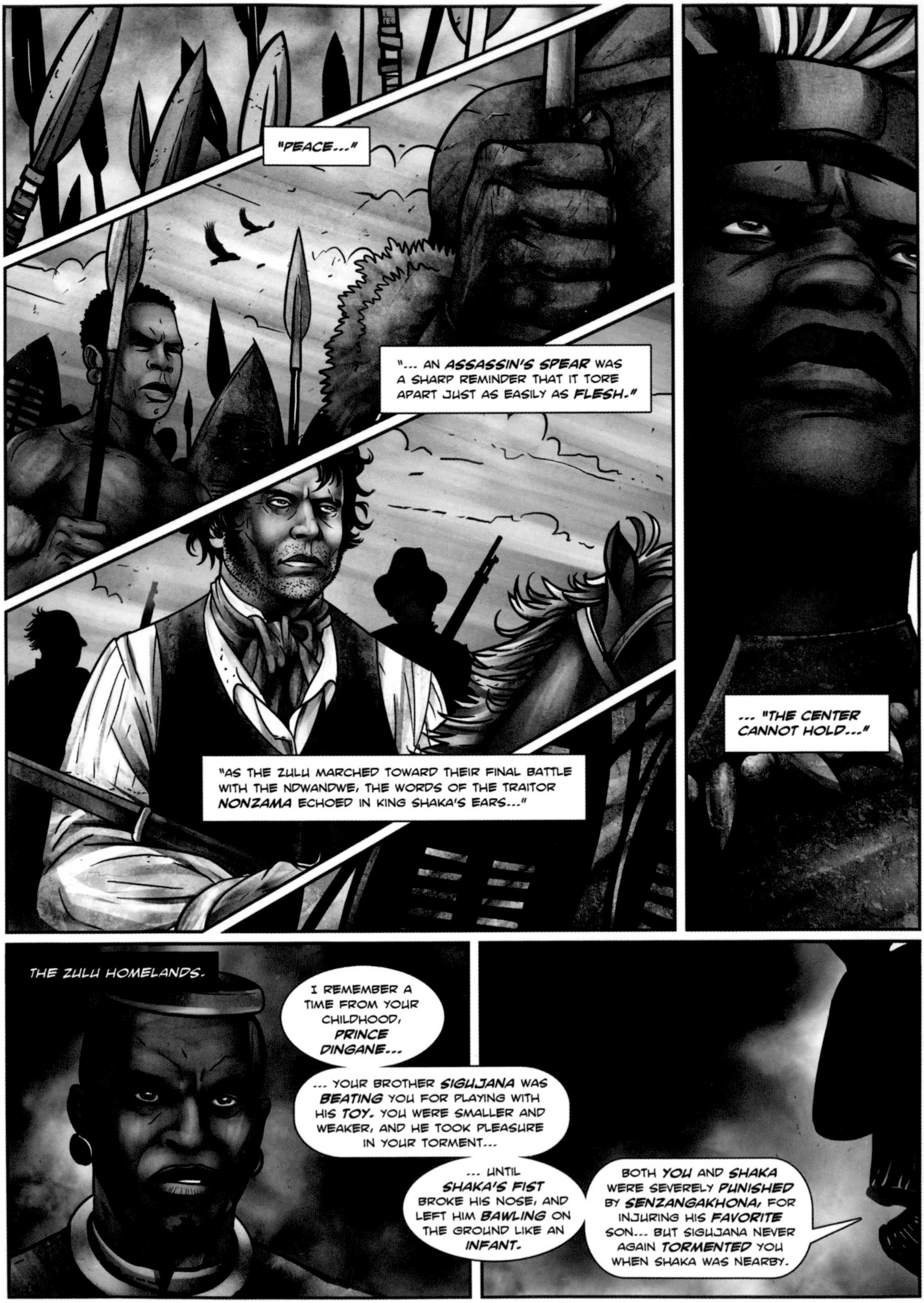
"PEACE..."
"... AN ASSASSIN'S SPEAR WAS A SHARP REMINDER THAT IT TORE APART JUST AS EASILY AS FLESH."
"AS THE ZULU MARCHED TOWARD THEIR FINAL BATTLE WITH THE NDWANDWE, THE WORDS OF THE TRAITOR NONZAMA ECHOED IN KING SHAKA'S EARS..."
... "THE CENTER CANNOT HOLD..."
THE ZULU HOMELANDS.
I REMEMBER A TIME FROM YOUR CHILDHOOD, PRINCE DINGANE...
... YOUR BROTHER SIGUJANA WAS BEATING YOU FOR PLAYING WITH HIS TOY. YOU WERE SMALLER AND WEAKER, AND HE TOOK PLEASURE IN YOUR TORMENT...
... UNTIL SHAKA'S FIST BROKE HIS NOSE, AND LEFT HIM BAWLING ON THE GROUND LIKE AN INFANT.
BOTH YOU AND SHAKA WERE SEVERELY PUNISHED BY SENZANGAKHONA, FOR INJURING HIS FAVORITE SON... BUT SIGUJANA NEVER AGAIN TORMENTED YOU WHEN SHAKA WAS NEARBY.

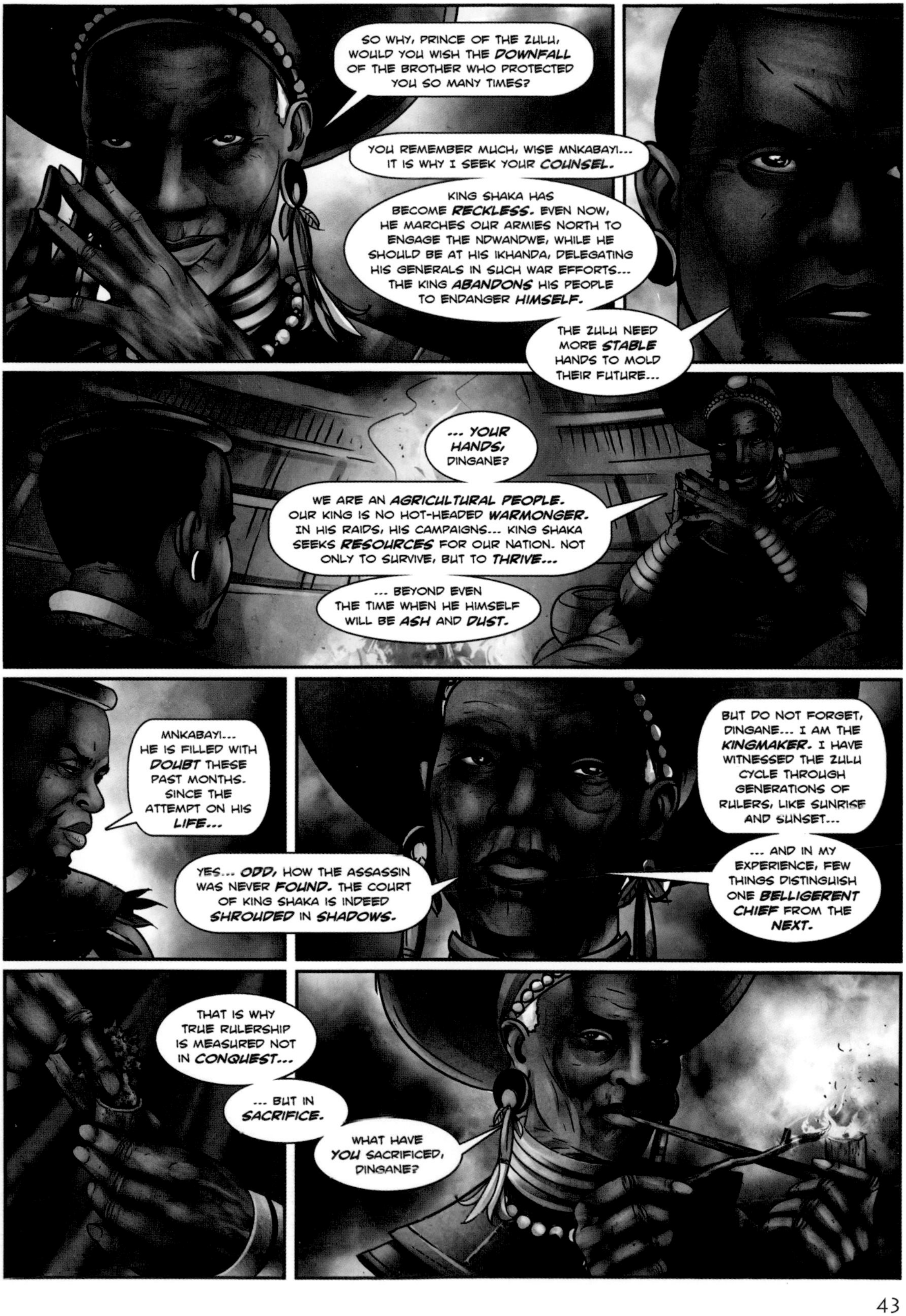
SO WHY, PRINCE OF THE ZULU, WOULD YOU WISH THE DOWNFALL OF THE BROTHER WHO PROTECTED YOU SO MANY TIMES?
YOU REMEMBER MUCH, WISE MNKABAYI... IT IS WHY I SEEK YOUR COUNSEL.
KING SHAKA HAS BECOME RECKLESS. EVEN NOW, HE MARCHES OUR ARMIES NORTH TO ENGAGE THE NDWANDWE, WHILE HE SHOULD BE AT HIS IKHANDA, DELEGATING HIS GENERALS IN SUCH WAR EFFORTS... THE KING ABANDONS HIS PEOPLE TO ENDANGER HIMSELF.
THE ZULU NEED MORE STABLE HANDS TO MOLD THEIR FUTURE...
... YOUR HANDS, DINGANE?
WE ARE AN AGRICULTURAL PEOPLE. OUR KING IS NO HOT-HEADED WARMONGER. IN HIS RAIDS, HIS CAMPAIGNS... KING SHAKA SEEKS RESOURCES FOR OUR NATION. NOT ONLY TO SURVIVE, BUT TO THRIVE...
... BEYOND EVEN THE TIME WHEN HE HIMSELF WILL BE ASH AND DUST.
MNKABAYI... HE IS FILLED WITH DOUBT THESE PAST MONTHS. SINCE THE ATTEMPT ON HIS LIFE...
YES... ODD, HOW THE ASSASSIN WAS NEVER FOUND. THE COURT OF KING SHAKA IS INDEED SHROUDED IN SHADOWS.
BUT DO NOT FORGET, DINGANE... I AM THE KINGMAKER. I HAVE WITNESSED THE ZULU CYCLE THROUGH GENERATIONS OF RULERS, LIKE SUNRISE AND SUNSET...
... AND IN MY EXPERIENCE, FEW THINGS DISTINGUISH ONE BELLIGERENT CHIEF FROM THE NEXT.
THAT IS WHY TRUE RULERSHIP IS MEASURED NOT IN CONQUEST...
... BUT IN SACRIFICE.
WHAT HAVE YOU SACRIFICED, DINGANE?

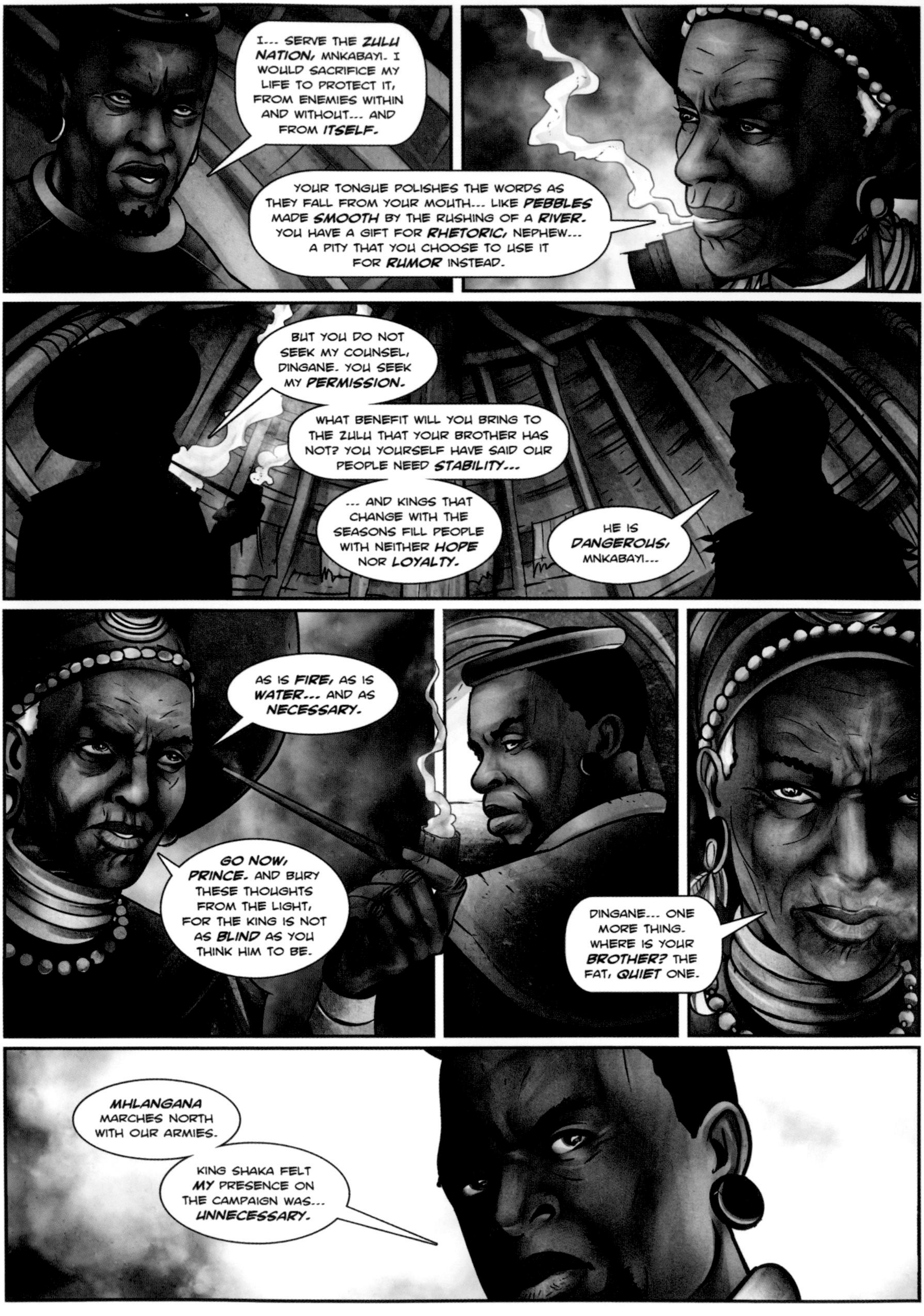
I... SERVE THE ZULU NATION, MNKABAYI. I WOULD SACRIFICE MY LIFE TO PROTECT IT, FROM ENEMIES WITHIN AND WITHOUT... AND FROM ITSELF.
YOUR TONGUE POLISHES THE WORDS AS THEY FALL FROM YOUR MOUTH... LIKE PEBBLES MADE SMOOTH BY THE RUSHING OF A RIVER. YOU HAVE A GIFT FOR RHETORIC, NEPHEW... A PITY THAT YOU CHOOSE TO USE IT FOR RUMOR INSTEAD.
BUT YOU DO NOT SEEK MY COUNSEL, DINGANE. YOU SEEK MY PERMISSION.
WHAT BENEFIT WILL YOU BRING TO THE ZULU THAT YOUR BROTHER HAS NOT? YOU YOURSELF HAVE SAID OUR PEOPLE NEED STABILITY...
... AND KINGS THAT CHANGE WITH THE SEASONS FILL PEOPLE WITH NEITHER HOPE NOR LOYALTY.
HE IS DANGEROUS, MNKABAYI...
AS IS FIRE, AS IS WATER... AND AS NECESSARY.
GO NOW, PRINCE. AND BURY THESE THOUGHTS FROM THE LIGHT, FOR THE KING IS NOT AS BLIND AS YOU THINK HIM TO BE.
DINGANE... ONE MORE THING. WHERE IS YOUR BROTHER? THE FAT, QUIET ONE.
MHLANGANA MARCHES NORTH WITH OUR ARMIES.
KING SHAKA FELT MY PRESENCE ON THE CAMPAIGN WAS... UNNECESSARY.

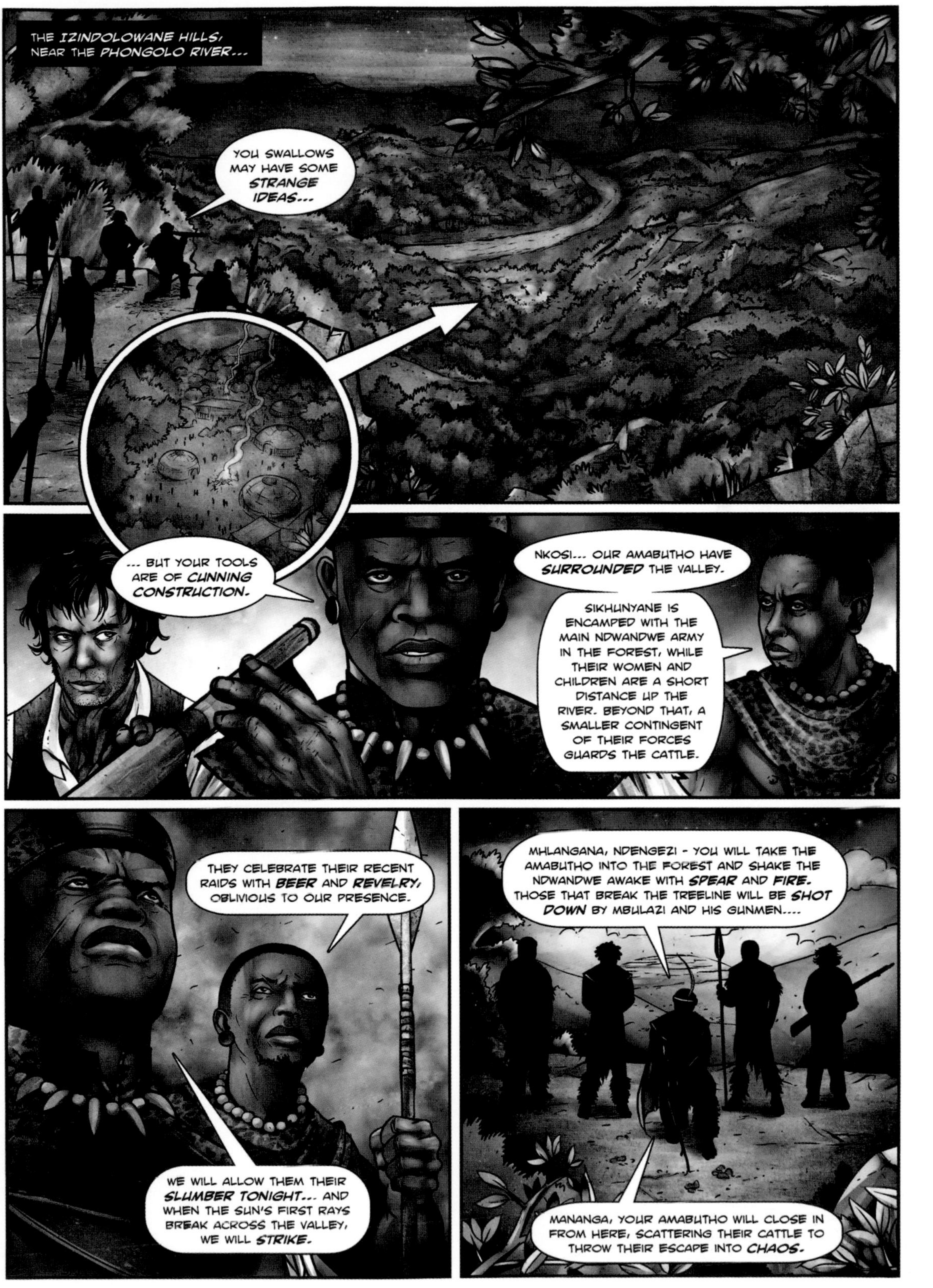
THE IZINDOLOWANE HILLS, NEAR THE PHONGOLO RIVER...
YOU SWALLOWS MAY HAVE SOME STRANGE IDEAS...
... BUT YOUR TOOLS ARE OF CUNNING CONSTRUCTION.
NKOSI... OUR AMABUTHO HAVE SURROUNDED THE VALLEY.
SIKHUNYANE IS ENCAMPED WITH THE MAIN NDWANDWE ARMY IN THE FOREST, WHILE THEIR WOMEN AND CHILDREN ARE A SHORT DISTANCE UP THE RIVER. BEYOND THAT, A SMALLER CONTINGENT OF THEIR FORCES GUARDS THE CATTLE.
THEY CELEBRATE THEIR RECENT RAIDS WITH BEER AND REVELRY, OBLIVIOUS TO OUR PRESENCE.
WE WILL ALLOW THEM THEIR SLUMBER TONIGHT... AND WHEN THE SUN'S FIRST RAYS BREAK ACROSS THE VALLEY, WE WILL STRIKE.
MHLANGANA, NDENGEZI - YOU WILL TAKE THE AMABUTHO INTO THE FOREST AND SHAKE THE NDWANDWE AWAKE WITH SPEAR AND FIRE. THOSE THAT BREAK THE TREELINE WILL BE SHOT DOWN BY MBULAZI AND HIS GUNMEN....
MANANGA, YOUR AMABUTHO WILL CLOSE IN FROM HERE, SCATTERING THEIR CATTLE TO THROW THEIR ESCAPE INTO CHAOS.

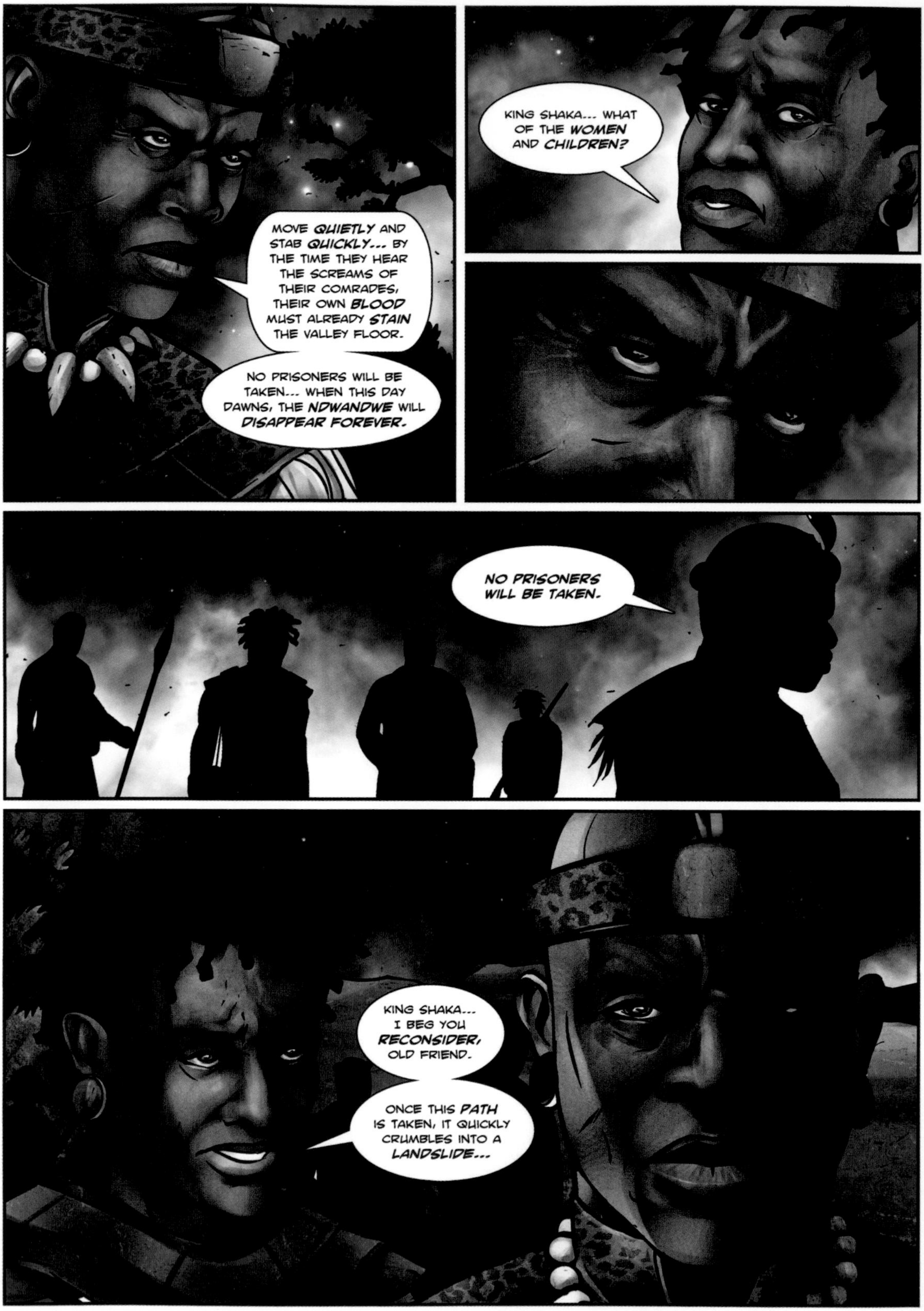
MOVE QUIETLY AND STAB QUICKLY... BY THE TIME THEY HEAR THE SCREAMS OF THEIR COMRADES, THEIR OWN BLOOD MUST ALREADY STAIN THE VALLEY FLOOR.
NO PRISONERS WILL BE TAKEN... WHEN THIS DAY DAWNS, THE NDWANDWE WILL DISAPPEAR FOREVER.
KING SHAKA... WHAT OF THE WOMEN AND CHILDREN?
NO PRISONERS WILL BE TAKEN.
KING SHAKA... I BEG YOU RECONSIDER, OLD FRIEND.
ONCE THIS PATH IS TAKEN, IT QUICKLY CRUMBLES INTO A LANDSLIDE...

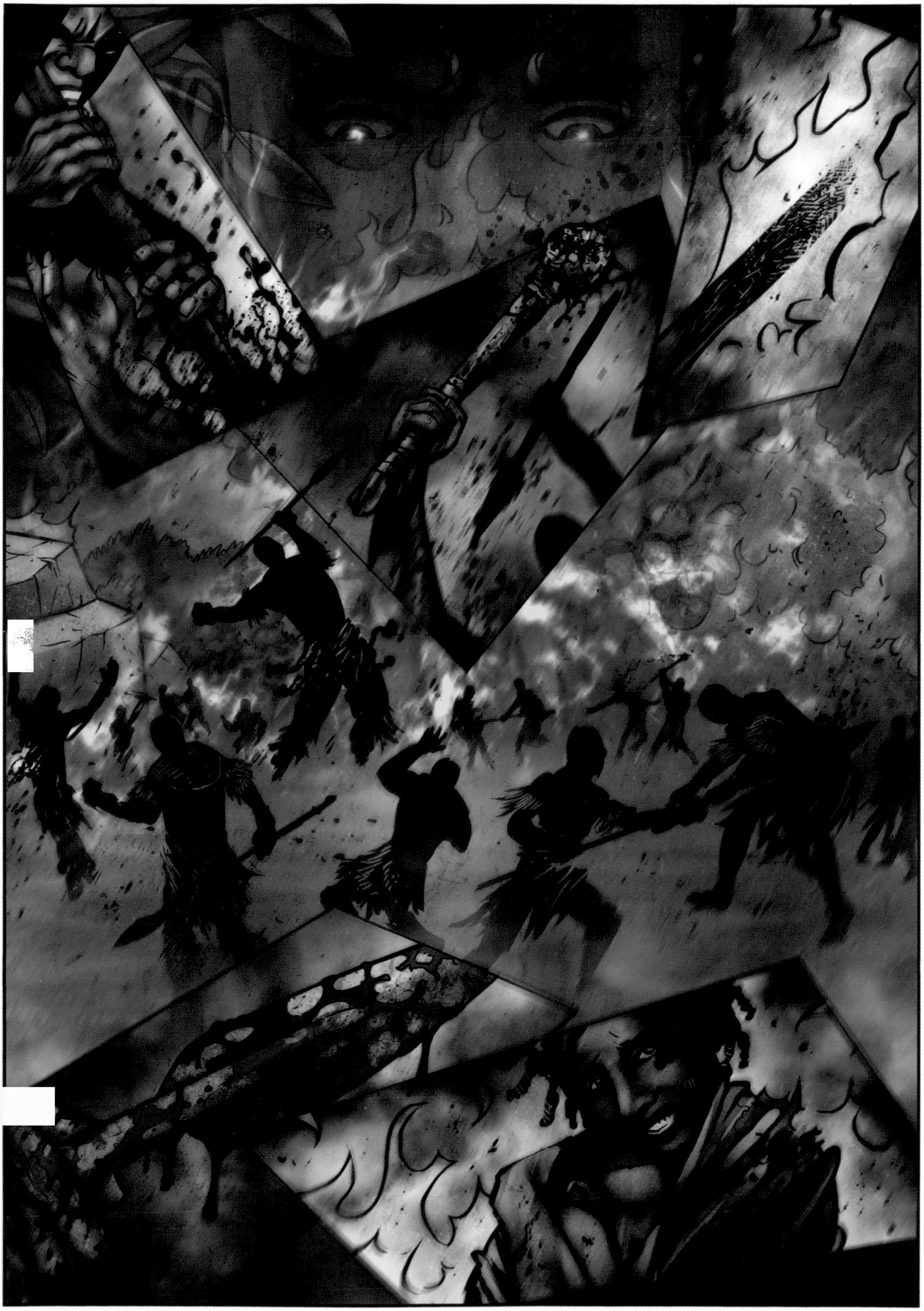

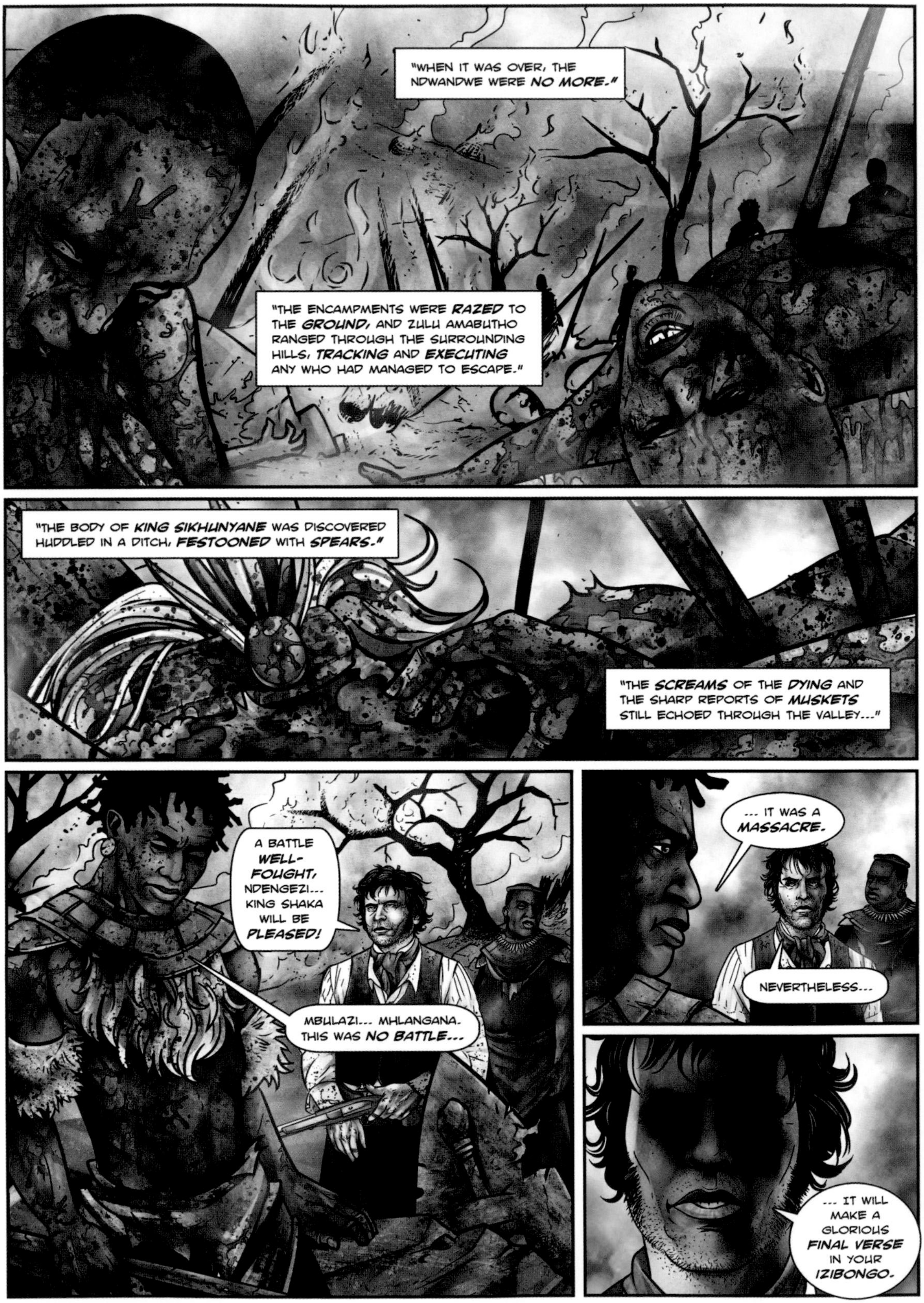
"WHEN IT WAS OVER, THE NDWANDWE WERE NO MORE."
"THE ENCAMPMENTS WERE RAZED TO THE GROUND, AND ZULU AMABUTHO RANGED THROUGH THE SURROUNDING HILLS, TRACKING AND EXECUTING ANY WHO HAD MANAGED TO ESCAPE."
"THE BODY OF KING SIKHUNYANE WAS DISCOVERED HUDDLED IN A DITCH, FESTOONED WITH SPEARS."
"THE SCREAMS OF THE DYING AND THE SHARP REPORTS OF MUSKETS STILL ECHOED THROUGH THE VALLEY..."
A BATTLE WELL-FOUGHT, NDENGEZI... KING SHAKA WILL BE PLEASED!
MBULAZI... MHLANGANA. THIS WAS NO BATTLE...
... IT WAS A MASSACRE.
NEVERTHELESS...
... IT WILL MAKE A GLORIOUS FINAL VERSE IN YOUR IZIBONGO.

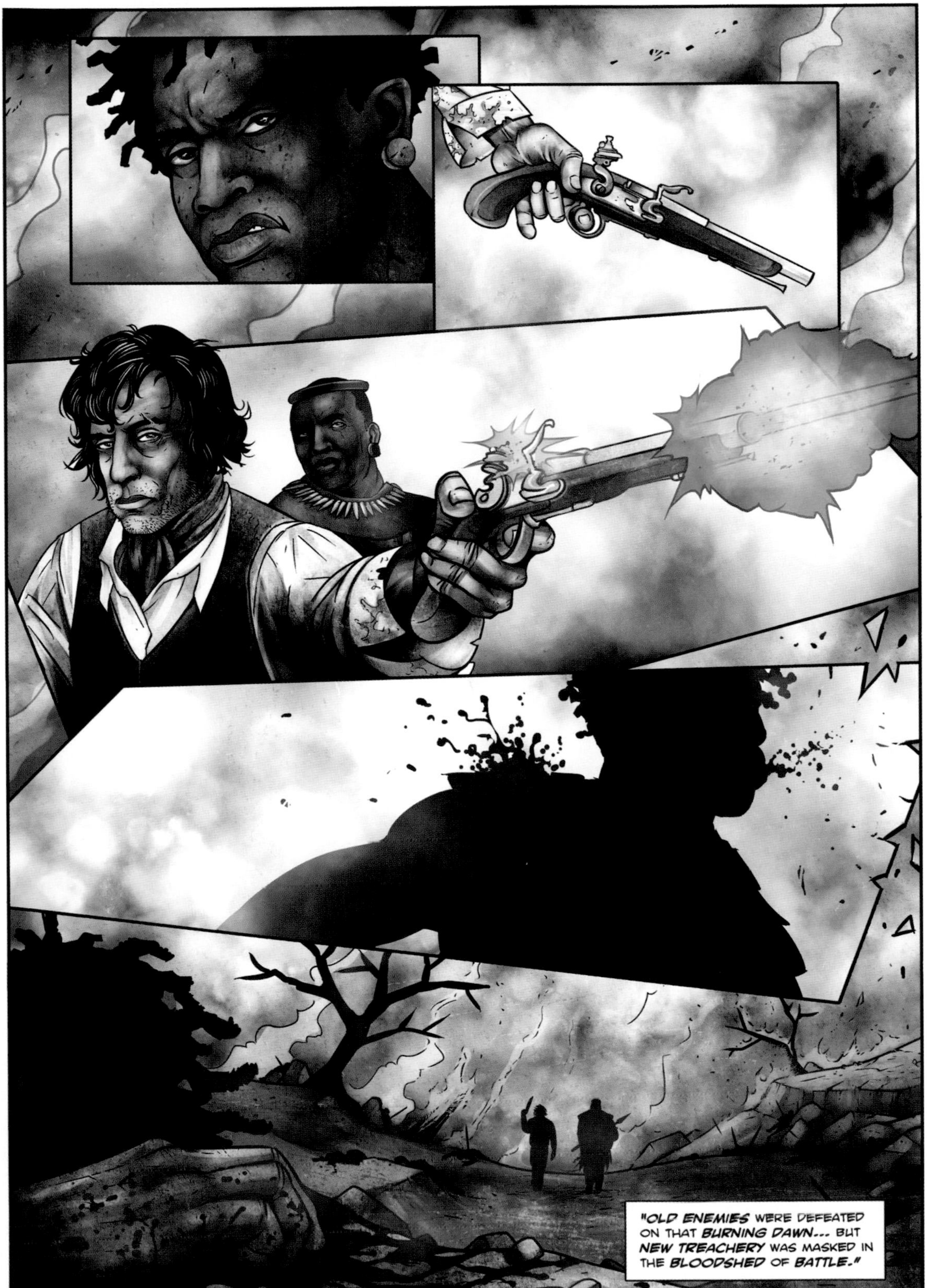
"OLD ENEMIES WERE DEFEATED ON THAT BURNING DAWN... BUT NEW TREACHERY WAS MASKED IN THE BLOODSHED OF BATTLE."

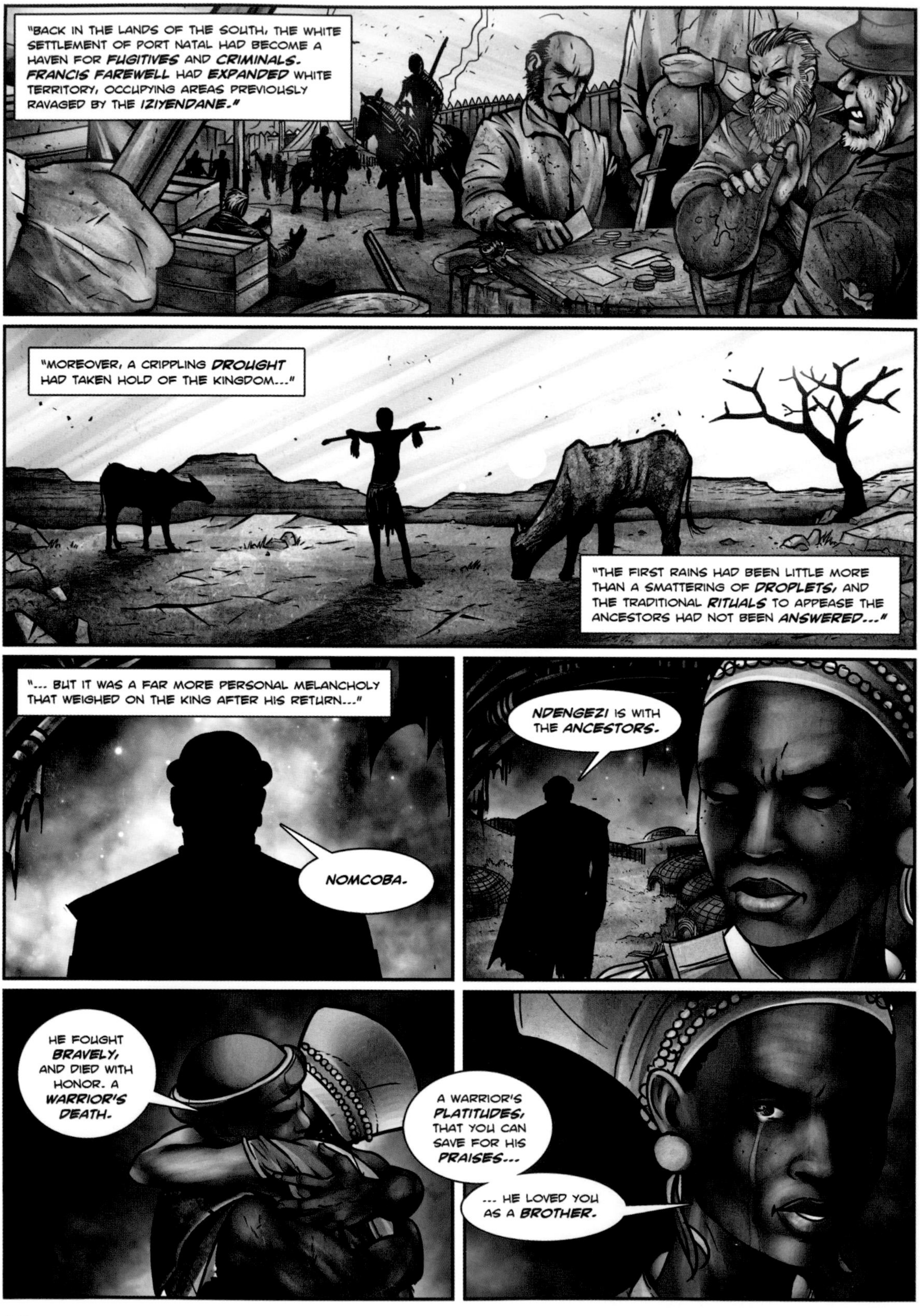
"BACK IN THE LANDS OF THE SOUTH, THE WHITE SETTLEMENT OF PORT NATAL HAD BECOME A HAVEN FOR FUGITIVES AND CRIMINALS. FRANCIS FAREWELL HAD EXPANDED WHITE TERRITORY, OCCUPYING AREAS PREVIOUSLY RAVAGED BY THE IZIYENDANE."
"MOREOVER, A CRIPPLING DROUGHT HAD TAKEN HOLD OF THE KINGDOM..."
"THE FIRST RAINS HAD BEEN LITTLE MORE THAN A SMATTERING OF DROPLETS, AND THE TRADITIONAL RITUALS TO APPEASE THE ANCESTORS HAD NOT BEEN ANSWERED..."
"... BUT IT WAS A FAR MORE PERSONAL MELANCHOLY THAT WEIGHED ON THE KING AFTER HIS RETURN..."
NOMCOBA.
NDENGEZI IS WITH THE ANCESTORS.
HE FOUGHT BRAVELY, AND DIED WITH HONOR. A WARRIOR'S DEATH.
A WARRIOR'S PLATITUDES, THAT YOU CAN SAVE FOR HIS PRAISES...
... HE LOVED YOU AS A BROTHER.

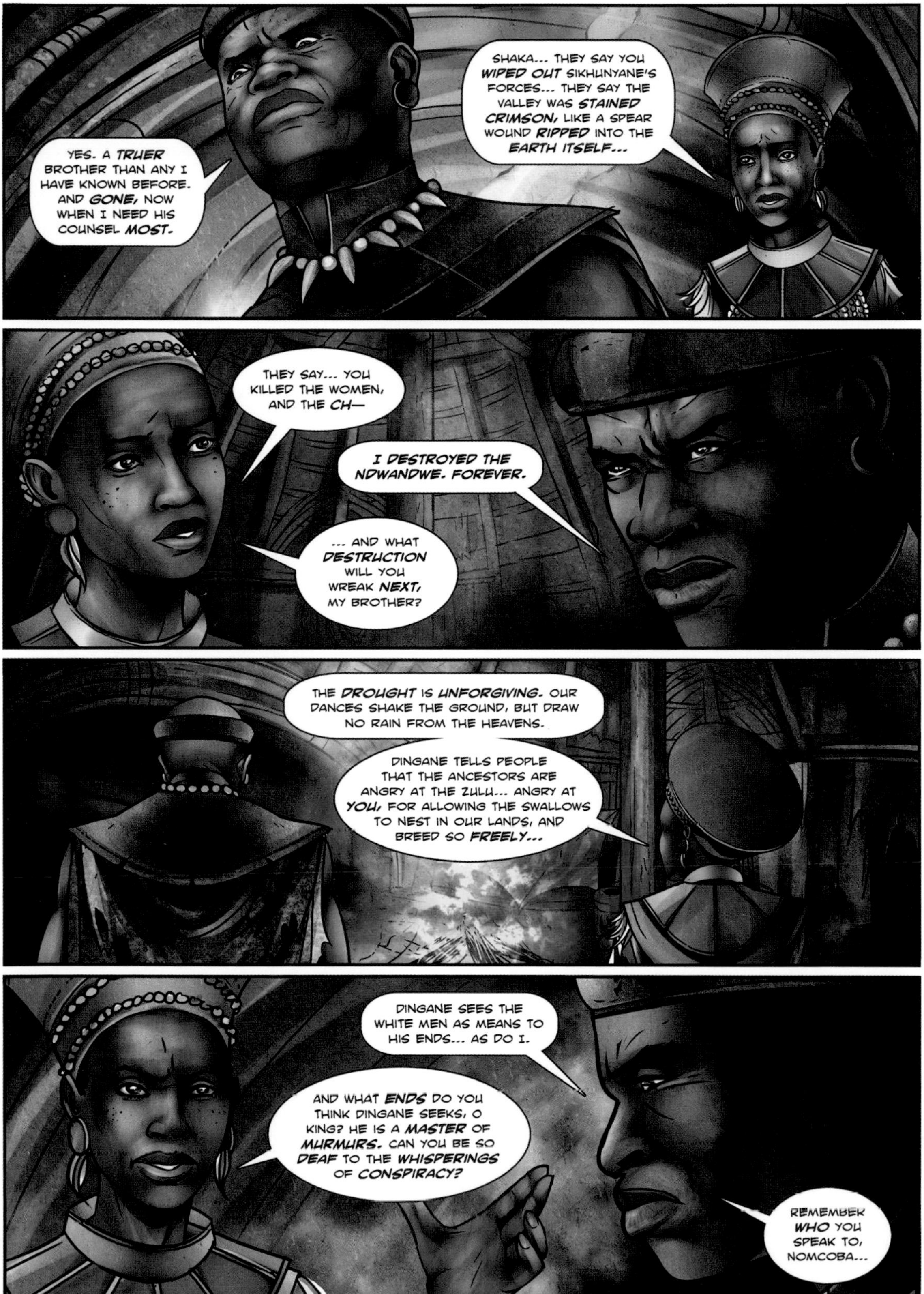
SHAKA... THEY SAY YOU WIPED OUT SIKHUNYANE'S FORCES... THEY SAY THE VALLEY WAS STAINED CRIMSON, LIKE A SPEAR WOUND RIPPED INTO THE EARTH ITSELF...
YES. A TRUER BROTHER THAN ANY I HAVE KNOWN BEFORE. AND GONE, NOW WHEN I NEED HIS COUNSEL MOST.
THEY SAY... YOU KILLED THE WOMEN, AND THE CH—
I DESTROYED THE NDWANDWE. FOREVER.
... AND WHAT DESTRUCTION WILL YOU WREAK NEXT, MY BROTHER?
THE DROUGHT IS UNFORGIVING. OUR DANCES SHAKE THE GROUND, BUT DRAW NO RAIN FROM THE HEAVENS.
DINGANE TELLS PEOPLE THAT THE ANCESTORS ARE ANGRY AT THE ZULU... ANGRY AT YOU, FOR ALLOWING THE SWALLOWS TO NEST IN OUR LANDS, AND BREED SO FREELY...
DINGANE SEES THE WHITE MEN AS MEANS TO HIS ENDS... AS DO I.
AND WHAT ENDS DO YOU THINK DINGANE SEEKS, O KING? HE IS A MASTER OF MURMURS. CAN YOU BE SO DEAF TO THE WHISPERINGS OF CONSPIRACY?
REMEMBER WHO YOU SPEAK TO, NOMCOBA...

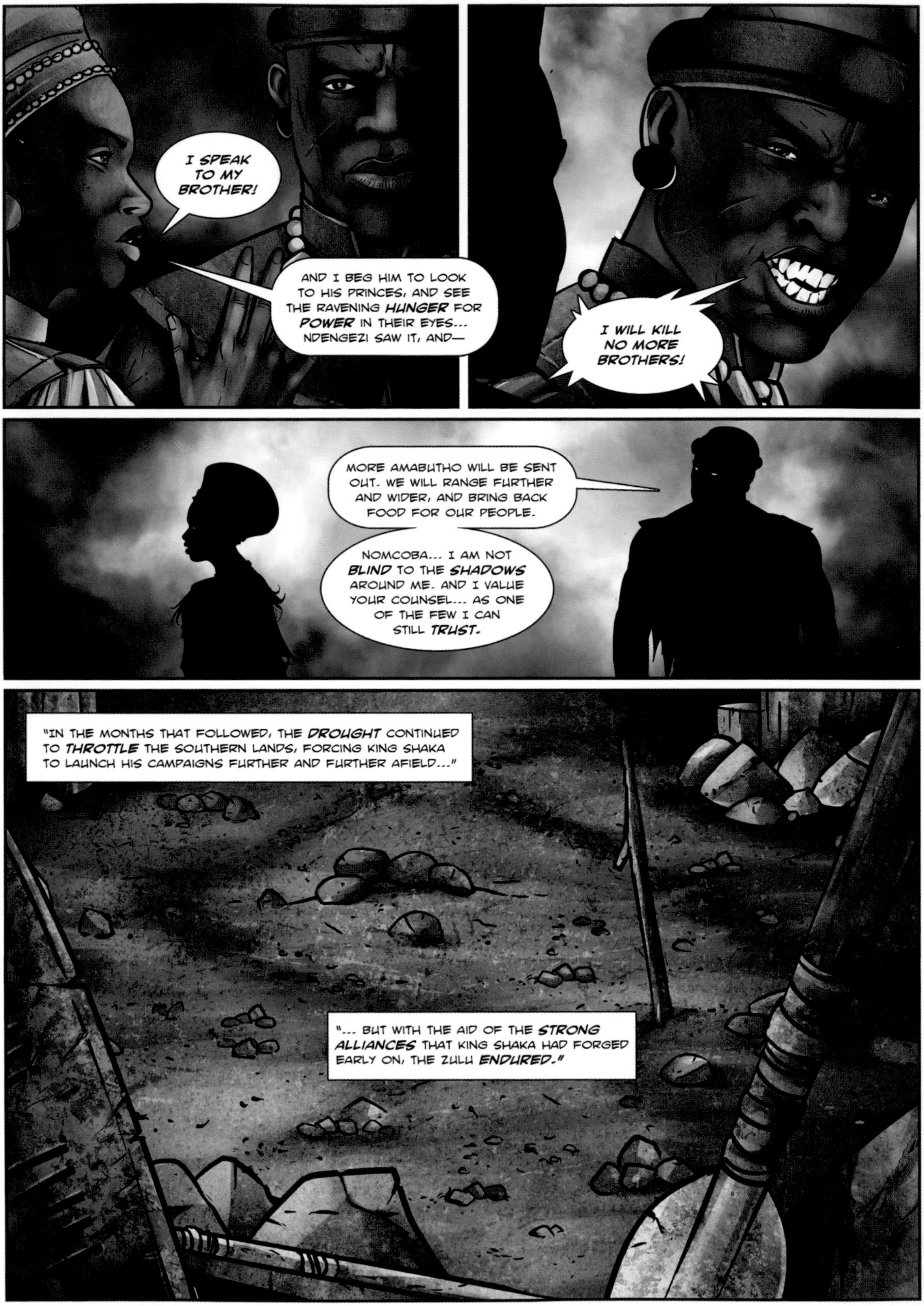
I SPEAK TO MY BROTHER!
AND I BEG HIM TO LOOK TO HIS PRINCES, AND SEE THE RAVENING HUNGER FOR POWER IN THEIR EYES... NDENGEZI SAW IT, AND—
I WILL KILL NO MORE BROTHERS!
MORE AMABUTHO WILL BE SENT OUT. WE WILL RANGE FURTHER AND WIDER, AND BRING BACK FOOD FOR OUR PEOPLE.
NOMCOBA... I AM NOT BLIND TO THE SHADOWS AROUND ME. AND I VALUE YOUR COUNSEL... AS ONE OF THE FEW I CAN STILL TRUST.
"IN THE MONTHS THAT FOLLOWED, THE DROUGHT CONTINUED TO THROTTLE THE SOUTHERN LANDS, FORCING KING SHAKA TO LAUNCH HIS CAMPAIGNS FURTHER AND FURTHER AFIELD..."
"... BUT WITH THE AID OF THE STRONG ALLIANCES THAT KING SHAKA HAD FORGED EARLY ON, THE ZULU ENDURED."

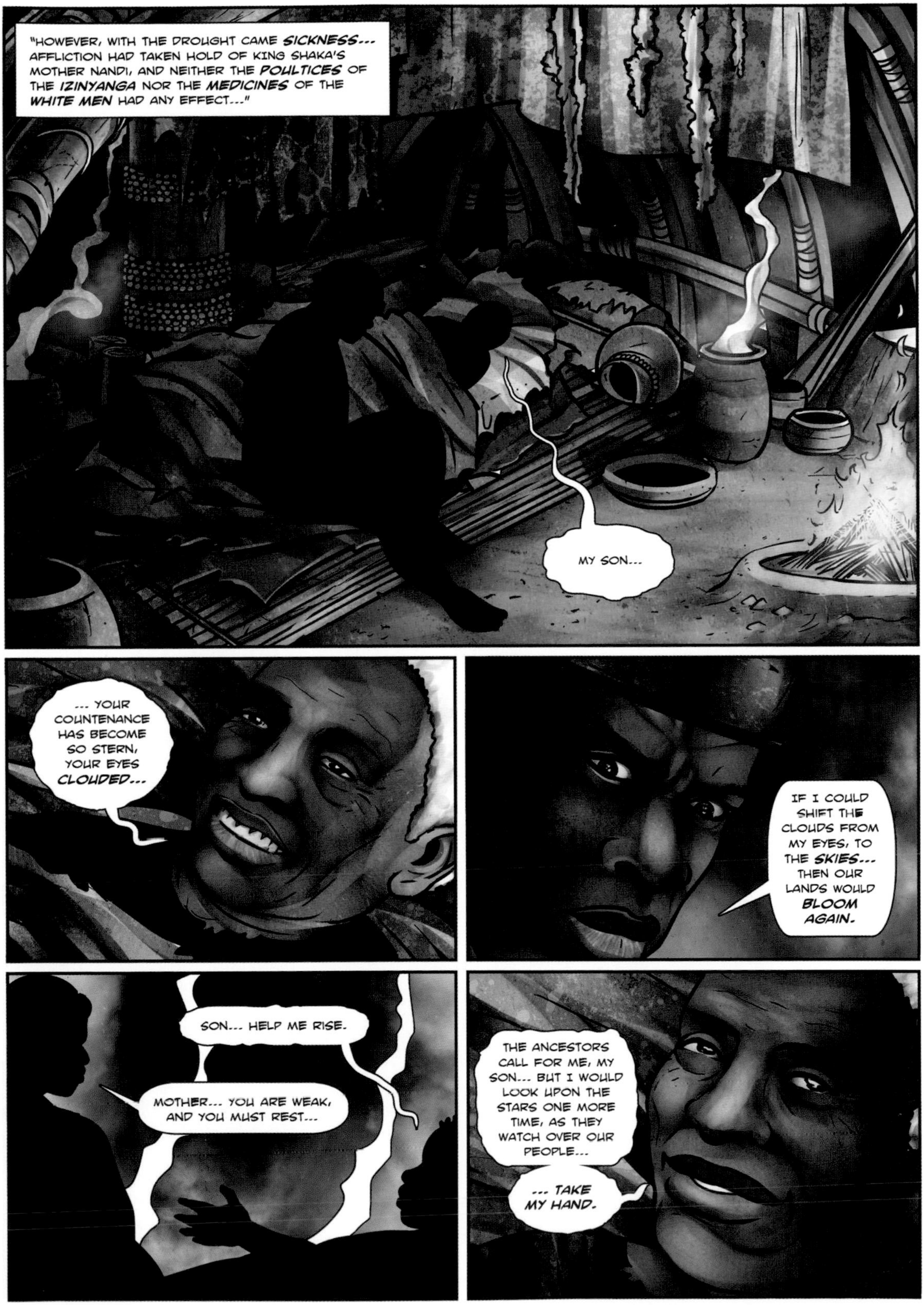
"HOWEVER, WITH THE DROUGHT CAME SICKNESS... AFFLICTION HAD TAKEN HOLD OF KING SHAKA'S MOTHER NANDI, AND NEITHER THE POULTICES OF THE IZINYANGA NOR THE MEDICINES OF THE WHITE MEN HAD ANY EFFECT..."
MY SON...
... YOUR COUNTENANCE HAS BECOME SO STERN, YOUR EYES CLOUDED...
IF I COULD SHIFT THE CLOUDS FROM MY EYES, TO THE SKIES... THEN OUR LANDS WOULD BLOOM AGAIN.
SON... HELP ME RISE.
MOTHER... YOU ARE WEAK, AND YOU MUST REST...
THE ANCESTORS CALL FOR ME, MY SON... BUT I WOULD LOOK UPON THE STARS ONE MORE TIME, AS THEY WATCH OVER OUR PEOPLE...
... TAKE MY HAND.

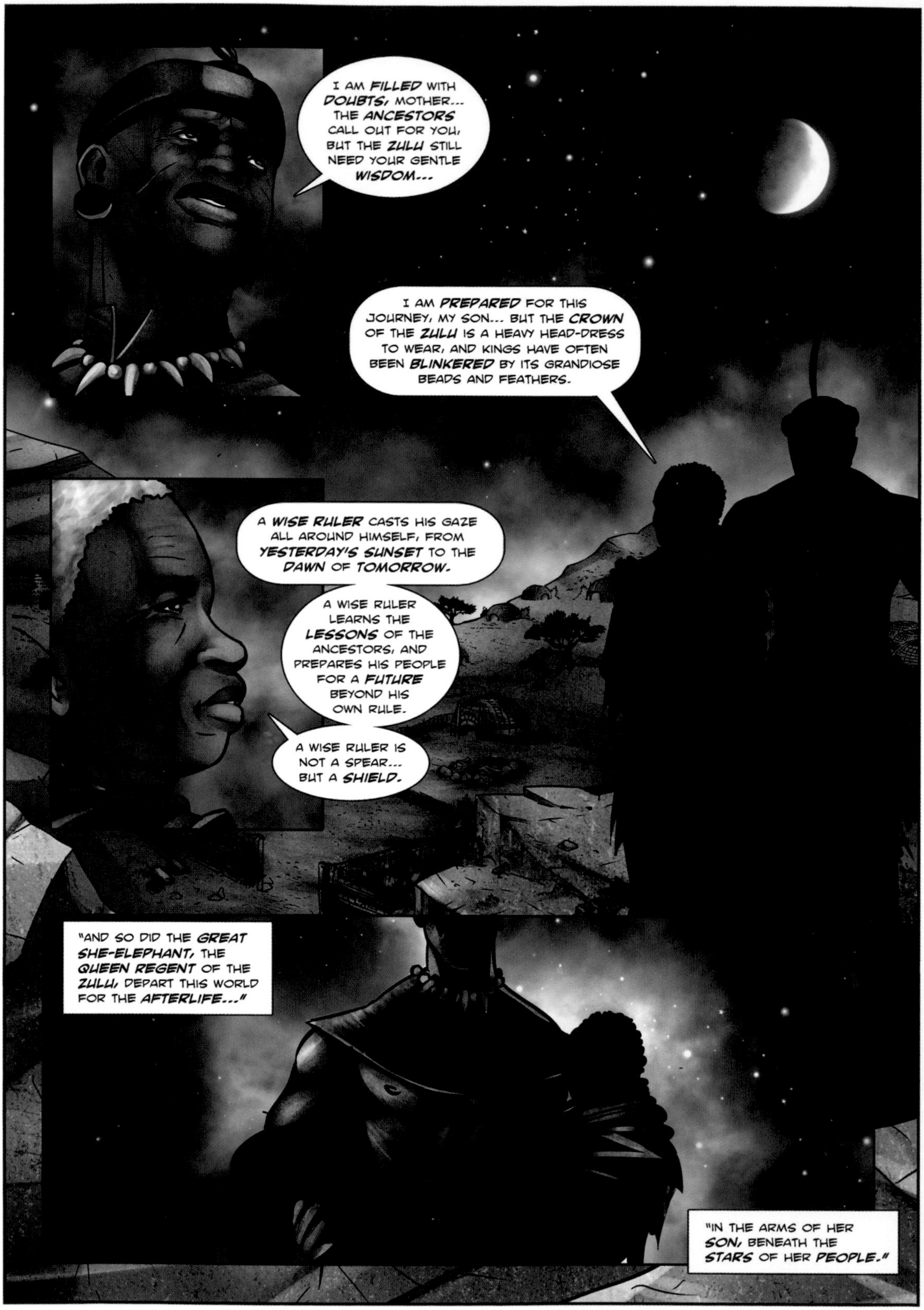
I AM FILLED WITH DOUBTS, MOTHER... THE ANCESTORS CALL OUT FOR YOU, BUT THE ZULU STILL NEED YOUR GENTLE WISDOM...
I AM PREPARED FOR THIS JOURNEY, MY SON... BUT THE CROWN OF THE ZULU IS A HEAVY HEAD-DRESS TO WEAR, AND KINGS HAVE OFTEN BEEN BLINKERED BY ITS GRANDIOSE BEADS AND FEATHERS.
A WISE RULER CASTS HIS GAZE ALL AROUND HIMSELF, FROM YESTERDAY'S SUNSET TO THE DAWN OF TOMORROW.
A WISE RULER LEARNS THE LESSONS OF THE ANCESTORS, AND PREPARES HIS PEOPLE FOR A FUTURE BEYOND HIS OWN RULE.
A WISE RULER IS NOT A SPEAR... BUT A SHIELD.
"AND SO DID THE GREAT SHE-ELEPHANT, THE QUEEN REGENT OF THE ZULU, DEPART THIS WORLD FOR THE AFTERLIFE..."
"IN THE ARMS OF HER SON, BENEATH THE STARS OF HER PEOPLE."

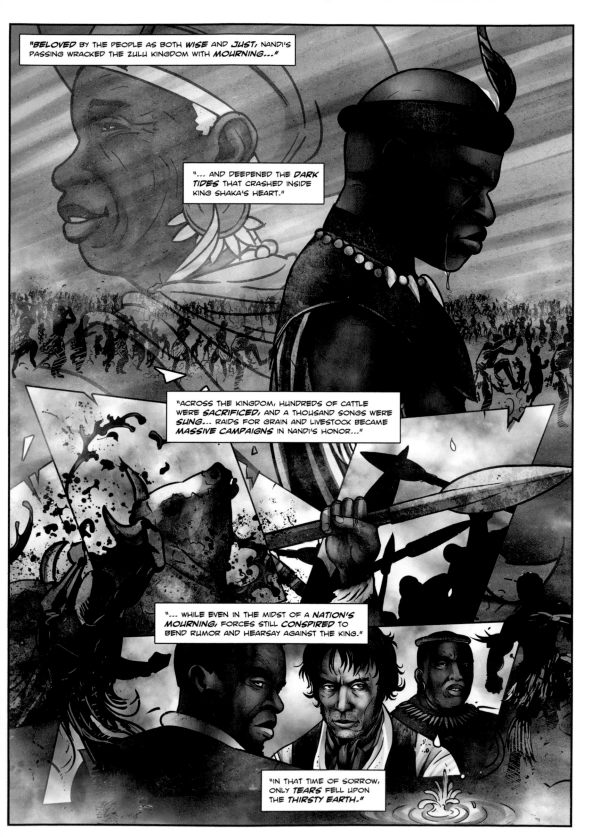

"*BELOVED* BY THE PEOPLE AS BOTH *WISE* AND *JUST,* NANDI'S PASSING WRACKED THE ZULU KINGDOM WITH *MOURNING...*"

"... AND DEEPENED THE *DARK TIDES* THAT CRASHED INSIDE KING SHAKA'S HEART."

"ACROSS THE KINGDOM, HUNDREDS OF CATTLE WERE *SACRIFICED,* AND A THOUSAND SONGS WERE *SUNG...* RAIDS FOR GRAIN AND LIVESTOCK BECAME *MASSIVE CAMPAIGNS* IN NANDI'S HONOR..."

"... WHILE EVEN IN THE MIDST OF A *NATION'S MOURNING,* FORCES STILL *CONSPIRED* TO BEND RUMOR AND HEARSAY AGAINST THE KING."

"IN THAT TIME OF SORROW, ONLY *TEARS* FELL UPON THE *THIRSTY EARTH.*"

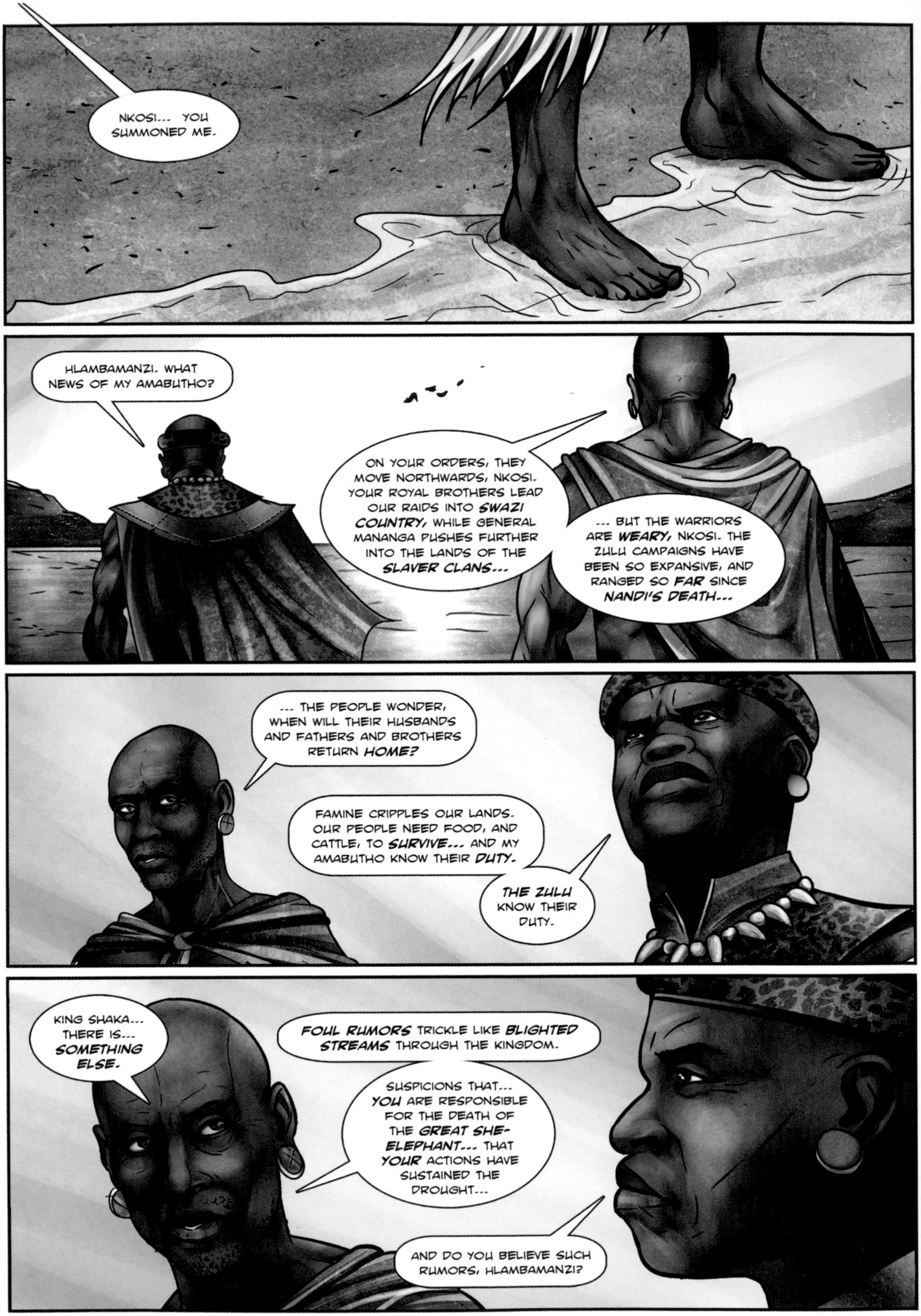
NKOSI... YOU SUMMONED ME.
HLAMBAMANZI. WHAT NEWS OF MY AMABUTHO?
ON YOUR ORDERS, THEY MOVE NORTHWARDS, NKOSI. YOUR ROYAL BROTHERS LEAD OUR RAIDS INTO SWAZI COUNTRY, WHILE GENERAL MANANGA PUSHES FURTHER INTO THE LANDS OF THE SLAVER CLANS...
... BUT THE WARRIORS ARE WEARY, NKOSI. THE ZULU CAMPAIGNS HAVE BEEN SO EXPANSIVE, AND RANGED SO FAR SINCE NANDI'S DEATH...
... THE PEOPLE WONDER, WHEN WILL THEIR HUSBANDS AND FATHERS AND BROTHERS RETURN HOME?
FAMINE CRIPPLES OUR LANDS. OUR PEOPLE NEED FOOD, AND CATTLE, TO SURVIVE... AND MY AMABUTHO KNOW THEIR DUTY.
THE ZULU KNOW THEIR DUTY.
KING SHAKA... THERE IS... SOMETHING ELSE.
FOUL RUMORS TRICKLE LIKE BLIGHTED STREAMS THROUGH THE KINGDOM.
SUSPICIONS THAT... YOU ARE RESPONSIBLE FOR THE DEATH OF THE GREAT SHE-ELEPHANT... THAT YOUR ACTIONS HAVE SUSTAINED THE DROUGHT...
AND DO YOU BELIEVE SUCH RUMORS, HLAMBAMANZI?

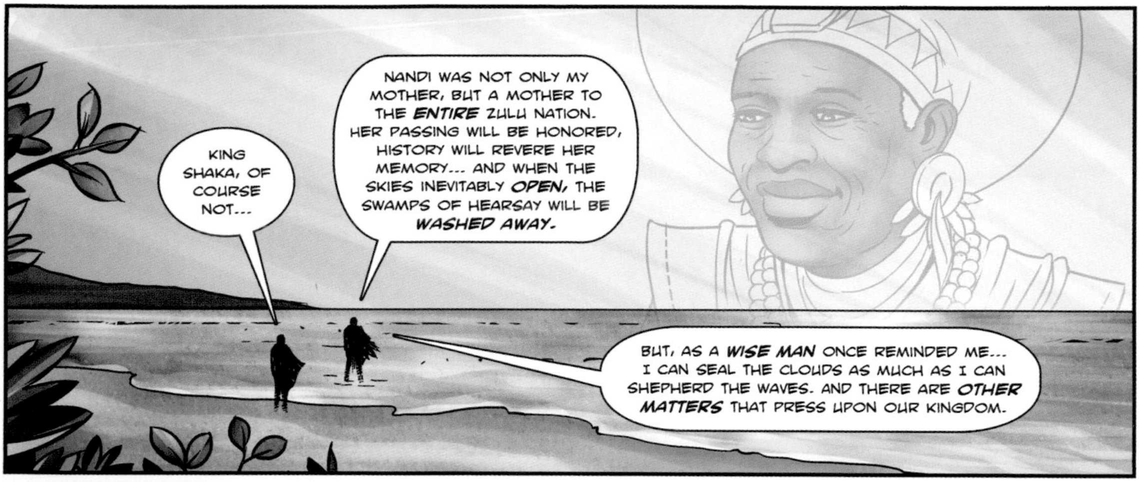

KING SHAKA, OF COURSE NOT...
NANDI WAS NOT ONLY MY MOTHER, BUT A MOTHER TO THE ENTIRE ZULU NATION. HER PASSING WILL BE HONORED, HISTORY WILL REVERE HER MEMORY... AND WHEN THE SKIES INEVITABLY OPEN, THE SWAMPS OF HEARSAY WILL BE WASHED AWAY.
BUT, AS A WISE MAN ONCE REMINDED ME... I CAN SEAL THE CLOUDS AS MUCH AS I CAN SHEPHERD THE WAVES. AND THERE ARE OTHER MATTERS THAT PRESS UPON OUR KINGDOM.

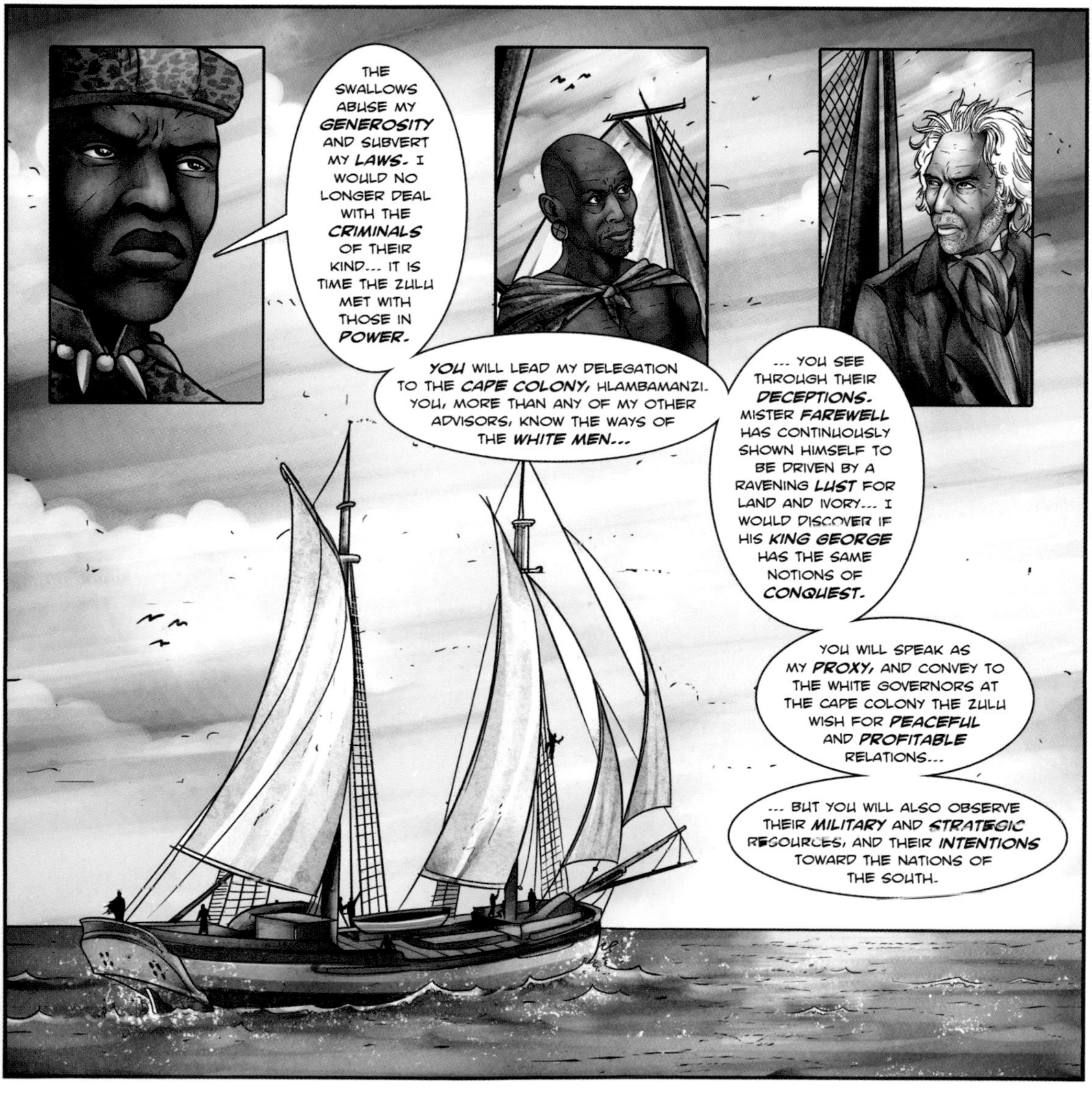

THE SWALLOWS ABUSE MY GENEROSITY AND SUBVERT MY LAWS. I WOULD NO LONGER DEAL WITH THE CRIMINALS OF THEIR KIND... IT IS TIME THE ZULU MET WITH THOSE IN POWER.
YOU WILL LEAD MY DELEGATION TO THE CAPE COLONY, HLAMBAMANZI. YOU, MORE THAN ANY OF MY OTHER ADVISORS, KNOW THE WAYS OF THE WHITE MEN...
... YOU SEE THROUGH THEIR DECEPTIONS. MISTER FAREWELL HAS CONTINUOUSLY SHOWN HIMSELF TO BE DRIVEN BY A RAVENING LUST FOR LAND AND IVORY... I WOULD DISCOVER IF HIS KING GEORGE HAS THE SAME NOTIONS OF CONQUEST.
YOU WILL SPEAK AS MY PROXY, AND CONVEY TO THE WHITE GOVERNORS AT THE CAPE COLONY THE ZULU WISH FOR PEACEFUL AND PROFITABLE RELATIONS...
... BUT YOU WILL ALSO OBSERVE THEIR MILITARY AND STRATEGIC RESOURCES, AND THEIR INTENTIONS TOWARD THE NATIONS OF THE SOUTH.

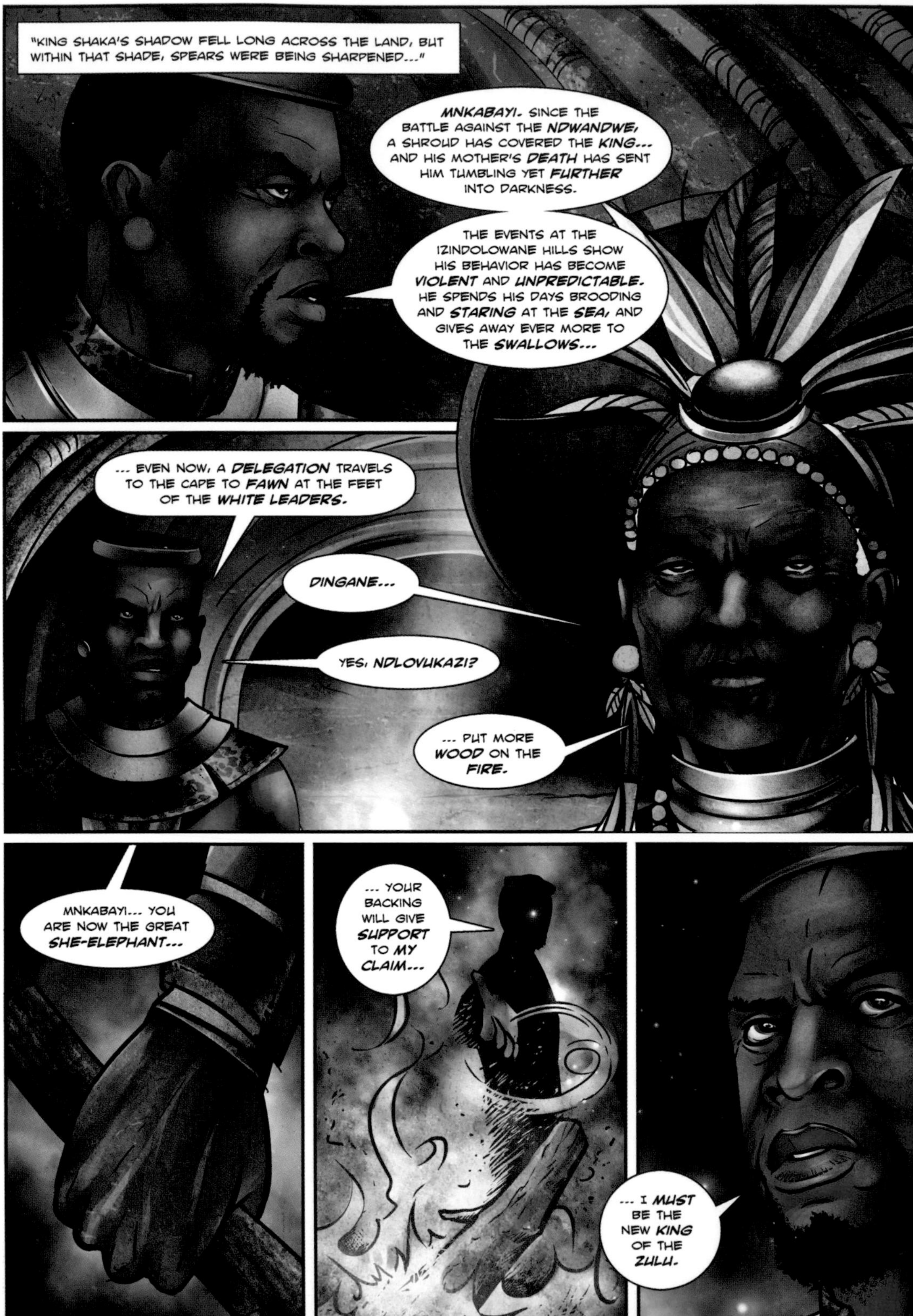
"KING SHAKA'S SHADOW FELL LONG ACROSS THE LAND, BUT WITHIN THAT SHADE, SPEARS WERE BEING SHARPENED..."
MNKABAYI. SINCE THE BATTLE AGAINST THE NDWANDWE, A SHROUD HAS COVERED THE KING... AND HIS MOTHER'S DEATH HAS SENT HIM TUMBLING YET FURTHER INTO DARKNESS.
THE EVENTS AT THE IZINDOLOWANE HILLS SHOW HIS BEHAVIOR HAS BECOME VIOLENT AND UNPREDICTABLE. HE SPENDS HIS DAYS BROODING AND STARING AT THE SEA, AND GIVES AWAY EVER MORE TO THE SWALLOWS...
... EVEN NOW, A DELEGATION TRAVELS TO THE CAPE TO FAWN AT THE FEET OF THE WHITE LEADERS.
DINGANE...
YES, NDLOVUKAZI?
... PUT MORE WOOD ON THE FIRE.
MNKABAYI... YOU ARE NOW THE GREAT SHE-ELEPHANT...
... YOUR BACKING WILL GIVE SUPPORT TO MY CLAIM...
... I MUST BE THE NEW KING OF THE ZULU.

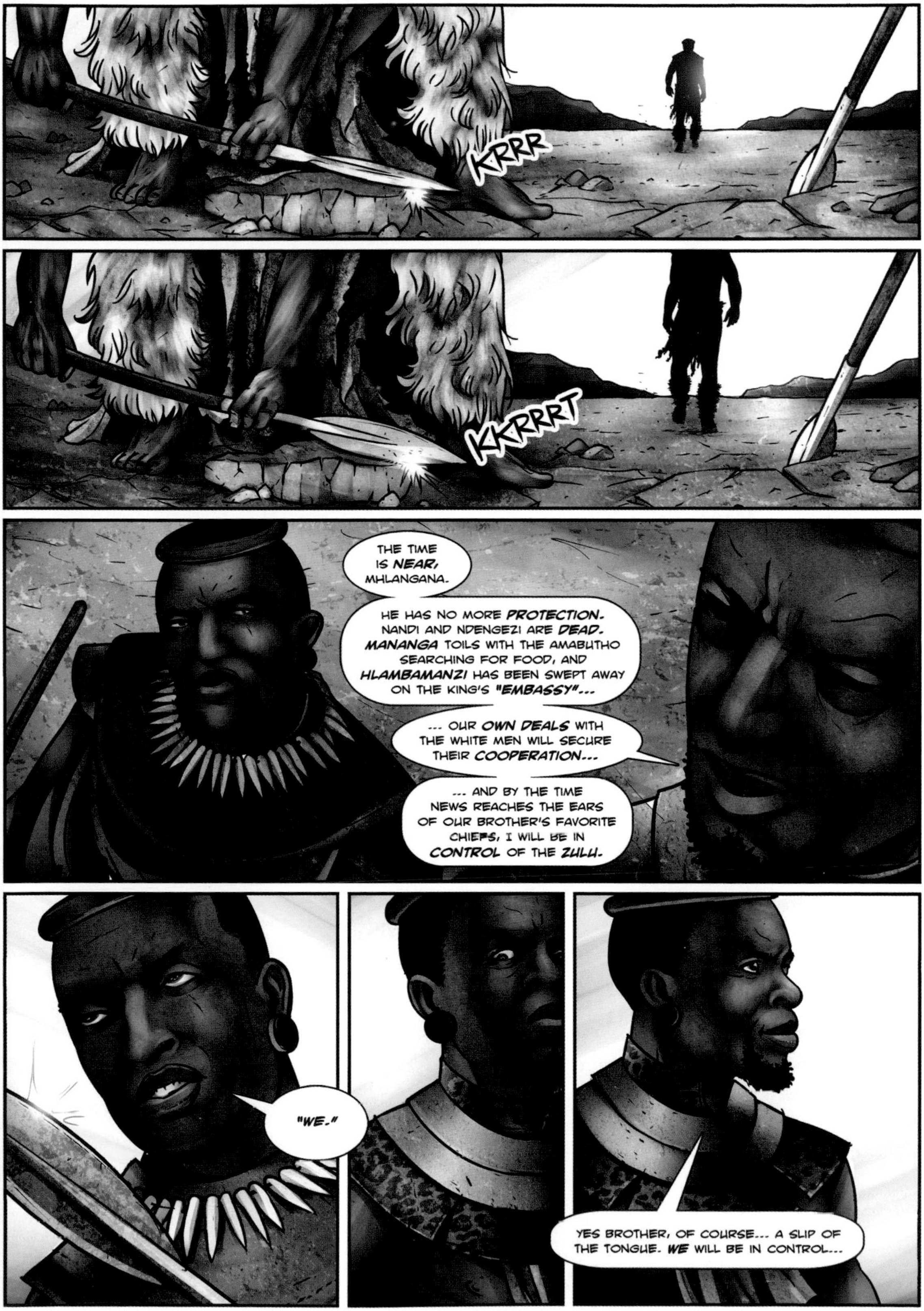
KRRR
KKRRRT
THE TIME IS NEAR, MHLANGANA.
HE HAS NO MORE PROTECTION. NANDI AND NDENGEZI ARE DEAD. MANANGA TOILS WITH THE AMABUTHO SEARCHING FOR FOOD, AND HLAMBAMANZI HAS BEEN SWEPT AWAY ON THE KING'S "EMBASSY"...
... OUR OWN DEALS WITH THE WHITE MEN WILL SECURE THEIR COOPERATION...
... AND BY THE TIME NEWS REACHES THE EARS OF OUR BROTHER'S FAVORITE CHIEFS, I WILL BE IN CONTROL OF THE ZULU.
"WE."
YES BROTHER, OF COURSE... A SLIP OF THE TONGUE. WE WILL BE IN CONTROL...

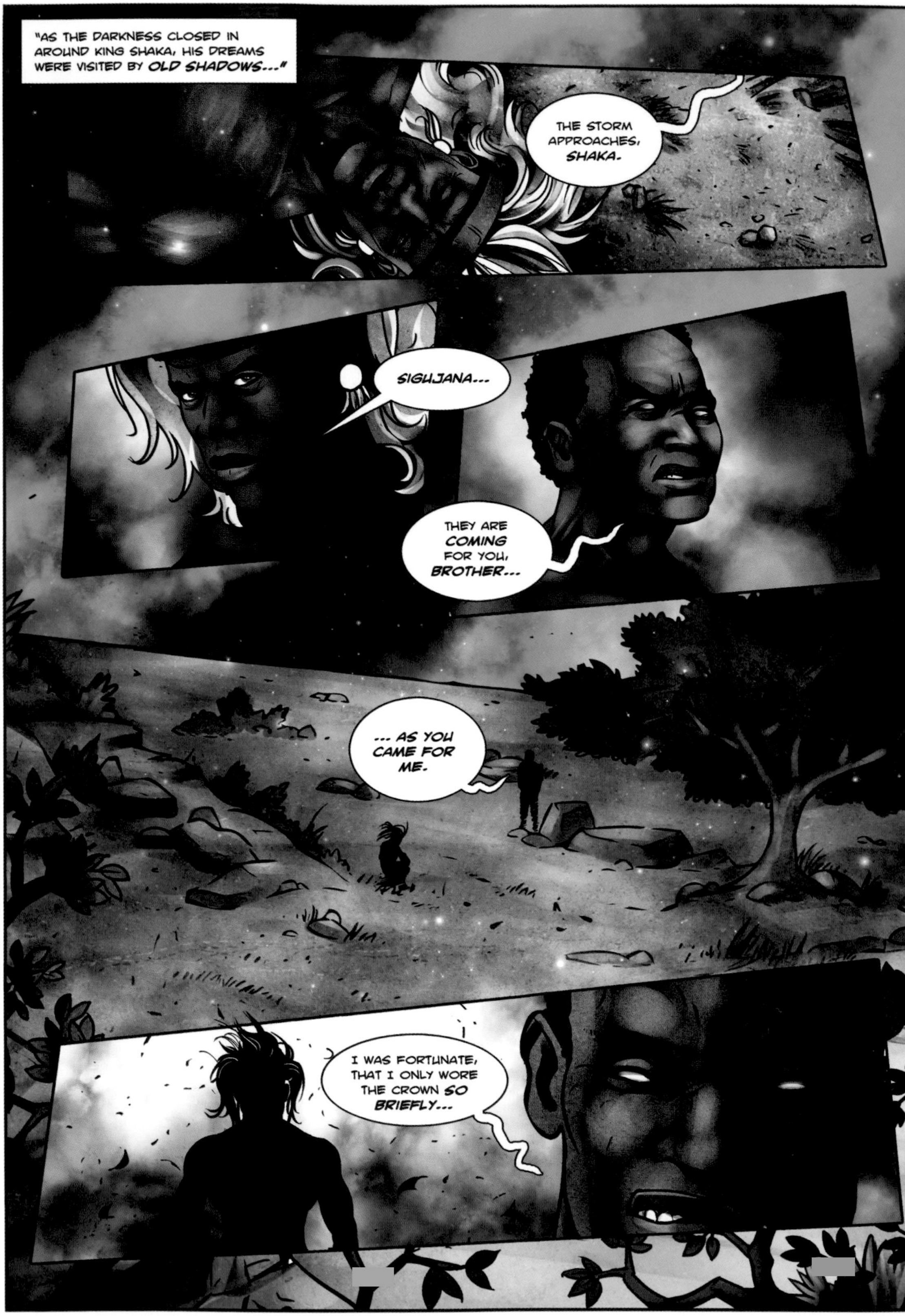
"AS THE DARKNESS CLOSED IN AROUND KING SHAKA, HIS DREAMS WERE VISITED BY OLD SHADOWS..."
THE STORM APPROACHES, SHAKA.
SIGUJANA...
THEY ARE COMING FOR YOU, BROTHER...
... AS YOU CAME FOR ME.
I WAS FORTUNATE, THAT I ONLY WORE THE CROWN SO BRIEFLY...

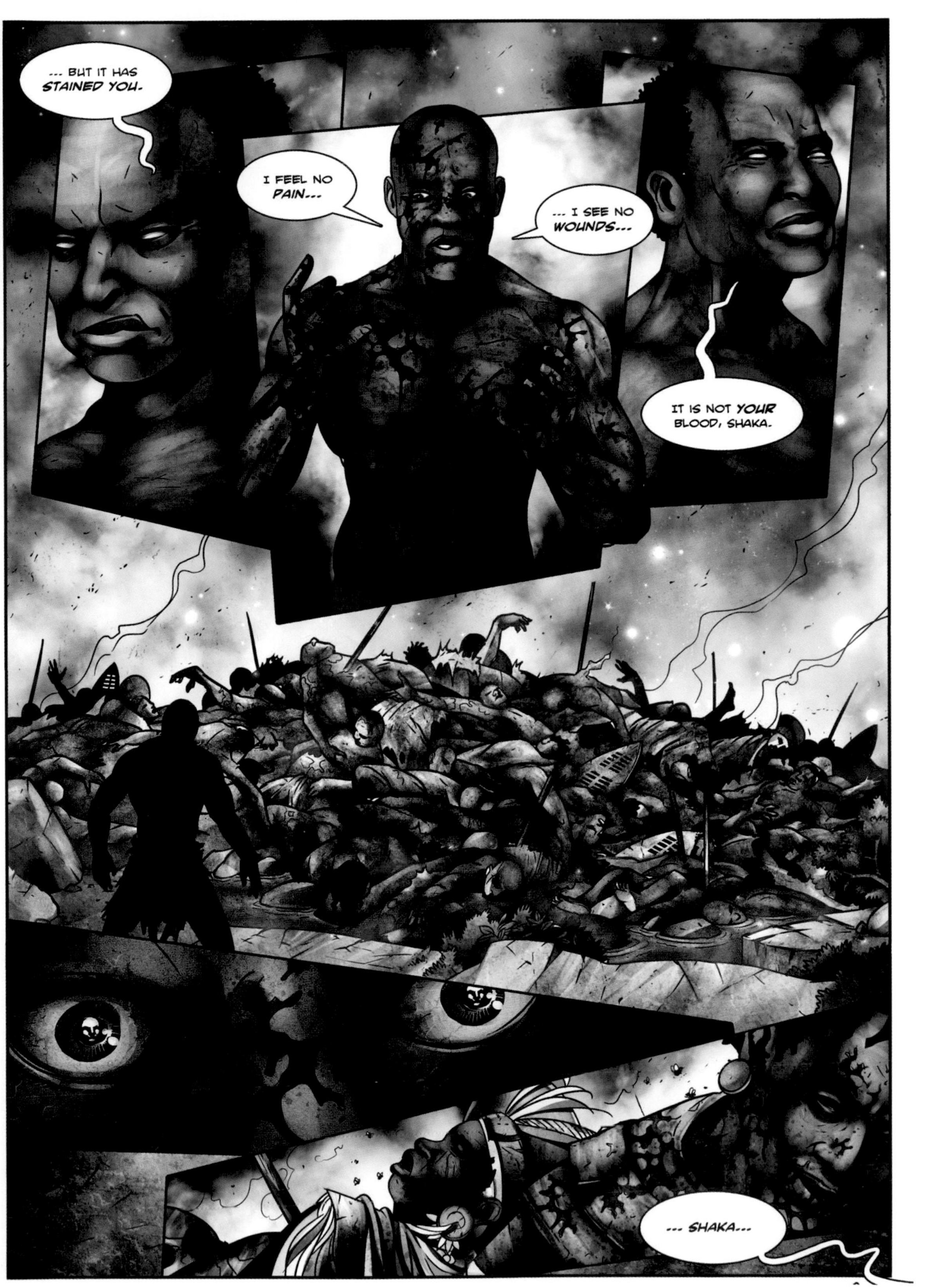
... BUT IT HAS STAINED YOU.
I FEEL NO PAIN...
... I SEE NO WOUNDS...
IT IS NOT YOUR BLOOD, SHAKA.
... SHAKA...

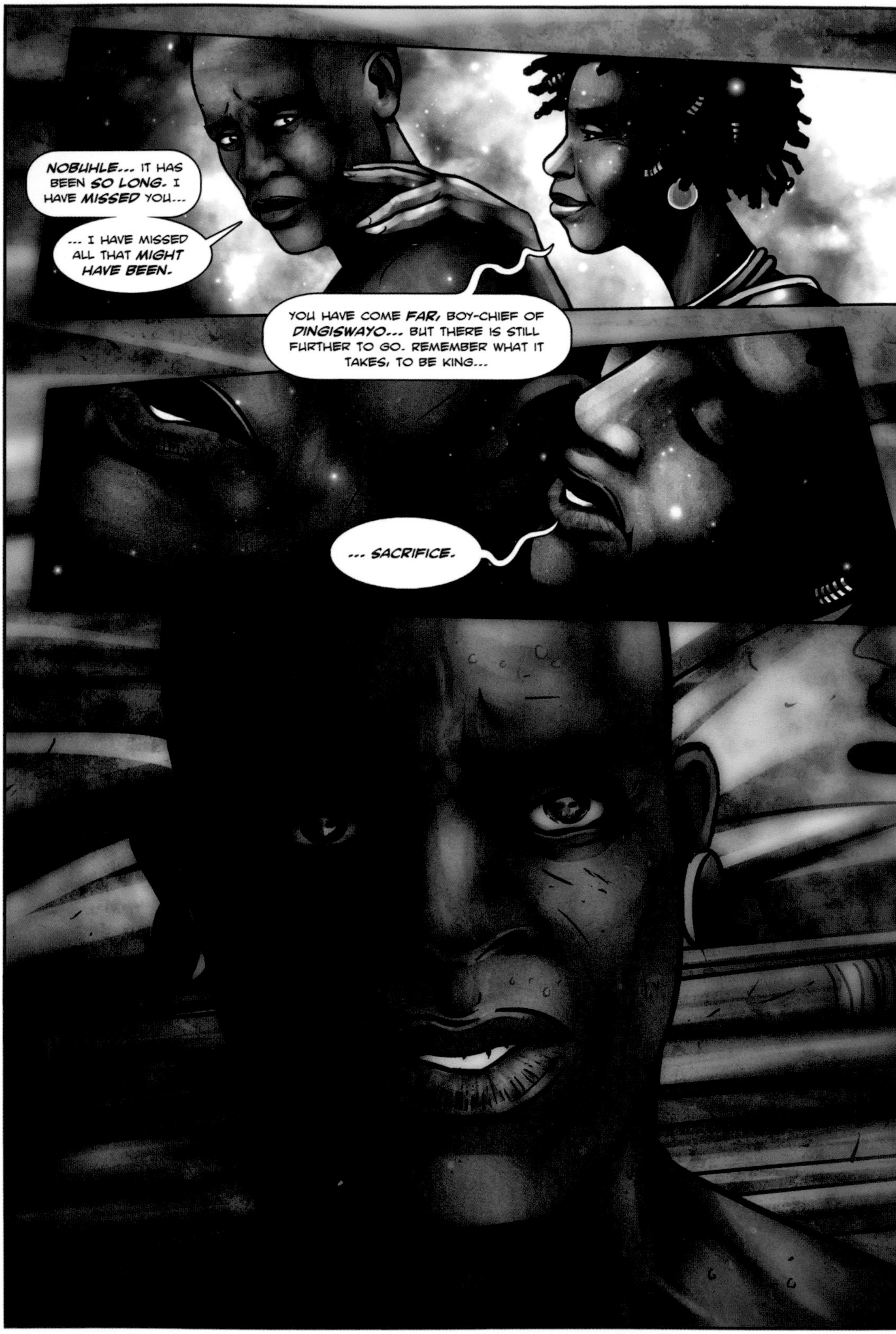
NOBUHLE... IT HAS BEEN SO LONG. I HAVE MISSED YOU...
... I HAVE MISSED ALL THAT MIGHT HAVE BEEN.
YOU HAVE COME FAR, BOY-CHIEF OF DINGISWAYO... BUT THERE IS STILL FURTHER TO GO. REMEMBER WHAT IT TAKES, TO BE KING...
... SACRIFICE.

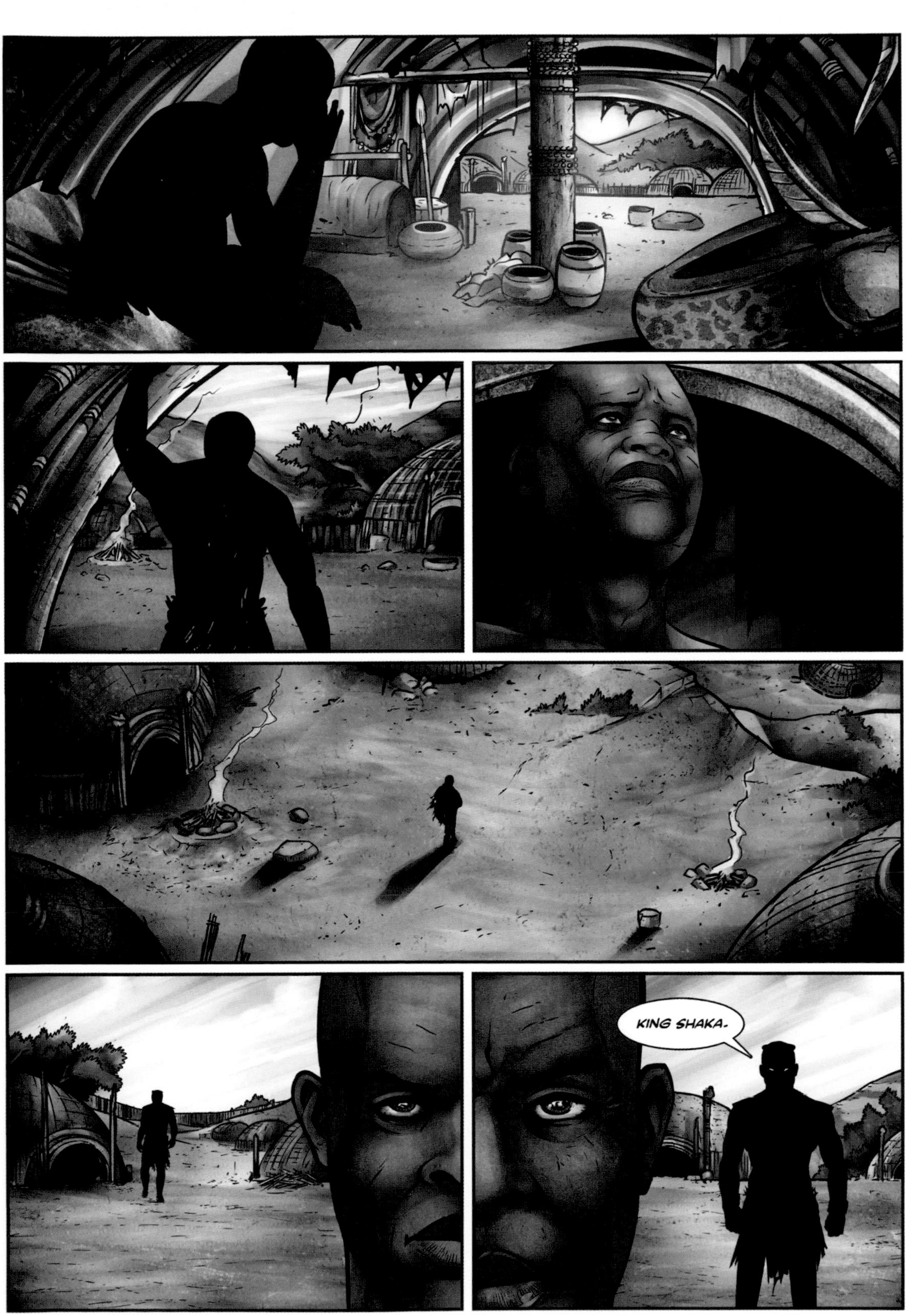
KING SHAKA.

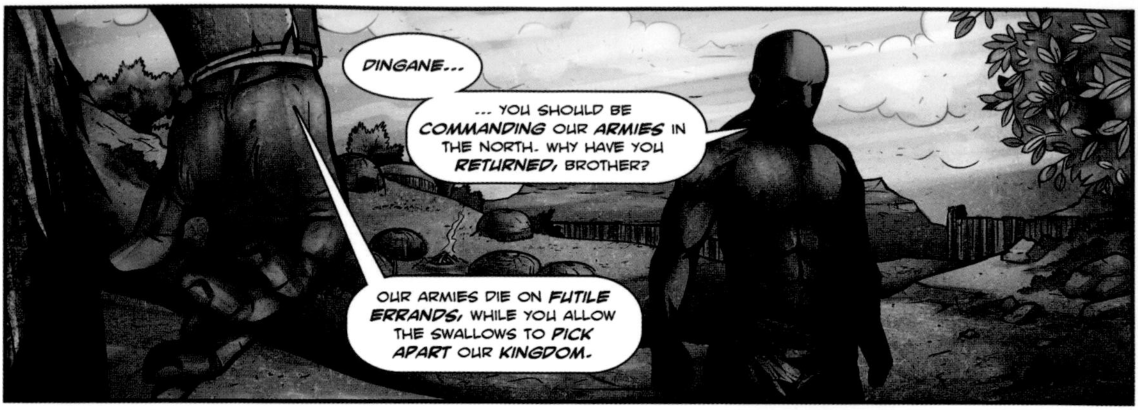

DINGANE...
... YOU SHOULD BE COMMANDING OUR ARMIES IN THE NORTH. WHY HAVE YOU RETURNED, BROTHER?
OUR ARMIES DIE ON FUTILE ERRANDS, WHILE YOU ALLOW THE SWALLOWS TO PICK APART OUR KINGDOM.

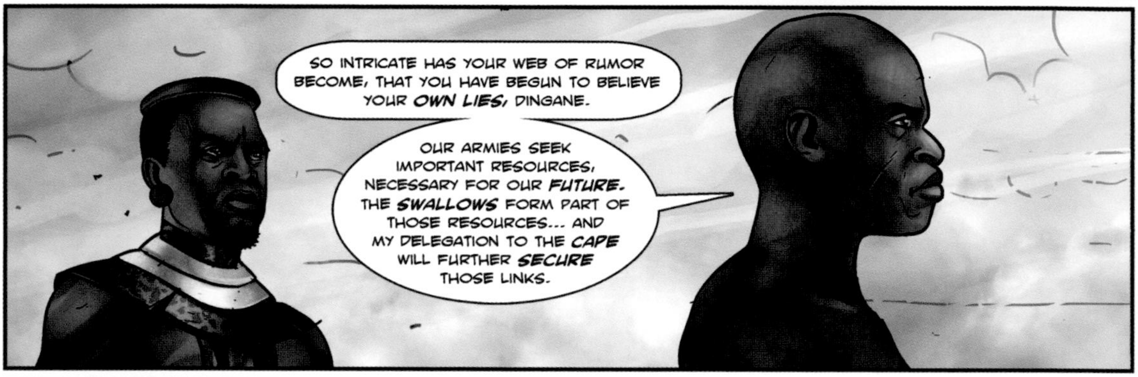

SO INTRICATE HAS YOUR WEB OF RUMOR BECOME, THAT YOU HAVE BEGUN TO BELIEVE YOUR OWN LIES, DINGANE.
OUR ARMIES SEEK IMPORTANT RESOURCES, NECESSARY FOR OUR FUTURE. THE SWALLOWS FORM PART OF THOSE RESOURCES... AND MY DELEGATION TO THE CAPE WILL FURTHER SECURE THOSE LINKS.

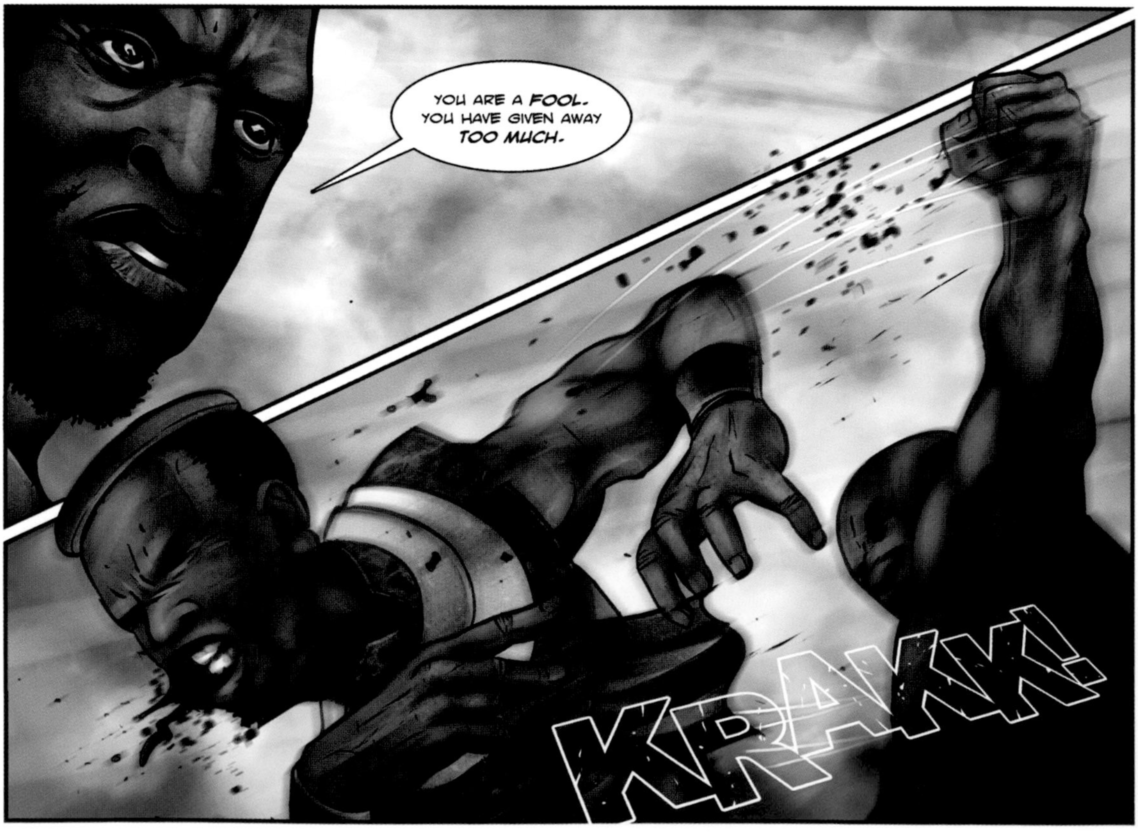

YOU ARE A FOOL. YOU HAVE GIVEN AWAY TOO MUCH.
KRAKK!

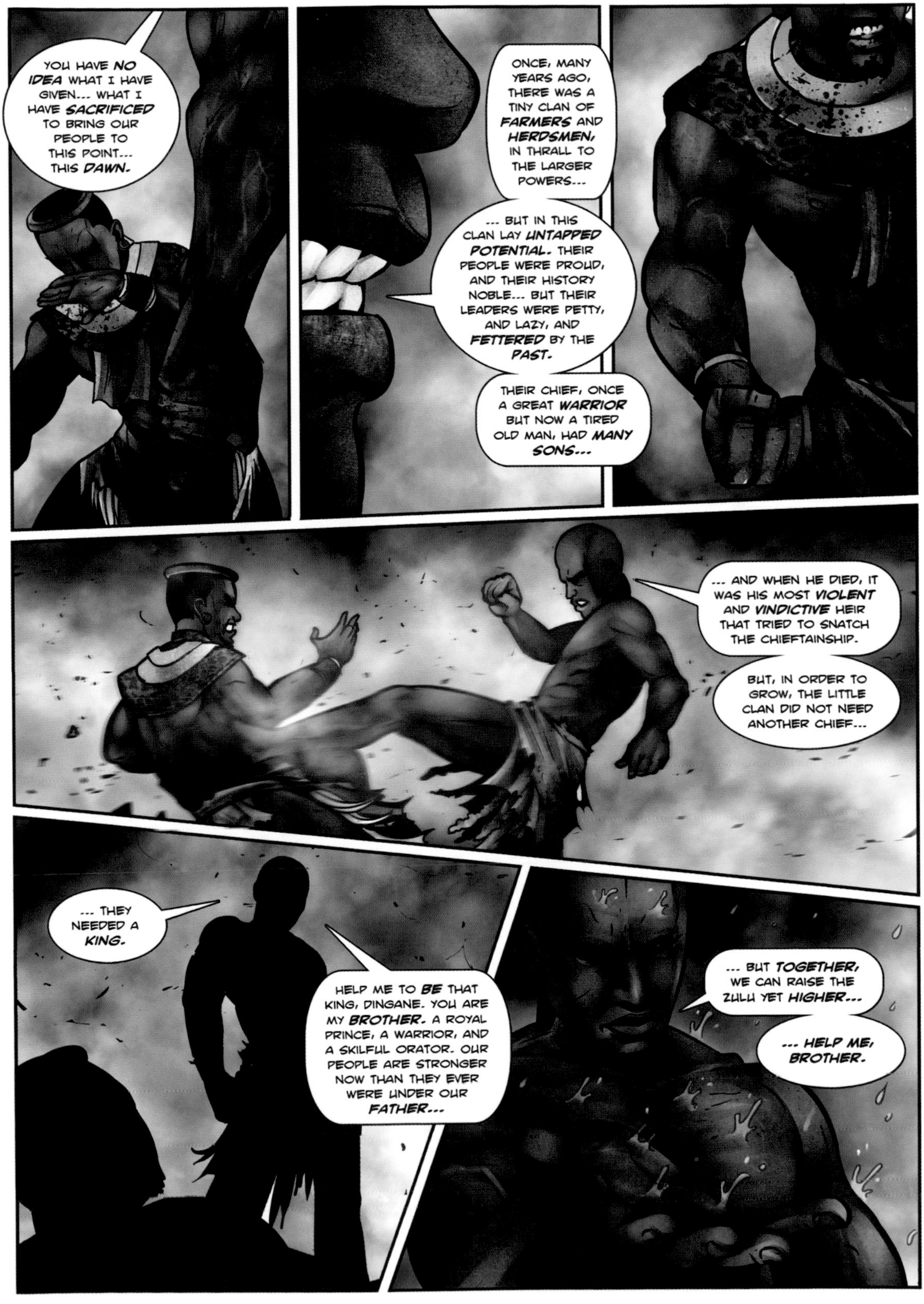
YOU HAVE NO IDEA WHAT I HAVE GIVEN... WHAT I HAVE SACRIFICED TO BRING OUR PEOPLE TO THIS POINT... THIS DAWN.
ONCE, MANY YEARS AGO, THERE WAS A TINY CLAN OF FARMERS AND HERDSMEN, IN THRALL TO THE LARGER POWERS...
... BUT IN THIS CLAN LAY UNTAPPED POTENTIAL. THEIR PEOPLE WERE PROUD, AND THEIR HISTORY NOBLE... BUT THEIR LEADERS WERE PETTY, AND LAZY, AND FETTERED BY THE PAST.
THEIR CHIEF, ONCE A GREAT WARRIOR BUT NOW A TIRED OLD MAN, HAD MANY SONS...
... AND WHEN HE DIED, IT WAS HIS MOST VIOLENT AND VINDICTIVE HEIR THAT TRIED TO SNATCH THE CHIEFTAINSHIP.
BUT, IN ORDER TO GROW, THE LITTLE CLAN DID NOT NEED ANOTHER CHIEF...
... THEY NEEDED A KING.
HELP ME TO BE THAT KING, DINGANE. YOU ARE MY BROTHER. A ROYAL PRINCE, A WARRIOR, AND A SKILFUL ORATOR. OUR PEOPLE ARE STRONGER NOW THAN THEY EVER WERE UNDER OUR FATHER...
... BUT TOGETHER, WE CAN RAISE THE ZULU YET HIGHER...
... HELP ME, BROTHER.

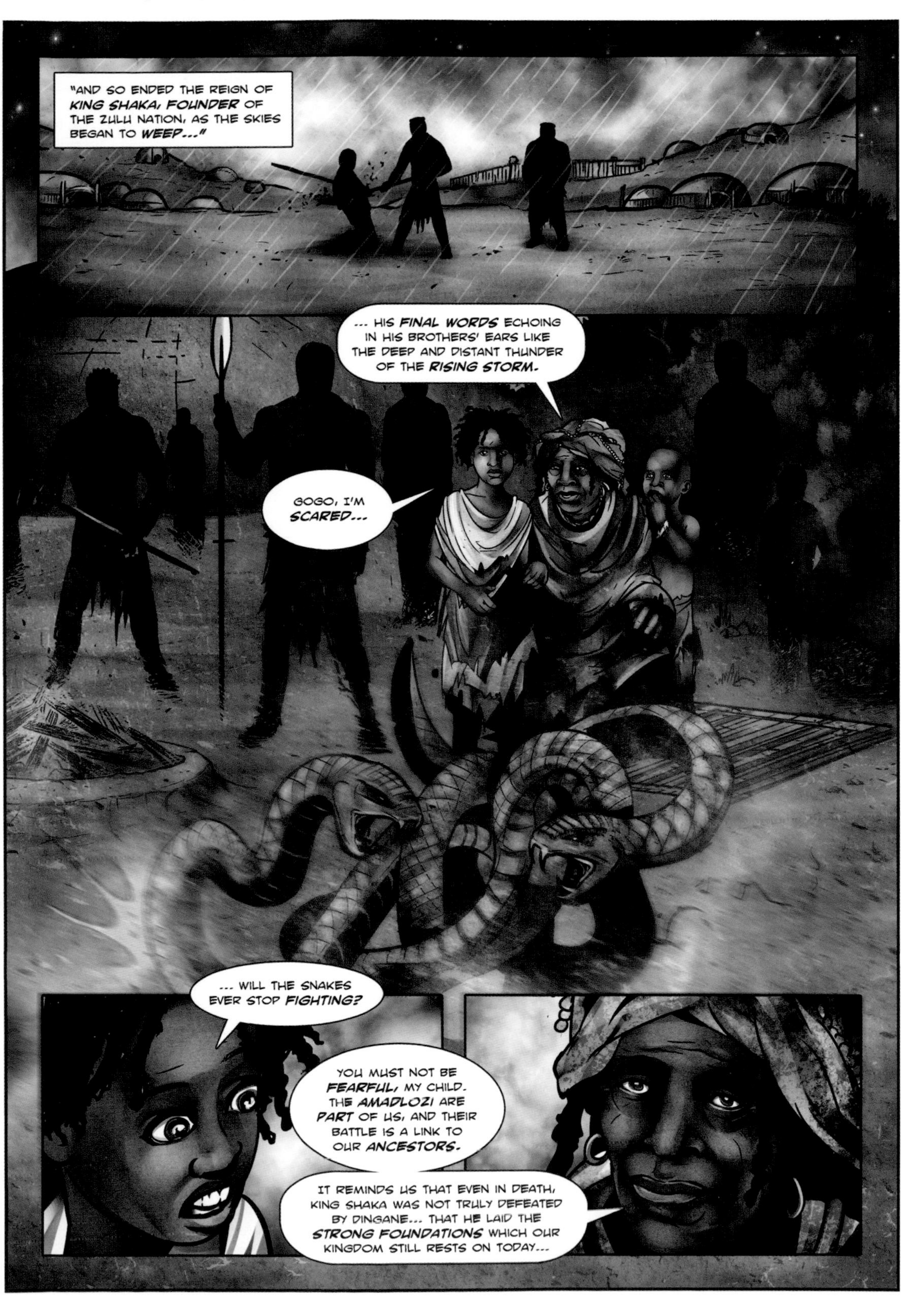
"AND SO ENDED THE REIGN OF KING SHAKA, FOUNDER OF THE ZULU NATION, AS THE SKIES BEGAN TO WEEP..."
... HIS FINAL WORDS ECHOING IN HIS BROTHERS' EARS LIKE THE DEEP AND DISTANT THUNDER OF THE RISING STORM.
GOGO, I'M SCARED...
... WILL THE SNAKES EVER STOP FIGHTING?
YOU MUST NOT BE FEARFUL, MY CHILD. THE AMADLOZI ARE PART OF US, AND THEIR BATTLE IS A LINK TO OUR ANCESTORS.
IT REMINDS US THAT EVEN IN DEATH, KING SHAKA WAS NOT TRULY DEFEATED BY DINGANE... THAT HE LAID THE STRONG FOUNDATIONS WHICH OUR KINGDOM STILL RESTS ON TODAY...

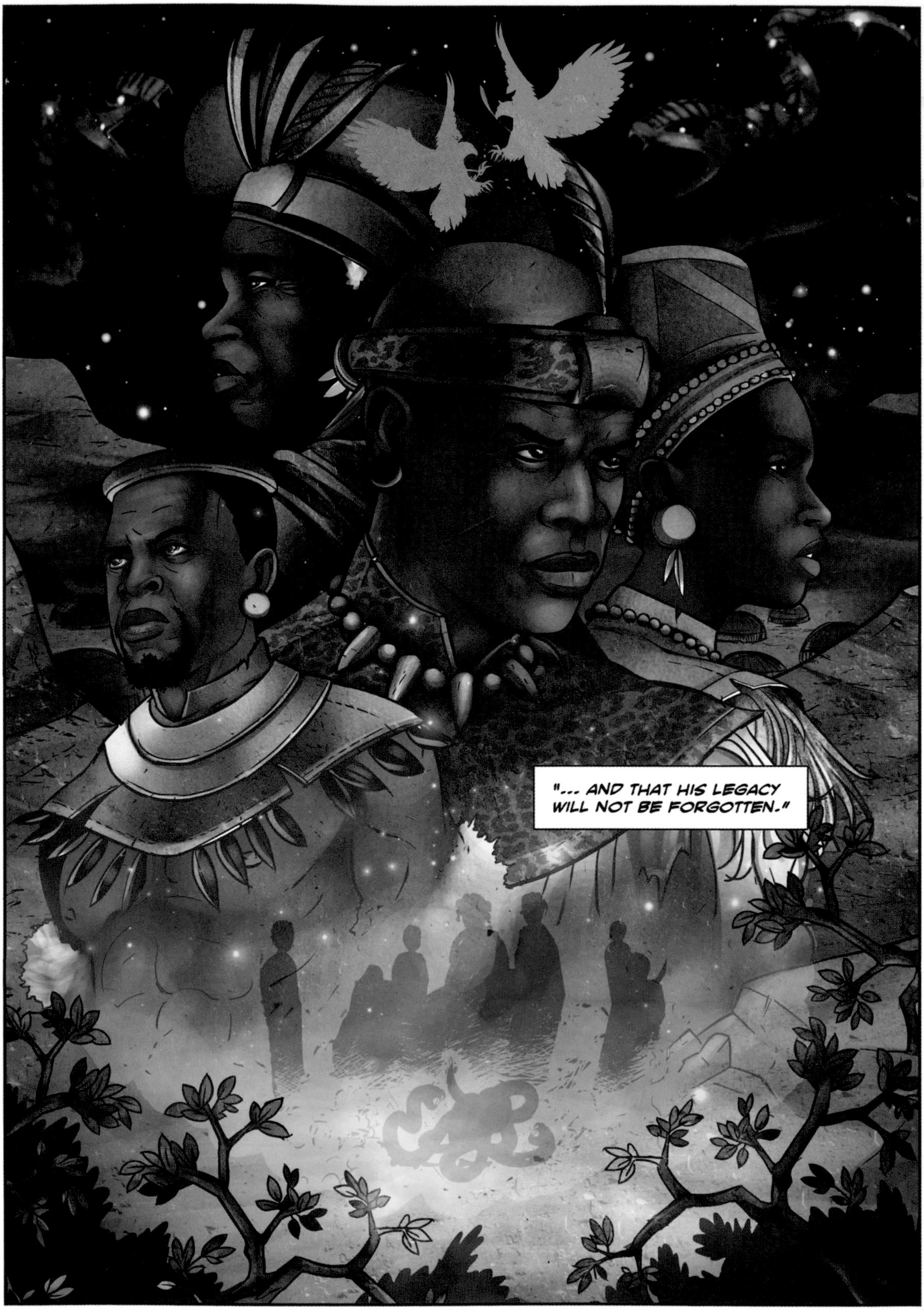
"... AND THAT HIS LEGACY WILL NOT BE FORGOTTEN."

THE STORY CONTINUES

During his reign, King Shaka established the Zulu people as the dominant power among the peoples of south-eastern Africa. After his death, many of his highly effective tactics were continued by his brother King Dingane and his successors. This made the Zulu a formidable force for the next fifty years, and a significant challenge to white settlers and British colonial ambitions.

When Dingane became king, he purged further threats to his rule. The executions included his brother and co-conspirator Mhlangana, proving King Shaka's alleged final words to be hauntingly prophetic.

The expansion of British control and Boer settlements gave rise to ongoing tension between the Zulu and the white newcomers, culminating in the Anglo-Zulu War, fought in 1879. The Zulu military tactics perfected by Shaka led to a humiliating rout of the British army at Isandlwana. Yet later in that year British firepower finally defeated King Cetshwayo's armies at Ulundi.

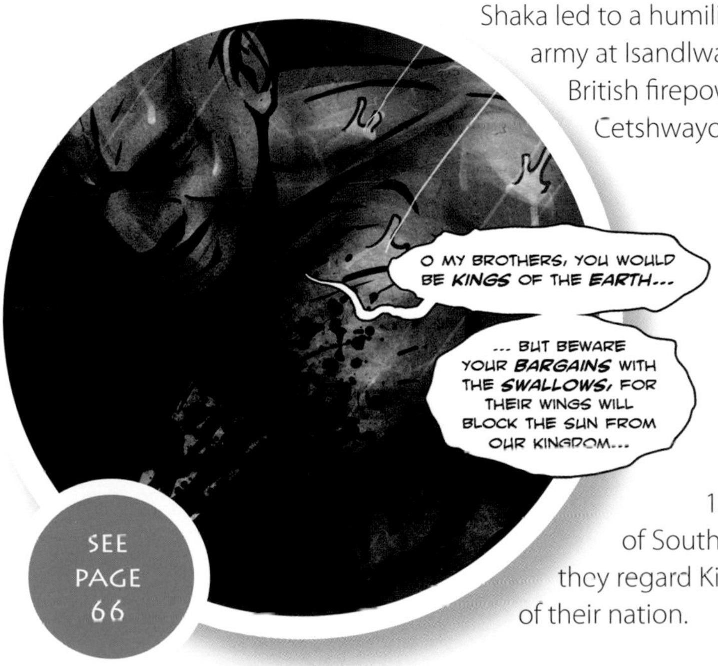
O MY BROTHERS, YOU WOULD BE KINGS OF THE EARTH...
... BUT BEWARE YOUR BARGAINS WITH THE SWALLOWS, FOR THEIR WINGS WILL BLOCK THE SUN FROM OUR KINGDOM...

SEE PAGE 66

King Shaka's legacy lives on. He established a succession of Zulu kings which continues to this day. The current monarch is King Goodwill Zwelithini and the Zulu people number some 12 million – almost a quarter of South Africa's population – and they regard King Shaka as the founder of their nation.

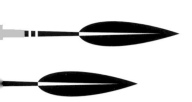

HOW ACCURATE IS THIS STORY?

King Shaka is a "historical fiction" based, as far as possible, on fact. But there are different versions of his story, and this is merely one "telling" of the story. Zulu culture had no written records at that time. It was an oral culture which transmitted its history through the telling and retelling of stories. It was only when Europeans arrived that details of Zulu culture were written down for the first time. These written records were produced mostly by European writers with their own very different "outsider" perspectives.

Oral history can be unreliable. As stories were passed down from each generation to the next, story tellers might exaggerate, select or embellish details. They might want to impress their listeners or portray a character's actions in a favorable light. The accuracy of their memories would differ. All these could lead to very different versions.

Written records can be just as unreliable. In most cases the writers would not have spoken the local language, did not understand the customs of the people they were writing about, and had very different ideas of land ownership and property rights. Most of the documentary records of King Shaka's time were authored by Europeans. In the past, they have been treated as historical fact. More recent research has revealed the ignorance or bias of the writers.

The diary of the Englishman Henry Francis Fynn is an example. His journal is

WILL YOU TELL US A *STORY* TONIGHT, GOGO...?

SEE PAGE 1

one of the more comprehensive written records relaying events and information about the Zulu kingdom in the 1820s and 1830s. Nonetheless, it is riddled with contradictions, exaggerations and even outright lies. This served the purpose of painting a picture of Fynn, Farewell and the other early white British settlers as explorers and pioneers. In reality, they were primarily traders and hunters with commercial obligations to merchants in the Cape, although they tried to avoid British trading regulations.

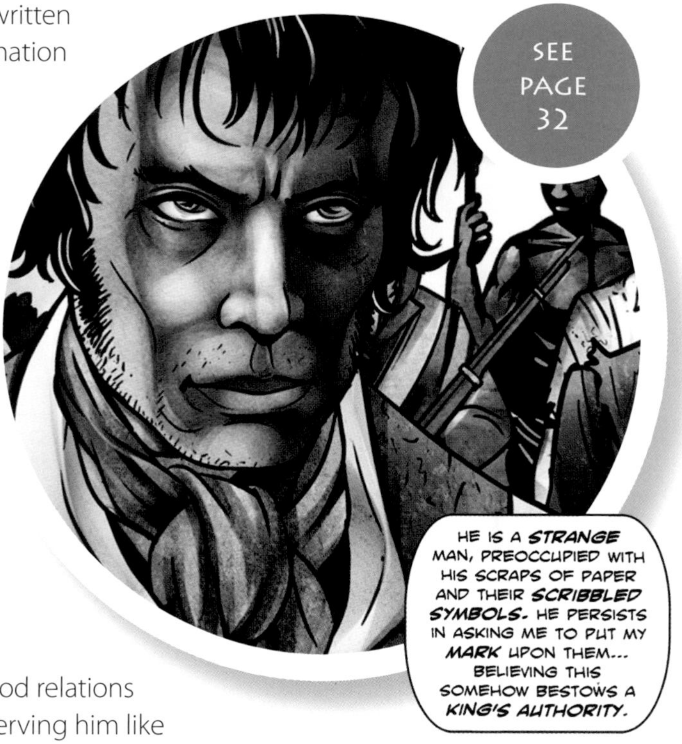
SEE PAGE 32
HE IS A STRANGE MAN, PREOCCUPIED WITH HIS SCRAPS OF PAPER AND THEIR SCRIBBLED SYMBOLS. HE PERSISTS IN ASKING ME TO PUT MY MARK UPON THEM... BELIEVING THIS SOMEHOW BESTOWS A KING'S AUTHORITY.

They did their best to maintain good relations with King Shaka, and this meant serving him like subordinate chiefs, which included military obligations. Other writings from white settlers must also be read with a discerning eye, as they were recorded by people who had their own agendas.

What really happened is, therefore, often difficult to prove. The best we can do is look at all available records and come to our own conclusions about the most convincing version of the truth.

For some aspects of King Shaka's life there are very few records or none at all. In *King Shaka* some elements of the story have been fabricated for the sake of exploring "what might have been." For example, the character of Nonzama, commander of the rogue iziYendane ibutho, was based on a real person. However, little is known of the reasons for his treachery. These reasons are imagined in the comic as a catalyst for King Shaka's own self-doubt and to dramatize the dilemmas of rulership.

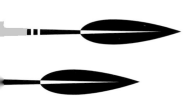

THE HISTORICAL SETTING OF KING SHAKA'S TIME

The events of *King Shaka* take place in the 1820s, soon after the story of *Shaka Rising*, and trace approximately the final eight years of the Zulu king's life.

Unreliable records notwithstanding, it seems that King Shaka was probably born in the early 1780s. To give some global context to his life, he was born shortly after America had gained independence from British Rule (1776), and before the French Revolution (1789).

When he was born, the Zulu were a small clan living approximately 200 kilometers (125 miles) north-east of the present-day port of Durban. After becoming king, he quickly elevated the Zulu to their position as one of the most dominant clans of southern Africa. He was the first Zulu leader to deal with European colonization and white settlement encroaching on his lands.

The timeline shows the succession of the three Zulu kings who held power after King Shaka's death, and the important historical events that punctuated their reigns.

KEY EVENTS IN ZULU HISTORY 1828–1879

Death of King Shaka

Dingane executes Boer delegation

1828 — King Dingane kaSenzangakhona, ruled 1828–1840

1837 — Boers invade the Zulu kingdom

1838 — Boers defeat Zulu forces at Ncome

1839

1840 — Boer republic of Natalia established south of Thukela River

SEE PAGE 23

Fynn and Farewell were among the first white arrivals to venture on to Zulu soil; but they were not the last. King Shaka's first embassies to the Cape Colony aimed to obtain military intelligence, but were also genuine attempts to open official relations between the Zulu and the British. Unfortunately, these efforts were consistently undermined by greed, misconceptions, treachery and fear on both sides.

After King Shaka's death, his successor King Dingane fared no better in creating relations with the British. By this

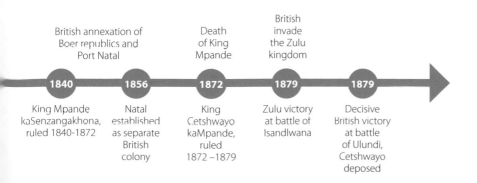

British annexation of Boer republics and Port Natal
1840
King Mpande kaSenzangakhona, ruled 1840-1872

1856
Natal established as separate British colony

Death of King Mpande
1872
King Cetshwayo kaMpande, ruled 1872–1879

British invade the Zulu kingdom
1879
Zulu victory at battle of Isandlwana

1879
Decisive British victory at battle of Ulundi, Cetshwayo deposed

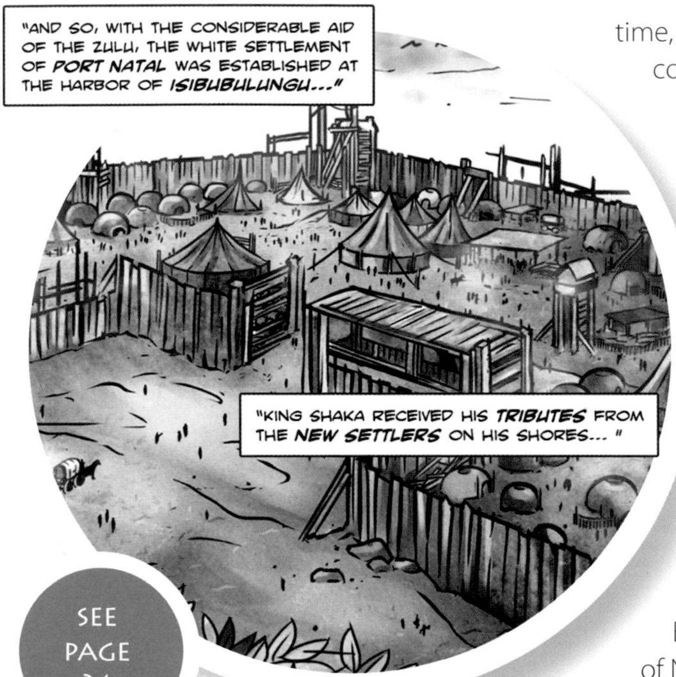
"AND SO, WITH THE CONSIDERABLE AID OF THE ZULU, THE WHITE SETTLEMENT OF PORT NATAL WAS ESTABLISHED AT THE HARBOR OF ISIBUBULUNGU..."
"KING SHAKA RECEIVED HIS TRIBUTES FROM THE NEW SETTLERS ON HIS SHORES..."

SEE PAGE 31

time, the Zulu were also increasingly coming into conflict with the Boers, Dutch settlers who had left the Cape Colony in the mid-1830s and sought to establish new republics of their own – one of which, the Republic of Natalia, occupied some Zulu territory. These conflicts escalated when King Dingane had an entire Boer delegation put to death, sparking a series of bloody battles between the Zulu and the Boers, culminating in The Battle of Ncome (popularly known as the "Battle of Blood River"). King Dingane's forces suffered a heavy defeat in this clash, and Dingane ceded the Boers all Zulu territory south of the Thukela River.

Soon afterwards his brother Mpande forged an alliance with the Boers. This enabled Mpande to overthrow King Dingane and become king himself. In 1843 the British annexed the Boer Republic of Natalia (including the land Dingane had ceded the Boers) as the colony of Natal and recognized the Zulu kingdom north of the Thukela.

This rising tide of white colonization displaced many thousands and led to much bloody conflict over the next decades. The independence of the Zulu kingdom finally came to an end in 1879, when British forces invaded KwaZulu (Zululand) and defeated the Zulu under King Cetshwayo. But this was only after the Zulu army had inflicted a humiliating defeat on the British at Isandlwana – the worst defeat ever suffered by a British force at the hands of an indigenous people defending their territory.

SEE PAGE 57

... YOU **SEE** THROUGH THEIR **DECEPTIONS.** MISTER **FAREWELL** HAS CONTINUOUSLY SHOWN HIMSELF TO BE DRIVEN BY A RAVENING **LUST** FOR LAND AND IVORY...

THE CHALLENGES OF LEADERSHIP

In 1824 the Zulu encountered white people for the first time when Henry Fynn and company were shipwrecked on the cost near isiBubulungu, later known as Port Natal, where they intended to settle and trade. The whites were woefully under-prepared to survive on this unknown coast, and would have perished without the considerable aid of the Zulu. Although King Shaka was wary of the new arrivals, he provided timber and a workforce to help build the settlement that would become Port Natal.

At different stages during his reign King Shaka had many different leadership roles to play. During the events of *King Shaka* he united local chiefdoms, led his people into battle,

SEE PAGE 46

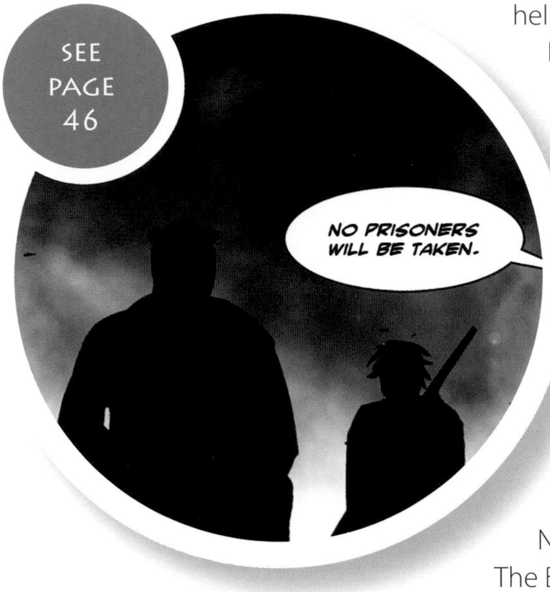
NO PRISONERS WILL BE TAKEN.

helped establish the white settlers at Port Natal in exchange for tributes of ivory and firepower, and ultimately sent a Zulu embassy to the Cape Colony in an attempt to open dialogue with the British.

King Shaka had to keep these roles and many more in a delicate balance with each other – a balance that was often very difficult to maintain. King Shaka's people wanted safety and prosperity. His brothers plotted for power. The Ndwandwe sought slaves and revenge. The British hunter-traders wanted access to ivory and a secure settlement. The Boers wanted to establish their own little republic on Zulu soil. Inside and outside the Zulu kingdom, turbulent change was taking place, and King Shaka had to prioritize where to focus his energies and resources. To protect his people's future he needed to adapt to a shifting socio-political landscape that no Zulu leader had faced before.

These issues, and the ways in which King Shaka chose to manage them, created an unavoidable separation between the king and his people. Those friends and family closest

KEY EVENTS DURING KING SHAKA'S REIGN

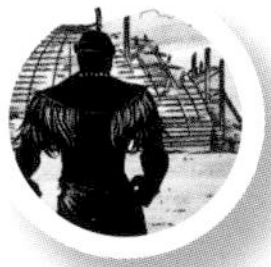

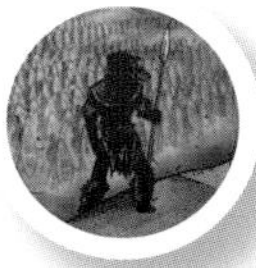

1819 Shaka defeats the Ndwandwe at the Mhlatuze River

1820 New Zulu capital is established at KwaBulawayo

1821

1822 Renegade iziYendane *ibutho* ravages the southern reaches of Shaka's kingdom

1823

to him – Nomcoba, Nandi and Ndengezi – were ultimately distanced, making King Shaka a legendary figure, but also a lonely one.

King Shaka upset much of the status quo for his people with his methods of rule, and this did not please everybody. However, it is undeniable that his reign laid the groundwork for the kings who followed him, and his legacy lives on even today.

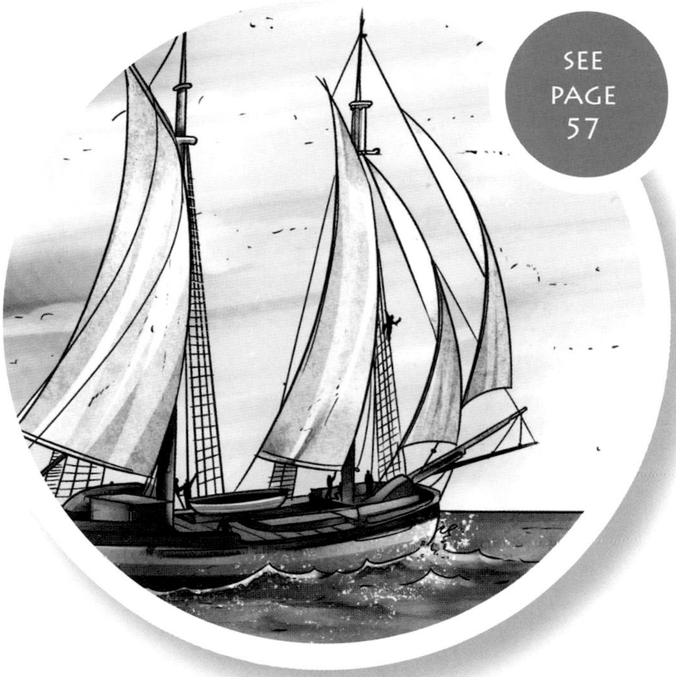

SEE PAGE 57

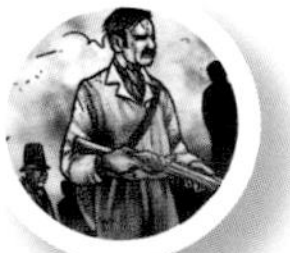

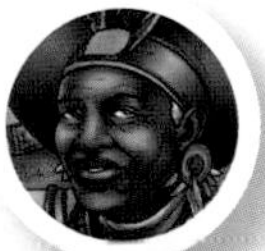

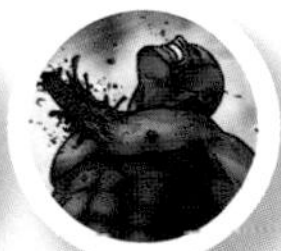

- **1824** Henry Fynn and company are shipwrecked on the coast near the Zulu homelands
- **1825** With Zulu aid, the white settlement of Port Natal is established at isiBubulungu
- **1826** The Ndwandwe are decisively defeated by the Zulu at the izinDolowane hills
- **1827** Nandi dies, and Shaka sends his first embassy to the Cape Colony
- **1828** Death of King Shaka

Zulu political structures

King Shaka's rise to power and period of rule can be seen as a departure from the existing system of localized chiefdoms – each consisting of a cluster of homesteads which housed extended family groups – in favor of a more complex state. When he took leadership of the Zulu, King Shaka united many of the disparate chiefdoms into one organized kingdom under his rule. He was able to command and extract labor from these allied chiefdoms both for military service and for building projects. In return he offered protection, helped resolve disputes, and allowed the various chiefs conditional autonomy over their own lands. King Shaka's rule was an elaborate but effective balance of social, political, and economic obligations, backed by military power.

SEE PAGE 11

"THE ZULU RULER HAD QUICKLY REALIZED THAT EVEN DURING TIMES OF CELEBRATION, THAT DANCE OF POLITICS NEVER ENDED... AND *PETTY RIVALRIES* AND *SIMMERING DISCONTENT* COULD BRING AN *EMPIRE* TO ITS *KNEES.*"

SEE PAGE 8

An important aspect of King Shaka's success in building the Zulu kingdom was his extensive use of the *amabutho* (singular: *ibutho*). Roughly translated as "regiments," these were more akin to mobile, multi-purpose labor forces that could number anywhere between a few hundred and several thousand men. Their numerous roles included raiding other chiefdoms or exacting tribute from them, establishing new *amakhanda* (royal military homesteads) and enforcing King Shaka's rule in outlying areas. Each *ibutho* had its own name and distinguished itself with specific colors and regalia. The iziYendane, for example, were known for their red shields and dreadlocked hair.

THE ROLE OF WOMEN

Zulu society in King Shaka's time was patriarchal, like most societies throughout history, and many still today. Men held power and authority over women, children and lesser-ranked men. A man was the head of his household. Yet women had a crucial part to play, and could be very influential in the politics of Zulu society.

The day-to-day roles of women included running the household, growing the crops, and raising the children. Typically this was done communally by all the women of a homestead. Women were also used as political devices: through marriage, clans could strengthen relations and form new alliances.

In *King Shaka*, we also see the key role played by the *amakhosikazi*, or female elders. High-ranking women in the

KING SHAKA HAS WELCOMED THESE *WHITE SWALLOWS* INTO OUR LANDS, AND ALLOWS THEM TO *NEST...*

SEE PAGE 27

royal house, such as King Shaka's mother Nandi and his aunt Mnkabayi, held considerable influence in society, and were often consulted for advice or guidance. Mnkabayi herself was known as "The Kingmaker," reputed by many accounts to have been instrumental in the succession of Senzangakhona, Shaka and Dingane to their positions as kings of the Zulu.

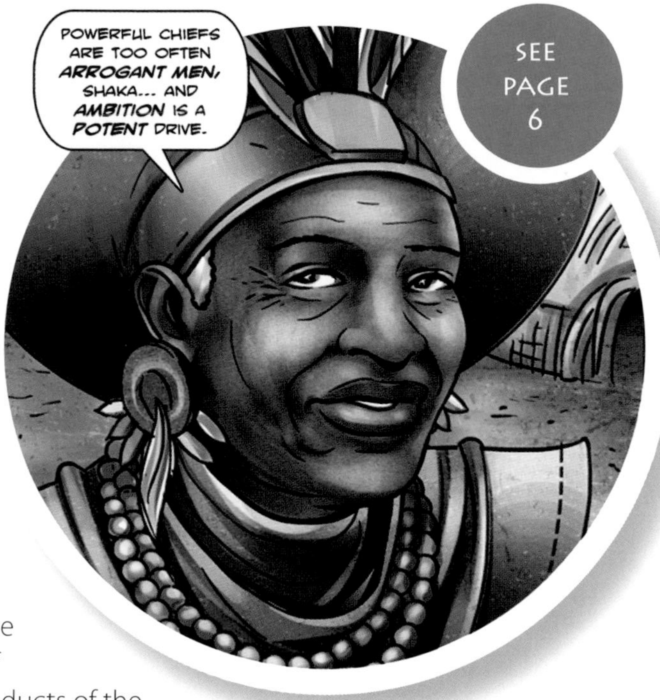
POWERFUL CHIEFS ARE TOO OFTEN **ARROGANT MEN,** SHAKA... AND **AMBITION** IS A **POTENT** DRIVE.

SEE PAGE 6

The role of the *amakhosikazi* also included overseeing marriage alliances, directing distribution of provisions and managing the products of the women's agricultural labor.

King Shaka's appointment of the *amakhosikazi* to his outlying royal homesteads (*amakhanda*) is an example of the king's unique shrewdness. While their presence as King Shaka's proxies would offset the ambitions of potentially troublesome chiefs, they could never, as women, be a direct genealogical threat.

Perhaps of understated importance was the role of elder women (such as Gogo) as storytellers. More than simple night-time tales for the children, these oral storytelling traditions formed an important generational history of the Zulu people at the time, a tradition that continues today.

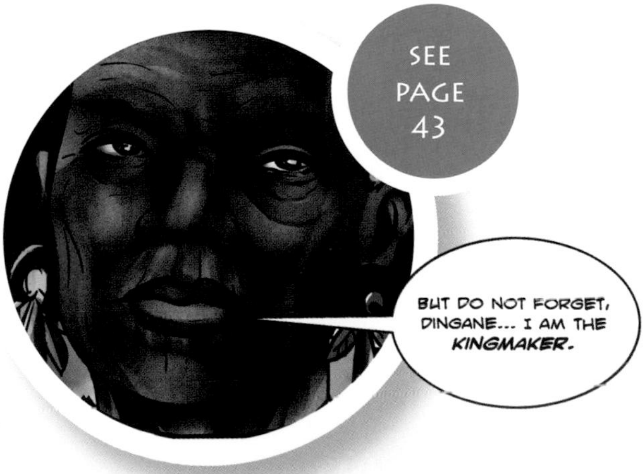
BUT DO NOT FORGET, DINGANE... I AM THE **KINGMAKER.**

SEE PAGE 43

SEE PAGE 52

I WILL KILL NO MORE BROTHERS!

Siblings

In this story we encounter King Shaka's sister Nomcoba, and his half-brothers Dingane, Mhlangana, and briefly, Sigujana. They shared a father but had different mothers.

If you have any siblings, you will likely be familiar with the close bonds that you form, as well as the rivalries that occur. The same was true of Shaka, Dingane, Mhlangana and Sigujana as they grew up together. Despite these bonds, there came a time when the brothers would kill each other to eliminate rivals and become king.

Compare this with the relationship King Shaka had with Nomcoba. The two trusted and cared for each other, and she saw King Shaka's reluctance to kill another brother – even though King Shaka probably suspected Dingane of conspiring against him.

THE ROYAL HOMESTEAD

The Zulu capital of KwaBulawayo, arguably King Shaka's most famous homestead (*ikhanda*), was situated some twenty kilometers (12½ miles) north-east of present-day Eshowe. While Henry Fynn's exaggerated records attest that it was between two and three miles in circumference, the reality is probably closer to about 350 meters (1150 feet) from the lowest gate to the royal enclosure, or *isigodlo*, at the top.

The *isigodlo* was the most tightly guarded area of a large Zulu homestead, furthest from the main gate. This is where the king would stay. The other inhabitants of the *isigodlo* were elderly female relations or widows of his predecessor, the king's wives (if he had any), maidens given in tribute to serve as the king's concubines and to marry out in return for a bride-price (*ilobolo*), and female servants, often captured in war.

SEE PAGE 24

Certain ceremonies would also take place within this royal enclosure. The operations of the *isigodlo* and its women were typically the responsibility of the *amakhosikazi*.

ZULU CULTURE AND BELIEFS

In Zulu culture, belief in the supernatural was an important aspect of their understanding of life and death. The spirits of the ancestors (*amadlozi*) were believed to influence health and human relations – for good or for bad.

Herbalists, known as *izinyanga*, could diagnose and treat physical ailments using medicines prepared from various plants. *Izangoma* were diviners believed to have direct contact with the *amadlozi* (ancestors) from whom they sought help to discern the future, grant favorable conditions, wish ill upon another person, and solve or create conflict within relationships. They also used medicines (*imithi*) in their treatments, prepared from plants and animal parts.

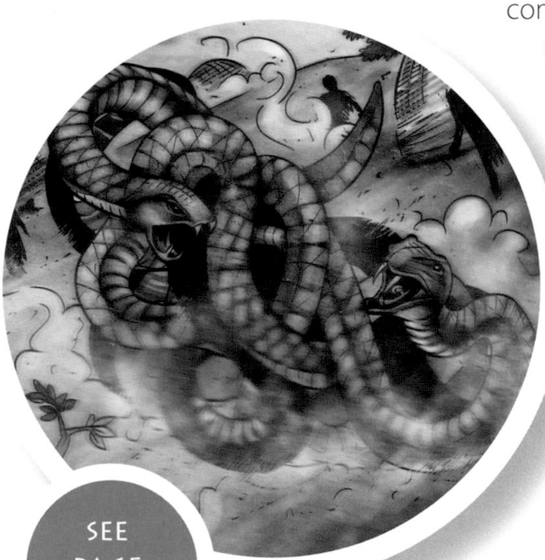

SEE PAGE 2

In the Zulu belief system, the realms of the living and the dead were inextricably linked. The *amadlozi* watched and communicated through signs and symbolism. Snakes in particular were a common vessel for *amadlozi* who wished to revisit the world of the living.

Ritual and ceremony were important parts of Zulu culture, and the *umKhosi*, or First Fruits Ceremony, was the grandest example of this. The umKhosi was typically an exuberant and impressive display of rain-dancing, ritual medicines, prayers to the ancestors, and cattle sacrifices to honor them. The king, as the great rain-maker, was ritually "strengthened" against his enemies and the allegiance of his subjects was reaffirmed.

LANGUAGE AND NAMING

The Zulu language, *isiZulu*, makes use of many idioms and metaphors. For example, instead of King Shaka saying, "You have stabbed me," he says to his brothers: "You have reddened your spears in my flesh."

Another example is the metaphor used to refer to the white settlers as swallows. Ndengezi asks King Shaka: "Is it wise to allow the white swallows to fly so freely?"

A popular custom was that of praise poetry, or *izibongo*, which made extensive use of idioms. The praise poet (*imbongi*) would sing the praises of a particular chief or warrior as a form of entertainment, as well as a chronicle of the person's deeds. Often praises were also co-opted from conquered chiefs and added to those of the victor.

King Shaka's praises were numerous and elaborate, often recognizing his royal lineage and exalting his heroic military prowess:

> *"He who beats but is not beaten*
> *The voracious one of Senzangakhona*
> *Whose spear is red, even on the handle."*

> *"He whose fame spreads*
> *Even as he sits."*

YOU ARE THE *RISING SUN*... BUT YOU ARE ALSO THE *SHADE.*

SEE PAGE 7

Even some of the white settlers began to amass their own *izibongo*, as they became increasingly involved in Zulu campaigns. The lines below are from the praises of Henry Fynn, and describe specific aspects of the man himself:

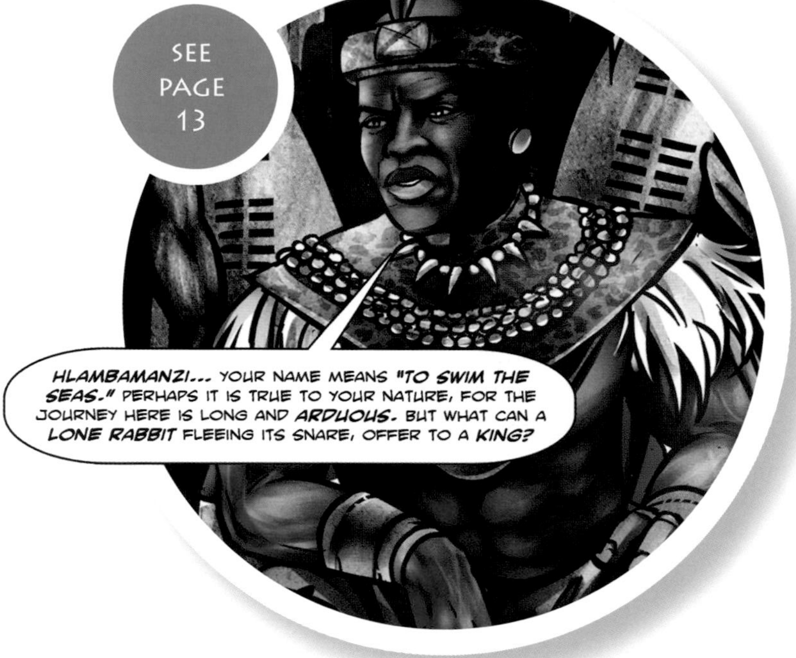
SEE PAGE 13
HLAMBAMANZI... YOUR NAME MEANS "TO SWIM THE SEAS." PERHAPS IT IS TRUE TO YOUR NATURE, FOR THE JOURNEY HERE IS LONG AND ARDUOUS. BUT WHAT CAN A LONE RABBIT FLEEING ITS SNARE, OFFER TO A KING?

"Feathers, now growing, now falling out..."
(A reference to Henry Fynn's bushy sideburns.)
"Tamer of the evil-tempered elephant..."
(Fynn's skill with firearms in hunting.)
"Who was pregnant with many young ones..."
(Fynn acquired several wives and fathered an unknown number of children during his time with the Zulu.)

Names of people and places were also often complex, themselves involving idiomatic descriptions. Two of the larger Zulu capitals during King Shaka's reign were KwaBulawayo and KwaDukuza, translated respectively (and somewhat ominously) as "The Place of Murder" and "The Place of Lost People."

King Shaka's own name has variations in the histories, depending on regional dialects. In the coastal lands south of the Thukela River, his name was pronounced "Tshaka." This would also explain why the early Port Natal settlers who were living in that area wrote "Chaka" in their written accounts, since that spelling indicates the "Tsh" sound. Those born upcountry in the lands of the Zulu usually spoke the king's name with the most commonly used pronunciation, "Shaka," which is the spelling we have chosen for this retelling of his legend.

The possible meanings of King Shaka's name reflect differing perceptions of the Zulu king. We cannot be certain of the true meaning – there are a number of versions of how he got his name, some less flattering than others. In Zulu territory there was a beetle known as "*itshaka*," which was believed to cause a bloated stomach symptomatic of intestinal distress. One story goes that, when Nandi became pregnant by Senzangakhona, she was said to be afflicted with this ailment, and King Shaka was given the name when he was born.

"*Itshaka*" also has another meaning, used to describe a girl who became pregnant out of wedlock, hence suggesting that King Shaka was illegitimate. This is quite possibly a convenient fabrication by later successors to vilify King Shaka and enhance their own reputations.

Another, somewhat more complimentary, version suggests that "Shaka" was not his birth name at all, but was actually bestowed later by King Dingiswayo, as part of the young warrior's praises: "*uSitshaka ka sitshayeki*" ("He who beats but is not beaten").

Whatever the truth may be, it is this last meaning that perhaps best reflects King Shaka's character.

QUESTIONS AND IDEAS FOR GOING DEEPER

The way in which the material in this book is organized uses the following pattern:

- You start by reading (and viewing) the story just as it is.
- Next, there are questions and ideas to help you get a deeper understanding of what you have read.
- Finally, you think about how this applies to life as you know it (your own life, or the world in which you live).

You have read the story of King Shaka's reign and his murder. You have focused especially on the challenges he faced as a leader in a time of change. The questions that follow will require you to think what his story has to do with your life and the modern world you live in.

CRITICAL THINKING QUESTIONS

How accurate is this story ?

- Some details in this storybook have been invented by the author. Does this mean that the story is not true?
- What is the difference between a fictional story and fake news?
- Is story telling important in your family? Why?

The history of King Shaka's time

- In what ways did the arrival of white settlers affect the Zulu people in King Shaka's time?
- How is your life affected by the history of colonial settlement?

The challenges of leadership

- King Shaka faced the dilemma of how to respond to the British settlers. What did he decide? What would you have done if you had been in his position?
- Think of a time when you had to make a difficult choice. Why was it difficult? How did you decide?

Zulu political structures

- During the Festival of First Fruits, King Shaka spent a lot of his time doing political work. Why did he need to do this?
- Are modern leaders and celebrities able to have private lives?

The role of women

- What effect did the key women in this story have on King Shaka's decisions?
- Why did King Shaka trust his sister's advice?
- In your community, do women have the same status as men? How do their roles differ? How do you feel about this?

Zulu culture and beliefs

- The Zulu people in King Shaka's time believed their ancestors (*amadlozi*) could influence their lives for good or bad. Find examples in this story. What do you believe about the role of your ancestors?
- In Zulu culture it is unacceptable to speak the king's name without his title. Dingane repeatedly refers to "Shaka" instead of calling him "King Shaka." What does this show about his attitude to King Shaka?
- In this story, people consulted herbalists and sangomas who sought wisdom from the ancestors for their health needs. In modern society, who are the people trained to care for our health and spiritual well-being?

Language and naming

- IsiZulu is a very expressive language. Look for examples of images that are used in this book.
- Imagery gives color to the language we use. Make a list of some images and idioms that we commonly use in English.
- How was your name chosen when you were born? Does it have a particular meaning?

GLOSSARY

Boer
Dutch settler (literally, "farmer")

Gogo
grandmother

ibutho (plural: **amabutho**)
age-grade regiment

idlozi (plural: **amadlozi**)
ancestral spirits

ikhanda (plural: **amakhanda**)
royal military homestead

imbongi (plural: **izimbongi**)
praise singer

imphepho
aromatic plant used as incense,
burned during Zulu ceremonies

inkosi (plural: **amakhosi**)
chief/king

inkosikazi (plural: **amakhosikazi**)
female elder, part of the royal
house, or principal wife

inyanga (plural: **izinyanga**)
traditional healer

isangoma (plural: **izangoma**)
diviner, witchdoctor

izibongo
praises, chanted in honor of a king
or influential person

isigodlo
the royal enclosure at the upper
end of the *ikhanda*; also the women
of the king's household

isiZulu
the Zulu language

iziYendane
the name of one of Shaka's
regiments (*isiYendane* is literally a
person with a strange hairstyle)

inkosi yami
my chief/my king

umKhosi
The annual Zulu Ceremony of the
First Fruits

umuthi (plural: **imithi**)
traditional medicine; more
specifically occult medicine for
ritual purposes

PRONUNCIATION

IsiZulu contains some sounds which are not used in English, but it uses letters from the English alphabet to represent them.

CLICK SOUNDS: C, Q, AND X

c   To make the sound of the letter "c," suck the tip of the tongue against the palate, just behind your front teeth and then pull it away. This makes a soft click sound. It is like the sound English speakers use to show sympathy ("tsk.")

q   To make the sound of the letter "q," suck the tip of the tongue against the roof of your mouth, and then pull it away suddenly. This makes a hard click, like the sound English speakers use to imitate the sound of a horse's hoof on hard ground.

x   To make the sound of the letter "x," suck the side of the tongue against the inside of your cheek, and then pull it away suddenly. This is the sound that English speakers use to call a horse.

ZULU PRONUNCIATION OF TH, PH AND KH

th   The English sound "th" (as in "thank" or "this") is not used in isiZulu. The letter combination "th" in isiZulu is sounded like the English letter "t." ("Sithole" sounds like "Sitole.")

ph   "ph" is pronounced like "p" and not like "f." (*Imphepho* sounds like "impepo.")

kh   "kh" is pronounced like "k" in "kick;" but "k" in isiZulu is pronounced more like "g," as in "gun." Thus "Shaka" sounds more like "Shaga."